SECRETS NEVER DIE

DAVID BRADWELL

SECRETS NEVER DIE

Would you confess to a murder you didn't commit?

A celebrity cold case gets solved when a convicted gangster confesses to a headline-grabbing murder.

But DSI Joe Leyland is not convinced. With the assistance of rogue former investigative journalist Clare Woodbrook, he begins to unravel a decade-old conspiracy that reaches right into the heart of the police. And as they start to delve deeper, they begin to discover secrets that very powerful people would kill again to hide.

Secrets Never Die is a gripping British conspiracy thriller, with twists galore and dashes of dark humour. It's book 2 in the bestselling Clare Woodbrook series.

ABOUT THE AUTHOR

David Bradwell grew up in the north east of England but now lives in Hitchin in Hertfordshire. He has written for publications as diverse as Smash Hits and the Sunday Times and is a former winner of the PPA British Magazine Writer of the Year Award. Aside from writing, he runs a hosiery company with web sites at www.stockingshq.com and www.tightsandmore.com.

Get in touch at:
www.davidbradwell.com

SECRETS NEVER DIE

A Gripping Conspiracy Thriller: Clare Woodbrook Book 2

Secrets Never Die was first published in 2021 by Pure Fiction
Copyright © David Bradwell, 2021
www.davidbradwell.com

ISBN: 978-1-914281-00-6

For Elaine Franklin.

Chapter 1

Friday, October 22nd, 1993

THE Red Lion Pub in London's Parliament Street is not the place to plan a murder, but if you're going to do it, you'd be wise to keep your voice down. It's a three-minute walk from New Scotland Yard, the headquarters of the Metropolitan Police.

"I'm not sure I agree with you," said the man leaning on the edge of the bar, its wooden rail providing a steadying influence during the third pint of the last forty-five minutes. Even hardened detectives need help occasionally.

"What are you saying, Dougie?" asked his former colleague, over the laughter, the chink of glasses, the scraping of bar stools on the wooden floor, and the general wall of conversation underpinning an atmosphere of bonhomie.

"I'm saying, Neil, I don't agree with you. Yes, you've got your celebrities and your God-knows-what, but you've got to admit, you must miss this. The absolute joy of nailing a bastard."

Neil Fearon put an arm round the shoulder of his former boss.

"You know what I do miss? I miss my mates. You, Wardy, Cov,

old Kenny Mason, God rest his soul. I don't miss the hours, the politics. Twats dishing out orders. But I'm glad you messaged me, it's great to see you again."

That was a lie. One of the primary reasons former Detective Sergeant Neil Fearon left the Force to set up his own security company was that he couldn't abide working for Detective Inspector Dougie Compton. Or Detective *Chief* Inspector as he was now. But this wasn't the time or place to revisit old grudges. Tonight was about celebrating the successful conclusion of a case that had baffled them all.

That was another lie. It hadn't baffled them all, but the truth had been successfully buried and now the secret could be quietly left to die. In an unexpected development, someone had confessed to the most notorious celebrity murder of a generation. And for the dozen or so detectives in the corner of the Red Lion, it was a great excuse for a party. Or a time to start thinking you'd finally got away with it, depending on your perspective.

Neil left Dougie and made his way through the crowd, past DS Alex Ward, DS Nick Brooks, DCS Terry Handley, and the former senior investigating officer DCI Brian Dalton. Brian had long since retired, but was having a day out in London to join in the celebration. Neil nodded, said hello, promised to be back in a moment, and finally reached his destination, where DCI Graham March was trying to chat up two young female detectives. Neither of the women had been involved in the case, but the drinks were free and flowing.

"Graham, you old fraud," he said, butting in. "Still suspended?"

March looked him up and down, then cracked a smile as recognition dawned.

"Neil Fearon! I thought you were dead. How are things in the security game?"

"Going well. You should think about it."

"Crossing to the dark side?"

"You've got all the skills. And rumour has it you might be looking for a new career."

March's smile disappeared as quickly as it had surfaced.

"You don't want to believe what you read in the gutter press," he said, with more than a hint of a snarl.

"Still, I'm surprised they let you in here."

"You always were a funny fucker. Make yourself useful and get another beer in."

"What are you having? Aside from a hard time with the ladies?" Neil nodded in the direction of the two detectives, who had seized their opportunity to make a hasty retreat.

"I was in there till you came along. The pair of them."

"The weird thing is, I genuinely think you believe that. Pint of Pride, is it? ESB?"

"Anything wet. Dougie's running a tab."

Neil nodded and made his way to the bar, chuckling to himself. Yes, there were things he missed. But, he thought as he edged his way to the front of the throng, there was even more he was glad he'd left behind.

Chapter 2

Saturday, October 23rd, 1993

I'D made an effort. A new black dress. New black suede heels. I'd even spent more time than usual on my hair and make-up, but none of it had worked. I just wasn't in the mood.

Wrapping my jacket around my shoulders, I headed out to the balcony. A cigarette wouldn't fix things, but it would at least take them off my mind for a few glorious, indulgent moments.

I inhaled deeply, leaning on the stone balustrade, watching the retreating lights of a riverboat heading south on the Rhine. It was so peaceful. So calming. Normally.

My mind drifted, thinking of those I'd lost, and wondering if anything could ever be worth the pain.

A sudden increase in the volume of music and laughter snapped me back into reality. I didn't turn immediately. Whoever had opened the door was welcome to join me. Everyone was an invited guest, and the balcony was big enough to share. But I wanted to savour my last moments of reflection before being dragged back into endless small talk.

"You are Clare Woodbrook?"

I blew smoke across the fields, then turned to find a staggeringly attractive blonde woman walking towards me with one hand extended, and two flutes of Champagne in the other. She looked stunning in an asymmetrical scarlet dress, with a cream faux fur stole to fend off the evening chill. I didn't know if her jewellery was real or costume, but it sparkled in the glow of the wall lamp. Her shoes matched the dress and added at least another four inches to her height. I guessed at early thirties.

"Iglika Lechkov," she said, as I accepted the handshake. "I thought you might like one of these."

"Iglika, of course," I smiled, accepting a flute, and immediately tried to put on my bravest of faces, while trying to hide my surprise. She was nothing like I'd imagined. My knowledge of Bulgaria was minimal, and expectations were heavily tainted by the thought of burly bodybuilders, with excessive facial hair. And that was just the women.

"You are coming to see me in Sofia," she said, as she let go of my hand, then joined me leaning on the stonework.

"I'm very much looking forward to it, and it's great to meet you at last," I said.

"And you." Her voice was captivating. Her English was excellent, with every word carefully enunciated, but with the edge of a deeply seductive accent. I was immediately impressed; maybe because I know how hard it is to master a language and speak it like a native. "There is still a lot to discuss."

I nodded.

"There is, but these events are strictly non-business. I imagine you're staying the weekend?"

"I fly back on Monday."

"Perfect. Maybe we can arrange some time tomorrow? I'd offer to take you for lunch but I'm not sure we'll be awake in time." That made her smile. "Maybe dinner, though? I'll show you Koblenz. Unless you have something planned?"

"No, that would be wonderful, thank you."

Some of my tension lifted as I took a sip of the Champagne, then rolled my shoulders before turning back towards her and making eye contact.

"Is this your first time here?" I asked.

"Yes, my first time ever at the Schloss, although I have wanted to come to one of the parties for a long time. I have heard they are ... loud."

I smiled.

"Not so much loud as lively once the fun starts. The first one can be a shock."

"I do not think I can be shocked." She winked and I felt an overwhelming maternal urge, even though I guessed we were a similar age. I didn't think I was shockable either, until I'd witnessed true debauchery with a German twist.

"How about you?" she asked.

"I've been living here since February so I've been to a few."

"Ah yes. You were rescued in Cologne. I heard all about you."

"That sounds ominous."

She smiled. It was infectious.

"I am sure we have all done bad things in our own way," she said. "The Blood Angel likes to recruit people with flaws."

"Indeed."

I'd researched Iglika. She'd grown up under communism, in a family connected to the government, and had been heavily involved in the black market before the Iron Curtain came down. I expected she knew about my own history in art fraud, with a side order of execution – even though that was, as I'd proved over and over, in self-defence. Still, the past was the past, and we were now working for an organisation that was trying to do good, albeit in occasionally questionable ways. We just had to avoid being arrested for previous misdoings in the process.

"Anders Hagström is here?" she asked.

"No, he doesn't come to the parties. I'm not sure they're his thing."

"That is a shame. I would like to meet him."

"You will, I'm sure. He's due to turn up at some point tomorrow."

Anders was the closest we had to a boss, even though he was insistent that we were all equal. The real mastermind was the Blood Angel herself, a near-mythical former Stasi spy and femme fatale. Nobody knew if she really existed any more. Except me. She'd taken me under her wing in more ways than one, but there was no question of ever revealing the secret of her identity.

Iglika offered me a cigarette, then held out a gold lighter that matched the bangles on her wrist.

"Something tells me you are not in the mood for a party," she said as I leaned in for a light. Was it that obvious?

"Not really," I said, at last.

"Because of what happened in Paris?"

So she'd heard about that too.

I nodded.

"It sounded heartbreaking," she continued, blowing smoke. "Although I am told you were brave."

I shrugged.

"I did what I had to do. I'd been trained, so it wasn't really bravery, and the end result was the loss of a colleague."

"I understand." She didn't need to say any more. I think we both understood. We lived in a dangerous world. But losing someone I cared about, who'd put his own life on the line to rescue me, had hit me hard. Not least because I'd doubted his intentions until the moment he'd died.

"I'm sure you'll have fun tonight, though," I said. "Don't let my mood stop you enjoying yourself."

The mischievous smile returned, along with another wink.

"I quite like the thought of a night of bad behaviour," she said.

"You're in the right place. Have you met anyone?"

"Not yet. Just the housekeeper and her husband this afternoon. Birgit and Walter. They are very friendly."

"They're lovely. Although Birgit keeps Walter well out of the way when the carnage begins."

She laughed.

"She sounds sensible."

I looked at the burning tip of my cigarette.

"We'll finish these and I'll take you in and introduce you to some people. I won't know everyone, but there'll be a few. The main thing is to remember that nothing that happens is ever discussed again."

"I have heard there is cocaine."

Instinctively I was on alert, naturally suspicious that someone might be planning to expose us. But it passed a split second later. Nobody would be here unless they'd been heavily vetted – especially after a traitor in our midst had caused so much hurt just a few weeks before.

"There's anything you want," I said. "Cocaine isn't really my thing, but you should know, nobody is going to judge you. These events are deliberately hedonistic. Despite the Blood Angel name, nobody is particularly angelic. At least not in every respect."

"I can imagine." She turned and leaned back on the balustrade, looking back towards the house. "This is what I do not understand. The human race is supposed to be the most intelligent species on earth. And yet there is tiny evidence of it. We have wars and kill each other. We do things we know are bad for us." She lifted her cigarette and looked at it before taking one last drag and flicking it away into the darkness. "Horses do not do that. Birds do not. Just us, and we are supposed to be the clever ones, but that cleverness comes with an urge to self-destruct."

"It's a good point," I said, hastily flicking my cigarette, too.

"It is all about ego," she continued. "We take risks because we want power. And yet when we achieve things we get bored, and we want to escape from ourselves."

Something was telling me that those who underestimated Iglika did so at their peril.

It was time to join the party. She put her arm through mine and we headed back inside.

The Schloss was a perfect venue for parties. It was a vast stone-built house that resembled a mini-castle, and hence the nickname. Even though the parties were nominally monthly, the previous one had been cancelled due to the events in Paris, so it was the first one since the end of August. As such, there were more people than normal. I didn't try to count them, but guessed at around forty, spread around half a dozen ground floor rooms, plus however many more were down in the basement gym and pool complex, or already in one of the many bedrooms. Iglika and I were among the youngest, although there was a smattering of fit young men and gorgeous young women whom I suspected had been drafted in specifically for the occasion.

It was lively, with background beats overlaid with lots of laughter, and conversations in languages that reflected the disparate origins of our colleagues. As soon as our glasses were empty, someone appeared with a bottle of Champagne and refilled them. I introduced Iglika to about a dozen people and then left her to mingle while I headed to the kitchen in search of our elderly housekeeper.

Birgit was sitting at the large table, reading a novel. She looked up as I entered. I closed the door behind me.

"Are you okay?" she whispered, in perfect English, even though, as far as everyone else was concerned, she only spoke German. Nobody – apart from possibly Anders – knew her true role. Or her past as an elite spy and killing machine, and the fact that she saw everything: the silent hand guiding us all, hidden in plain sight. Also, by common consensus, her husband Walter was deaf, but I knew the truth there as well. They were all secrets I'd die to protect if they asked me to. Or at least put up a good fight.

I wasn't sure how to answer, but I knew she'd see right through any attempt to add non-existent gloss.

"I'm kind of okay, and kind of feeling a bit blue," I said, after a moment. "I'm sure things will get better in time."

She put down her book, removed her reading glasses, then stood up and gave me a much-needed hug.

"They will," she said, brushing the hair from my eyes, so she could look straight into them. "Can I get you anything? More Champagne?"

I smiled.

"I think I've already had far too much," I said. "These shoes were hard enough to walk in when I was sober. The best thing is probably to go to bed and leave everyone to have fun. I just wanted to come and say goodnight. And to say thank you again, for everything."

"It's me that should be thanking you. You keep me young."

I kissed her on the cheek and then headed back for one last glance at the party. Iglika was having an interesting time, in among a group of three men and two other women. She tried to beckon me to join them, but I shook my head, blew her a kiss, and headed for the stairs.

It wasn't just the events of Paris. It was an awareness this was my new life, whether I liked it or not. It was a long way from the hustle and bustle of a busy daily newspaper office. I missed that. I missed the interaction, the deadlines, the humour, the social life. I missed my home. I missed England. I missed my former protégé Danny Churchill and his flatmate Anna Burgin. But tomorrow would be a new day, and while I might have a hangover, plenty of others would be feeling far worse.

I removed my make-up and headed to bed with a book, feeling a mixture of old, sensible and melancholy. My mind was still processing the memories of a fallen colleague. My last thought before falling asleep was that I would never let his passing be in vain.

Chapter 3

Sunday, October 24th, 1993

THE morning after a party always felt strange. Although colleagues occasionally visited the Schloss while on business in the nearby cities of Frankfurt, Cologne and Düsseldorf, I was the only full-time resident – apart from Birgit and Walter – and I'd come to think of it as my private home. After a party, however, the evidence of other people's excesses was everywhere, from the empty glasses and overflowing ashtrays, to the occasional mysterious stain on the furniture. The cleaning crew were excellent, though, and they'd have it back to normal long before the hardest-partying visitors surfaced to witness the mess they'd left behind.

Despite no longer having a personal trainer, I was determined to maintain my fitness, not least because I knew the cigarettes were working their hardest in the other direction. So, before breakfast I hit the pool for forty lengths, to try to blow away my headache.

It was partially successful, and a hot shower and couple of ibuprofens finished the job. By just after 10am, I headed to the kitchen in search of breakfast. Birgit was bustling around, working hard, but stopped to give me another hug. She told me to sit at the table and then delivered coffee, and a selection of delicious-looking pastries. Periodically, Walter appeared and took plates of food, juice and coffee upstairs to the bedrooms.

I was nearly finished when Iglika arrived, looking fragile and distinctly less polished than the night before. She put her hand over her face when she saw me, then started to laugh, before wincing.

"You could have warned me," she said with something approaching a smile. Her voice still had the delicious accent, but it was now overlaid with a seductive throatiness.

"Good night, was it?" I asked, pulling out a chair for her.

"I think so. I ... Oh God. Bits of it are coming back to me."

"It certainly sounds like a good night, then." I fought hard to suppress a chuckle but failed.

"I seem to remember doing things I have never done before and which even now I am not sure are physically possible." She rested her elbows on the table then dropped her head into her hands with a groan.

"Don't worry about it," I said. "We all have needs. We all deserve to have fun." I turned to Birgit and added "I've got a patient for you" in German, which made Birgit smile, and Iglika glance up as though I'd said something astonishing. I expect it was the shock of an English person actually speaking another language.

I arranged to meet Iglika in the drawing room at noon and then left Birgit to work her magic. There was plenty to do. I was due to fly to Sofia in two days' time, according to the current plan, and homework was required, both on the city itself, and in terms of what I was likely to find when I got there.

Iglika was to be my guide, but I was responsible for brokering deals with factory owners who'd inherited the means of production in the post-communist age, but had no idea how to make a profit. It was a fantastic opportunity to act as an intermediary between the Bulgarian industrialists and rich western investors who were looking for new opportunities in the post-perestroika east. For a hefty commission, obviously. That said, I knew there would be challenges. Not least from criminal gangs who wanted to muscle in on the same golden goose.

I wasn't expecting trouble, at least not on the first visit, but experience suggested it was never far away. If I came up against a threat of violence, it was my responsibility to nullify it with minimal fuss, and the minimum amount of evidence left behind. I'd come a long way from the investigative journalist who lapsed into criminality in a moment of madness. Preparation was potentially a life-saver, especially when I couldn't rely on the police to help me. I was on the wanted list in more countries than I dared to count.

My mobile phone burst into life while I was midway through reading a CompuServe article about Sofia's various styles of architecture.

"Anders," I said, with genuine joy in my voice. "How are things? Are you still coming to see us?"

"I am, but it won't be till later this evening now." I never tired of his German accent, even if it wasn't as sexy as Iglika's Bulgarian one. "I hope that's okay."

"Of course."

Anders Hagström was an elder statesman who automatically engendered respect. Like all of us, he'd done bad things, but his were for the most noble of reasons. He'd suffered horrors I could barely imagine. His parents were killed when he was young, on the night the British Royal Air Force dropped three thousand tonnes of bombs on his home city of Dresden, during the Second World War. Then further tragedy struck when his wife and children were killed trying to escape from East Germany during the darkest days of the communist era. Despite that, and the trauma that followed, he was now a voice of sanity within the Blood Angel organisation.

"Iglika is here and desperate to meet you," I said. "I'd love you to join us for dinner if you're here in time. I'm taking her into town."

"No, you two have fun. It may be close to ten by the time I get there."

"Is everything okay?"

"Everything is fine." Was his hesitation real or did I imagine it? "We can discuss it later."

Something in his tone was unsettling, but it was pointless asking him to elaborate on the phone.

We ended the call and I returned to CompuServe. But a moment later my phone rang again. Expecting Anders had forgotten something, I didn't look at the number before hitting the button to connect the call.

It was a careless mistake. Because I recognised the voice at the other end of the line as soon as he said my name.

Chapter 4

ALTHOUGH Detective Superintendent Joe Leyland was the closest I had to a friend in the Metropolitan Police, I was aware that officially he was still supposed to be trying to arrest me for fraud and murder. He was due to retire soon, and it would be an extremely popular climax to a distinguished career. With his colleagues, anyway. Not so popular with me.

"Joe," I said, trying to gauge his mood from his tone of voice. "How's London?"

"Are you thinking of coming back?"

"No, I was being polite and friendly. You know me."

"That's a shame. And yes, but try not to remind me."

"Charming," I chuckled, lying back on the bed. "Are you calling about my amnesty?"

"It depends on your definition of amnesty." That sounded hopeful. "If Amnesty is the name of a perfume, I might be able to pick you up some, next time I'm in Boots."

That sounded less so.

"Joe, don't be horrible. I'm a nice person. You know that really."

"Nice people don't murder their accomplices."

"Self-defence. Anyway, how can I help you?"

I checked my watch. As much as I enjoyed talking to Joe, as long as he was exercising a certain level of restraint vis-a-vis handcuffs, it was getting close to noon, and I still had to finish my preparation for Iglika.

"What are you up to?" he asked.

"At this moment, getting ready for a meeting, but I'm hopefully about to head to Sofia."

"Sofia?"

"Bulgaria."

"I know where Sofia is. I was just a bit surprised. Dare I ask why?"

"You can ask. I probably won't tell you."

"Fair play. When are you going?"

"Tuesday, I think. That's what the meeting's about."

"Tuesday this week?"

"Yes. Do you want to come with me? You should see the yellow brick roads. It's famous for them."

I heard a sigh.

"That's a shame," said Joe.

"Why is that a shame? Are you too busy?"

"What? No, I was hoping you'd be in London. I need a favour. A chance for you to earn some brownie points."

Despite the unfortunate timing, something stopped me declining the request immediately. For the last couple of months I'd been trying to convince Joe that I could be more help to him if I was left to roam free, providing intelligence, rather than spending all day staring at the walls of a prison cell. Despite a minor success helping him with a recent murder case, I sensed he didn't fully support my viewpoint. If there was ever an opportunity to persuade him, I'd do everything in my power to leap at it. Potentially it could mean being allowed to go home without constantly watching over my shoulder – for police at least. I'd still have to be careful of one or two others.

"So you've decided to trust me?" I asked.

"I've decided to be very cautious around you. And delay claiming the medal I'd get for bringing you in."

"You've got enough of those already. How urgent is the favour? Can it wait a week?"

"Very urgent, so no."

Typical. I looked at my watch again, though I didn't really know why.

"How long will it take?" I asked. I doubted it would be ten minutes.

"A few days."

"It's a big favour then?"

"You're running quite a big deficit in the brownie points department."

"Can you tell me what it is?"

"I can. When you get here."

"And you're sure it can't wait a week?"

"Can your trip to Sofia?"

At times of stress, I tend to let my eyes wander and start counting things. This time it was the checks on my skirt. The Sofia trip was important. Others were depending on me. It was my first big business assignment, and there was no way I could afford to mess it up. I needed to start repaying Anders and the others for the faith they'd shown in me. For rescuing me, both from the police (so far) and a killer hell-bent on revenge (likewise).

But Sofia wasn't absolutely *confirmed* for Tuesday. There was a possibility I might be able to rearrange it. The risk, of course, was that it would put us a week behind other parties in the negotiations. And if our potential Bulgarian partners decided to strike deals with seriously bad guys in the interim, it would be unfortunate – and potentially dangerous for everyone when I was forced to unpick them.

Had I been more established, I wouldn't have hesitated. Equally, though, I wanted to prove my worth to Joe, and if I rejected this opportunity, I might never have another again.

That whole thought process took less than three seconds.

"Can you give me half an hour?" I said. "I'll need to move a couple of things but I'll call you."

"Don't do that. I'll call you," said Joe. "It'll be an hour. I'll be sorting out your hotel room."

"Wooah! I haven't said yes yet."

"No, but you will."

I hate it when people know me that well.

"I might not now, just to assert my independence," I said.

Joe laughed.

"Your desire to maintain your independence is exactly why you'll agree."

Chapter 5

I GLIKA was reluctantly okay about delaying the Sofia trip for a week, but was adamant that any longer would put our proposals in serious jeopardy. I got the message. Plans were made, then I gave her the guided tour of Koblenz, before stopping for dinner at a wonderful French restaurant overlooking the Rhine.

I introduced her to Anders when we got back to the Schloss, and then we all stayed up till the early hours, making plans, discussing scenarios, and trying to second-guess the dangers we might face.

Joe still hadn't told me exactly what his favour entailed, but it would be something that required discretion. So, the following morning I packed a selection of equipment that might come in useful, together with enough clothes to potentially stay a week. I thought about dyeing my hair again. It had been dark brown a while, but I decided against it. Joe had seen me recently, and there was no real reason to change it yet. I already looked very different to how people would remember me in London.

The safest option was to take my car and catch a ferry to the UK rather than trying to book a flight, to minimise the potential for difficult questions in customs. Shortly after lunch, I set out for the five-hour drive from Koblenz, through Belgium and France, to Calais.

It was late evening by the time I finally pulled my Mercedes 500 SL into a parking space outside a cosy-looking hotel, in Dulwich, south London. Joe had booked a room under his own name, but informed reception that a woman would be checking in. He'd known better than to ask for the name on my passport, which was just as well. He'd have struggled to spell Kaarina Mäkinen, and it was better he didn't know all of my aliases, in case he ever turned against me. He understood the risk I was taking by returning to London, though, and knew that I'd do everything in my power to minimise it.

Having collected my key, I made my way to the lift, with a suitcase in each hand. As I waited for it to arrive, I sensed someone approaching me from behind, but before I'd had a chance to react, he had a firm grip on my upper arm.

"Clare Woodbrook. Detective Sergeant Nick Brooks."

Well, that hadn't lasted long. I dropped the bags, getting ready to fight, disappointed that Joe would have stooped so low as to have me arrested the moment I arrived.

To his credit, DS Nick Brooks anticipated my reaction and his grip loosened.

"Don't worry," he said. "DSI Joe Leyland sent me to meet you. Can I give you a hand with the bags?" He picked them up and took them into the lift.

"What was with the arm grip?" I asked as the doors closed behind us.

"Save the questions till tomorrow," he said. "I'm only here to make sure you check into your room okay."

It was an annoying response. Immediately my hackles were up. The short lift journey gave me a chance to look at him properly. Mid-thirties, about six feet tall, clearly fit, smartly dressed, with a smattering of stubble. Overall, reasonably suave, probably fancied himself a little too much. Humourless. Intrinsically and immediately irritating.

The doors opened on the third floor, and I led the way to my room, but made no attempt to open the door.

"Is that your real name or did you choose it for the comedy?" I said, turning to him.

"What do you mean, comedy?"

"Nick the policeman? It's funny, isn't it? Albeit a bit Jim Davidson."

"Are you saying you're a fan of Jim Davidson?"

"Obviously not. Of all things you could level at me, that's towards the top of the ones I'd most vehemently deny, but ... oh, forget it. Let's move on. Lovely to meet you. Thank you for bringing my bags. We're here now. You can go again."

He stood firm.

"I need to see you into your room."

I sighed. It had been a long day, with a lot of driving. I was tired. I didn't want an argument. But I wasn't about to let a stranger into my room, no matter what he said his name was. He hadn't even shown me his ID.

"I'm a big girl," I said. "I know how keys work. Let's not fall out."

"DSI Leyland was insistent."

"And I'm equally as insistent I can manage on my own."

"He said you might be awkward."

I was all for heading back downstairs, getting back into the car and driving home.

"I'm not going to ask why he was insistent," I said. "Because, as you just pointed out, I've got to save the questions till tomorrow. But let me give you one last chance to piss off voluntarily before I make the decision for you. Okay?"

He still didn't move.

Neither did I.

He was much taller than me, and I really didn't want to cause a scene, but I would if I had to. The only thing stopping me was the thought I was supposed to be on my best behaviour.

Eventually he broke the silence.

"I'm going to be watching you," he said. "I know what you've done. And just so you know, not everyone shares the opinion that you should be allowed to go free."

"Thank you for clarifying. Duly noted."

He took an envelope from his inside jacket pocket.

"Instructions for tomorrow," he said. "Don't be late."

And with that, he finally turned away. I waited until the lift doors had closed behind him before taking out my keycard.

Something told me I would need to watch DS Nick Brooks very carefully too.

Chapter 6

Tuesday, October 26th, 1993

JOE had arranged a meeting room in an anonymous-looking Regus office block, not far from my hotel. I wasn't keen on the 8am start, but partly to make a point to Nick, I made sure I was there on time. I wasn't sure of the dress code either, but opted for a reasonably presentable white shirt, beige high-waist Donna Karan pencil skirt, and knee-length boots with opaque Falke tights, all topped off with my favourite trench coat.

Joe opened the door himself, then stood aside so I could enter. Nick was already seated at a big oval table. Beside him, a woman I didn't recognise stood up and made her way towards me.

"Clare, this is DC Emily North," said Joe. "I believe you've already met Nick."

"I have." I nodded in his direction, trying not to scowl, but then smiled at Emily as I shook her hand. She was young, slim, about five foot seven or eight, with green eyes behind round tortoiseshell glasses. Her dark brown hair was tied back, giving her a severe, no-nonsense look, and she was dressed in a navy trouser suit that was smart, but practical rather than super-stylish. Her make-up was minimal, if there was any at all. Unlike Nick, she didn't inspire immediate antipathy in me.

Joe indicated a chair on the opposite side of the table. I took off my trench coat and folded it over the back of an adjacent one before sitting down, facing the other three as though at a particularly surreal job interview. Emily offered me a cup of tea, which she poured while Joe collected his thoughts.

"Can I just point out, I'm a bit nervous here," I said. "There are three of you, and if I need to make a quick getaway, you're all between me and the door."

"You're safe," said Joe. He looked tired but was still imposing. He was balding, and what little hair was left appeared even greyer than just a few weeks before. His reading glasses lay on top of a notepad on the table in front of him.

"Even so."

I cast a glance at Nick, who'd locked his eyes on me in some kind of death stare. He was dunking a biscuit in a cup of tea, but with his attention on me, it snapped off and fell into the cup.

"Oopsadaisy," I said. Emily let out a giggle, which immediately made me warm to her. As she pushed my cup across the desk towards me, Joe cleared his throat.

"I haven't got long, but for the avoidance of doubt this conversation didn't happen," he began.

"Chatham House Rules?" I said.

"What?"

"Participants are free to use the information received, but the identities of all participants must remain a secret."

"Very definitely not."

"So I can reveal your identity?"

His brow creased into a frown.

"Not funny. Breathe a word of anything that's said during this meeting to the wrong person, or in fact even think about it, and you'll be inside faster than a wasp turns up at a picnic."

"I don't do picnics," I said.

"Something else really fast then."

"Too many wasps," I whispered to Emily, with a wink, and got a smile in return. My attention turned back to Joe. "Understood. I'm on best behaviour."

"I hope so, although in your case these things are relative."

"Oooh."

Joe smiled, but Nick continued with the ice stare. I wondered why he was there, but was in no hurry to find out. It was time to start getting serious. I decided not to pursue the arm grip issue.

"We have an unsolved case from 1985," Joe began.

"Okay. A murder?"

He nodded.

"Who? And why?"

"Why was he killed or why was it unsolved?"

"Both."

"Both of those are difficult. It was a radio DJ, occasional TV presenter. You might have heard about it. Rex Dexter?"

The name was familiar.

"It was big news, wasn't it?" I said. "Wasn't he stabbed in a car park?"

"He was."

"But nobody was ever caught?"

"Exactly. There were lots of conspiracy theories but very little forensic evidence."

"Which pointed to a professional hit?"

Joe shrugged.

"It was one line of enquiry."

"And you're reinvestigating? Have you got new leads?"

He hesitated.

"Yes and no."

"Yes you're reinvestigating but no, you haven't got any more leads?"

He shook his head.

"It's bigger than that. Somebody just confessed to it."

"Wow." That took me aback.

"It's going to be announced at a press conference in the next couple of days."

"That's good, isn't it?" I glanced at all three of them, but none showed signs of celebration.

Joe took a deep breath before answering.

"He didn't do it," he said.

"Oh." That didn't make much sense. "How come? And who was it? Although if you're announcing it at a press conference, that suggests someone's taking it seriously."

"Let's just say it seems to suit a certain agenda to finally bring it to a close," said Joe.

"The man who's confessed is called Eddie Whitfield," added Nick, finally deeming me worthy of a contribution.

"He's already in prison," added Emily.

All three of them were looking at me as though I was going to perform a magic trick, but I had no idea why, or exactly what they expected of me.

"Okay. And who's Eddie Whitfield?"

"He's been in and out of the nick for years," started Joe. "Burglary, occasional violent disorder. The big one was a failed attempt at robbing a security vault. He was part of a gang, but we had a man on the inside, and as soon as it started, they all got caught red-handed."

"So he's not a fan of the police then?"

Joe shook his head.

"This was all back in '85. It was the week after Rex Dexter got killed. So in theory, he could have done the murder because he was still free at the time. But in all the investigation, his name never once came up as a suspect. And he was very much your baseball-bat-and-monkey-wrench kind of hard man. Not particularly subtle. Whoever killed Rex Dexter inflicted one fatal knife wound and left behind an almost complete lack of evidence."

"Okay. I can see why there'd be a doubt. So why's he confessing now, especially if he didn't do it?"

"He's got cancer," said Nick. "He's got days to live. And not many of them. It could be any moment."

I took the opportunity to dunk one of the proffered digestives into the cup of tea to give myself a moment to think. The fact it remained whole was a small victory over Nick. I made sure he noticed.

"Is it the morphine talking, then?" I asked. "Believe me, I've seen people in the final stages of cancer, and the painkillers are extreme."

"Your father?" asked Joe.

I nodded.

"And others, but he was the first."

"I'm sorry to hear that," said Nick, showing a level of compassion that took me by surprise. If it was genuine.

I shrugged.

"There's nothing anyone can say or do. It happens. It's a tragedy, but all I'd say is that by the end it's a relief, because you know the pain has ended. But it does underline the point – if he's on heavy doses of morphine, he won't be in his right mind."

Emily picked up a remote control and clicked it at a television that was standing against the end wall.

"This is his confession," she said.

The camera was focused on a frail-looking man, in what looked like his prison cell. After a moment's hesitation he started to speak, looking directly into the lens, rather than reading from a script.

"By the time you're watching this I may well be dead, but I want to go to my grave with a clear conscience, and make my peace with God. And before I start to lose my mind, I owe it to all of the people I've hurt to clear

up a mystery that has troubled the Metropolitan Police for the last eight years.

"On the night of Friday 26th July, 1985, the DJ Rex Dexter was killed with a single knife wound in the car park of his radio station, Sound Of London FM.

"I take no pride or comfort in this confession, but for the sake of passing into the next life with no more secrets, it is with a heavy heart that I must now acknowledge my guilt for that murder. I know this will come as a surprise. I know that I was never considered a suspect, and I know that I could have died without ever confessing, but I am a changed person to the man I was back then. I have nothing to lose by making this confession, but everything to gain. God will be my only judge and jury and it is my hope that by taking responsibility for my actions, it will help my quest for His forgiveness.

"I didn't know Rex aside from what I'd seen on TV. I'd never met him until that day. It was a chance meeting. It wasn't planned. I can't explain my state of mind eight years ago, but I would like to apologise to his friends and family for his death.

"I would also like to apologise to the Metropolitan Police for the amount of time and money they've spent investigating his murder. I know I should have come forward earlier, but I had other things on my mind back then. But over the last eight years, I've had a lot of time to consider the sins in my past and while I cannot bring the dead back to life, I can at least hopefully give some peace to the living by finally revealing the truth.

"May God bless you all. Amen."

The tape stopped. Emily turned off the TV. It felt like the temperature in the room had dropped by a few degrees.

"When was that made?" I asked after a moment.

"Six months ago," said Joe. "Before things got too bad."

"But it's only come out now?"

He nodded.

"Was he coerced?"

"There's no sign of it."

"Do you believe the religion thing?"

"Apparently that bit's true."

"Who made the video?"

"According to his son, he asked for a camera, and then filmed it himself. He gave strict instructions that nobody was to watch it until he was in the final stages."

"And I take it he's too ill to go and interview now?"

"Correct."

"And what does the son say?"

"He isn't a fan of the police, so at the moment he's saying nothing."

Joe looked at his watch.

"I've got to go to a meeting," he said, "so let me summarise this for you."

"Okay."

"The three of us don't think he did it. But that's not a popular opinion. As far as everyone else is concerned, the video is proof. It's the end of a long-running, notorious case. There was a big team who got a lot of flak for failing to find the killer, so they're extremely happy to have it off the books. And it's been explained to me by senior management, in no uncertain terms, that any further discussion or investigation would be extremely unwelcome. A line has been drawn. That's it. Finished. Along with strict instructions not to spend another minute or another pound of our budget giving it any more consideration."

"Which is why we're here?"

"Like I said at the start, this meeting didn't happen. Emily and Nick feel the same as I do. But none of us can work on this in any kind of official capacity. I'm going to leave you with them and they can give you all the background."

"That sounds like you want me to do it for you."

He smiled and started putting on his jacket.

"I couldn't possibly ask that. It would be foolish, reckless, possibly dangerous, and almost certainly illegal."

"It sounds like I'm made for it."

"I was hoping you'd think that. There's no pressure, obviously."

"Obviously."

"Although it would help us to continue to turn a blind eye and not arrest you."

"That's very kind."

His hand was on the door handle. "I know you're only here till the weekend, so I won't expect miracles."

"Best not to. It's already Tuesday."

"Although you're good at miracles. Rising from the dead and all of that. We won't leave you to do it all by yourself. But see what you think when they've given you the details. I'll call you first thing tomorrow. About 7am."

"Take care, Joe," I said.

He waved as the door closed behind him. I sat back in my chair, wondering what on earth I'd got myself into now.

Chapter 7

AFTER Joe left, I thought the others might take over, but they both turned their attention back to me, compelling me to take the initiative.

"Just to clarify: you're both on board with this, but equally can't be seen to be helping?" I said.

Nick nodded.

"In a word."

"Fourteen words, actually," said Emily.

I gave her a second glance.

"Did you just count them?" I asked.

"It's okay. I've got a thing about numbers."

"Evidently."

Nick looked like he'd seen it all before.

"Emily is a force of nature," he said, which was one way of putting it. "We're both working on live cases. I've got a murder–"

"And I'm mainly on a missing child," interrupted Emily.

"And before you ask," Nick continued, "we're not in a position to discuss details of those, not that it's relevant anyway. And also, so you understand, they have to be our priority. Even being here today was problematic. We'll do our best to be available if you need someone to talk to, but we can't guarantee it."

"You say that as though I've already agreed to take this on," I said. Nick shrugged, not denying it. I made it my mission to one day see him smile. "You both know Joe well? You've both worked with him before?"

"Of course," he said.

"That's good." I sighed, wondering quite where to start. I had a confession, an impossible case, a miserable bastard and a numbers geek. It wasn't going to be easy.

"Just to recap, then," I said. "You want me to help prove that Eddie Whitfield's confession was nonsense, and in the process, single-handedly solve a murder that's baffled the finest minds of the Metropolitan Police, with all of the resources at its disposal, for the last eight years. All while keeping a low profile because Joe's generosity in terms of the temporary amnesty probably doesn't extend to your colleagues – especially given that this is all strictly forbidden."

"If you don't think you're up to it, say so now," said Nick.

"No, I'm just getting a feel for the boundaries."

"I must just say," interrupted Emily, "it's an absolute pleasure to meet you. You're a legend. Joe told us all about you."

"That's not a good thing."

"No, it is! I think what you did was amazing." She was beaming.

"Selling stolen pictures and faking my own death?"

"No," she laughed. "But everything else, before and since. When you were an investigative journalist. I read some of your stories in the archive. And Joe told us about everything you did in Paris."

I frowned. Joe wasn't supposed to know *everything* I'd done in Paris. Technically I'd helped him solve a murder and risked my life in an attempt to save those of my friends and colleagues, but

I'd only given him the edited highlights, minus the gun bits. I hoped she was referring to those.

"I'm a big admirer," she continued. "I can't believe I've actually got to meet you. He told me how you shot the guy through the roof."

God.

"Well, that's very, er, *flattering*," I said, not quite sure what to make of it, and keen to change the subject. "In the meantime, can we go back to the beginning? Refresh me on the actual murder?"

"Of course." She was still beaming. It was quite endearing in a way. Yet terrifying in others.

Nick handed me a thick manila envelope.

"That's a summary," he said, with a look that suggested he'd love nothing more than to see me fail.

I felt the weight of it. "It must be about three hundred pages."

"Three-hundred-and-twelve," said Emily, predictably, passing me the VHS tape of the confession alongside.

"It's not everything," Nick continued, "but it's a copy of all of the most relevant information, forensics for what they're worth, witness interviews, background information. It should keep you busy, but if you need anything more specific, I'll give you private numbers for both of us. Again, for what they're worth."

I let out a deep breath.

"So that's the homework," I said. "For now, though, can you talk me through the basics?"

He nodded. That was something.

"Rex Dexter, as you probably know, was a DJ and occasionally presented kids' pop shows on TV. He left the BBC in '84 to be one of the launch presenters on Sound Of London FM. It was a new commercial station, and he had the breakfast show."

"I used to listen before I went to school," added Emily. "All my friends did."

"How old are you now?" I asked, hoping it wasn't impolite, but assuming she'd be overjoyed at more number action.

"Twenty-four," she said.

That made me feel old. It's true what they say about the police getting younger.

"It was actually my first case as a DC," said Nick. "I think that's the main reason why Joe started to speak to me about it. Assuming I'd have some kind of inside line."

"And do you?"

He shrugged. "Not really. I was new and inexperienced so I got tasked with lots of the tedious stuff."

"Okay." It could still be useful to have someone who'd worked on the original case, assuming he'd actually want to help me. But equally I imagined he'd have already relayed all of his evidence to the original team.

Something else was bothering me. "If I remember rightly, he got stabbed as he left the station, in the car park. But wasn't that in the late evening? What was he doing there at night if he presented the breakfast show?"

"There'd been a shake-up," said Nick. "He made some on-air comments about one of the other DJs, implying alcoholism. The other DJ got fired, and Rex Dexter's punishment was to move to the evening slot."

"Do we have a name for the other DJ?"

"Alfie Pattison."

"And does Alfie Pattison have an alibi? It sounds like he had a motive."

"He did. He was on air at the time, at another commercial station, in Nottingham."

"Ah." Still, I wouldn't rule him out yet. His Nottingham show could have been pre-recorded, especially if it was a smaller station. I kept that thought to myself for the moment.

"Were there any other suspects?" I asked.

Nick nodded.

"A fair few. He had some property investments with a business partner, but when interest rates spiked and recession hit in the early eighties, they lost a fortune, and it all ended acrimoniously."

"Not good."

"He was highly paid, so he coped better than his business partner."

"So the partner, was he a suspect as well?"

"She was. It was a woman, Sophie Harper. But she had a watertight alibi too."

There was no surprise there, but I made a mental note to look into it.

"Any other debts apart from the property ones?"

"No, no gambling or anything like that as far as we could tell," said Nick.

"And the other contenders?"

"He'd fallen out with the press – one journalist in particular. That started with a profile piece when the station launched, but some comment questioning the sincerity of his charity work offended him, so he took them to task on air. There were also rumours he was asking for backhanders from record pluggers, which in itself was nothing out of the ordinary, but he fell out with some of those and refused to play the bands they represented."

"Wow," I said. "I had no idea. I remember him bouncing around on children's TV, as though he didn't have a care in the world. He was quite the wheeler-dealer."

"There was more," Emily added. "He was going through a particularly bitter divorce, which was his own fault as he was fairly notorious for putting it about. He had a new semi-permanent girlfriend, but her previous partner was far from happy about it."

"I'll add 'charmer' to that, then." I hoped she realised I was being ironic. "Any others?"

"Not that we focused on," said Nick, taking over. "But all of the ones we've mentioned were categorically ruled out. There was always the possibility that it was a random killing, perhaps a mugging, or a case of mistaken identity. Or someone else altogether that never crossed our radar. But none of the evidence was ever conclusive."

"So it could have been Eddie Whitfield?"

"Possibly, but like Joe said, there's nothing to link them, and it wasn't Eddie's MO. I worked the case, and never once heard his name in any of the briefings."

I could see why the case had gone unsolved for the last eight years. Nothing was immediately jumping out at me, and obviously all of the suspects would have been interviewed, all of the alibis checked.

"Was a mugging likely?" I asked.

"No," said Nick. "Again, it was a very clean hit. It was a single knife wound."

"And did you recover the knife?"

"It was left in him."

Ouch.

"What about forensic evidence?"

"Minimal," said Emily. "There was the knife itself, but there weren't any prints. It was a fairly common kitchen knife, for sale all over the country. It had been a dry day, but by the time the body was found there'd been a downpour."

"And the car park was outside?"

She nodded.

"No security guard or CCTV?"

"There was a security man on the gate but he said he hadn't noticed anything," said Nick. "I interviewed him myself. There again, all he seemed to do was read fishing magazines in his little hut, and occasionally open the barrier when anyone beeped at him. And no, no CCTV."

I was fighting the urge to have a cigarette, partly to give myself something to focus on rather than an increasingly bleak conundrum, and partly because it was a long time since I'd had one. I resisted for the sake of the others. Emily, particularly, didn't look the type.

"Just a thought," I said instead, "there's no way Rex Dexter could have been involved in Eddie's security vault heist? I know that sounds ridiculous but strange things happen."

"No," said Emily. "Like Joe said, we had an undercover detective in the gang so we knew everyone who was involved."

I sat back, took a deep breath and sighed. Then reached for my tea, but to my dismay, realised I'd already finished it.

"One more thing," I said. "The two events happened quite close to each other, so presumably the investigations were running simultaneously. Was there any crossover? Anyone who worked on both cases?"

Nick shook his head.

"They were different ops. Dexter was a murder enquiry. Whitfield was caught before it ever got that far. It was all undercover."

I realised I was counting the number of grains in the wood of the table, but forced myself to stop.

"There is one obvious question," I said after a moment. "One big unknown."

"Which is?" asked Nick.

"How on earth you expect me to be of any assistance. I imagine the police spent millions of pounds on the original investigation, with huge resources in terms of manpower. I'm just me. I'm only here for a week, maximum. I don't want to put myself down or anything, but I must admit, I'm not optimistic."

Emily started to laugh.

"We had exactly the same conversation with Joe," she said. "But that's when he told us all about you. He thinks you'll bring a fresh perspective."

"And the whole point is that we have to be incredibly subtle about this," added Nick. "Apparently you're good at disappearing when you need to."

I didn't know if he was taking the piss or paying me a compliment, but it sounded a bit snide. Joe had offered me an opportunity to prove myself, to justify my liberty. But the warning klaxon was sounding loud inside my head.

"Can you give me a minute?" I asked.

They both nodded. I headed to the door. I needed a moment on my own outside. The lure of a Silk Cut was overwhelming. And it was either that or run.

Chapter 8

THERE was a fresh pot of tea when I returned, sucking on a mint, in the vague hope they wouldn't realise what I'd just been doing. Not that it really mattered whether they approved or not. I got the impression that Nick especially had already made his mind up about me.

"Initial thoughts?" he asked with a frown when I'd retaken my seat.

I weighed up my options, then decided on positivity.

"The thing that's changed is Eddie Whitfield's confession," I said. "Either he's telling the truth, which I agree is unlikely, or he's confessed for a reason. If we can find out what that is, we'll be getting somewhere."

Their expressions were expectant, but neither spoke. Presumably they'd already thought of that.

"Let's look at the possibilities," I continued, feeling the urge to start writing on a non-existent flipchart. As if reading my mind, Emily passed me a notepad and a pen.

"First of all, three possible motives for his confession, off the top of my head," I said. "To be mischievous. To protect someone. Because he did it."

"We're working on the basis that we can rule out the third," said Nick.

"Of course. So, why would he be mischievous? Does he strike you as the sort of person who'd want to cause trouble?"

"He does. But even so, that would be a weird way of attempting to do it. I can't see any possible benefit. If anything, it helps the police because it clears up an unsolved murder."

"Even though there's potentially a miscarriage of justice?"

Nick nodded. "The killer's still out there, but everyone seems more concerned with a positive headline."

I understood his frustration. Maybe I'd misjudged him. He genuinely seemed bothered by the situation, although it still felt like he resented me.

"So, that leaves the third option. Is he protecting someone? He takes the fall so the case gets closed and the real killer can sleep easily at night."

"Possibly," said Emily.

It was my turn to nod.

"We'll keep that one open, then," I said. "Other options: has he been paid by someone? Is he repaying a debt? And the most pertinent question of all: why now? Is it genuinely because he wants a clear conscience or because he's got nothing left to lose?"

"We can discount the clear conscience thing, if we've rejected the possibility of him being the killer," said Nick. "And as for nothing left to lose, he's going to die at any minute."

"Exactly," I said. "But he could have released the video six months ago, as soon as he recorded it. The logical reason to wait till now is that he's in no fit state to be questioned about it."

"Which makes us think he knows it wouldn't withstand scrutiny," said Emily, echoing my thoughts entirely.

Another issue was nagging at me, but I wasn't sure it was wise to voice it.

"You look like you want to say something," said Emily. She

might have only been young, but I could see that she was going to be a very successful detective. I fought the urge to smile.

"Why?" I said.

"Why what?" said Nick.

"Why are the police so keen to take this at face value? Why the rush to have the press conference? Is it really just for a positive headline?"

"We've been getting a lot of stick over the Stephen Lawrence case," he said. "From certain perspectives, some good news would be extremely welcome."

I'd read about Stephen Lawrence in English newspapers while I was in Germany. He was a black teenager who had been murdered at a bus stop in April, in a racially motivated attack, but the charges had been dropped due to lack of evidence, and the suspects freed. It had all the makings of a national scandal, raising issues about racism within the heart of the Met.

"Really, though? You really think they'd use this to brush the Lawrence case under the carpet? That's immensely disappointing if so."

Nick opened his hands as if to suggest it was entirely likely. Emily appeared agitated. It was my turn to suggest that *she* wanted to say something.

"Personally, I'm not comfortable with the headline theory," she said, at last. "It suits somebody to stop investigating."

"It certainly suits the killer," I said.

She nodded. She was good. I could see where this was heading.

"Which implies an almighty cover-up," I said, my voice softening.

"Maybe," she said.

It was beginning to make sense. Joe knew that I couldn't abide corruption, especially in the police. I'd investigated a Detective Chief Inspector called Graham March for the newspaper, and handed Joe my evidence of all his wrongdoings before departing for criminal pastures new.

If Joe suspected a conspiracy now, it was no wonder this meeting was so top secret.

And no wonder he knew I wouldn't be able to resist it. It was everything I'd lived for – until my moment of madness.

Nick announced that he had to leave and get back to work. It was our cue to end the meeting. They both gave me their numbers on business cards, and I told them mine. At least the one that Joe knew about. They each wrote them in their notebooks, which was unsettling in a brief-glimpse-into-being-questioned kind of a way.

As we were leaving the office, Emily pulled me aside. Once we'd watched Nick reach reception, she started to speak.

"Don't worry about him," she said, nodding at his retreating back. "He might seem like he doesn't like you, but he's good."

"It's okay. I'm used to people not liking me."

"Really?" She sounded surprised. "Well, if it means anything, I think you're great. I have to be a bit careful, because I can't exactly tell people you're a role model, but honestly, you fascinate me." She blushed as she said it. I was beginning to think she had a little crush, which was flattering, unexpected, and definitely needed to be discouraged. "It's true what we said. We are busy, but I will do everything I can to help you. It'd be a privilege to work alongside you, and see how you approach things."

Thankfully there was nobody else around to overhear us.

"Emily, that's lovely for you to say, and I do appreciate the help. But really, I'm going to be a disappointment if you think I'm something special. I was an okay journalist, but I'm not a detective. I'll do my best, and I would love to get to know you, too. But I suspect I'll learn as much from you as the other way round."

"Oh, shhh. I'm new. I've not even been a detective a year yet. What are your plans now?"

I didn't really have a plan, I told her, other than to return to my hotel and start reading the evidence.

"Okay. I wasn't involved in the original case, so I could do with reading it all too. Shall I come to your hotel this evening and see what we make of it together? Two pairs of fresh eyes have got to be better than one."

"Good plan." Was it a good plan? I gave her the benefit of the doubt. "What time do you finish?"

"Who knows? I've got a meeting now, but the afternoon depends on what develops on the case. I'd hope to be with you by six, though. Maybe half-past."

"Perfect."

We shook hands at the front entrance before setting off in opposite directions. I liked Emily, but she had a certain naivety that worried me. Still, her enthusiasm was endearing, if that's all it was.

I headed back to my hotel. It was too early for lunch, and there was an awful lot of reading to do. It was strange to be back in London, on my own. A police car went shooting past, its siren blaring. My initial instinct was to dive for cover, but I had to trust Joe. As far as he'd told me, the only three people who knew I was in the city were himself, Nick and Emily. Assuming I could trust them, I had nothing to fear.

Who was I trying to kid? I knew from experience that when you feel safest, that's the most dangerous time of all.

Chapter 9

EMILY saw Nick waiting outside a coffee shop, a block away.

"Do you have to be so unfriendly?" she asked, as soon as she was within earshot.

"Me?"

"Yes, you. I know you don't approve of her, but she's here to help."

Nick snorted.

"Come on," he said. "Let's get back. We're both late."

She fell into step alongside him, but he reached out his hand to hail a passing black cab. Once they were safely in the back, she tried again.

"What is your problem?"

"I don't have a problem."

"I'll put it another way, then. What are you so worried about?"

Nick turned to face her.

"I don't have a problem, and I'm not worried, okay?"

"So what's the matter?"

"Jesus."

Emily moved as far away as the bench seat would allow, and gave her attention to the window. If he was going to be like that, she'd ignore him. Eventually Nick broke the silence.

"I just don't like the thought that we're relying on someone like that. Never mind the risk of the thing. I know Joe speaks very highly of her, but I find it hard to look past what she's done and what we should be doing about it, if we valued our careers. Okay?"

"So it's an ego thing?"

"What?"

She had to choose her words carefully, aware she could be overheard by the driver.

"You couldn't get a result. And you're worried that some woman who's not even in the job will come along and do it for you?"

"For fuck's sake. That's got nothing to do with it. In case you've forgotten, it's our duty to stop people like that. Not to bloody humour them."

"I haven't forgotten, but I trust Joe's judgement. If he's prepared to give her the benefit of the doubt, then I think we should too."

"Which is exactly what I am doing, *Constable*. But it doesn't mean I like it."

Emily returned to the window. Arguing would be futile. After a few minutes, the cab pulled up outside their station. But as she emerged onto the pavement, she let out an internal groan.

"Hello, something you're not telling me?" said a man she really hadn't wanted to catch her. She knew what it probably looked like.

"Nothing sordid, before you start," she said, with a grin. "Jonathan, this is DS Nick Brooks. Nick, this is DS Jonathan Hubbard. Although you probably already know each other."

"Not had the pleasure," said Jonathan, extending his hand.

Then he turned back to Emily. "Come on, we're late for a briefing."

She followed him inside. It was time to get back to the day job. She'd worry about everything else later.

———

Nick hadn't even made to it to his desk before a colleague stopped him.

"Where the hell have you been?" asked DS Alan Beattie. Alan was a good friend. It was said more out of concern than any sense of chastisement. "The boss wants you."

"God."

"Chin up, mate."

"Can I at least take my coat off? It's not even 10 o'clock."

Alan raised an eyebrow, looking past Nick in the direction of DCI Dougie Compton's office.

Nick turned. He knew he was in trouble.

"Good afternoon, Sergeant," his boss bellowed across the room. "What the bloody hell time do you call this? A word, please, if it's not too much of an inconvenience to your overactive social life."

"Wish me luck," said Nick, under his breath, before heading to his DCI's office. Once in, he closed the door behind him. He didn't want his colleagues to hear the inevitable dressing-down, even though it was hardly a novelty for any of them.

"I've been calling you," snarled Dougie. "Where the hell have you been? And what bit of you being duty bound to answer my calls, the second I make them, do I need to reiterate the most? The fact that I'm your superior officer, or the fact that I'm running a murder investigation and it might just be the case that I need some information from you in order to find the fucker who did it?"

"Sorry, sir, I was out, chasing up a lead," said Nick.

"What lead? And don't even think about sitting down."

"It was a waste of time. An old guy phoned in, thought he saw something, but it was nothing. I would have sent someone else but it was on the way in."

"Did you take a statement?"

"There was nothing to take."

"Fuck's sake. That's even worse. And Joe Leyland. What did he want with you?"

That was unsettling.

"Nothing, sir," said Nick.

"That's obviously shite. I've seen the pair of you chatting on the stairs like you're the best of buddies."

"I know him, yes. He's a senior officer. If he asks me what I'm up to, it's only polite to stop and have a conversation. I wouldn't tell him anything confidential."

"Do you think I'm fucking stupid, son?"

Nick sighed. It was pointless protesting. It would be someone else's turn within the hour.

"I'm sorry I missed your calls," he said instead. "I genuinely didn't hear the phone, but if there's something urgent I'm here now."

Dougie's eyes narrowed, his glare hardening.

"You don't get it do you? Luckily for your job prospects, I didn't actually phone you. But the point is, I might have done. And in future, if you want to fuck about, you do it in your own time. Understood?"

"Yes, sir." Nick had to stop himself lip-syncing the next bit. He knew exactly what was coming.

"Listen son, I can be good for your career or I can be your worst nightmare. Your choice. What's it to be? Now piss off and get back to work."

Nick nodded, then turned to leave. He could see a pile of new paperwork on his desk, but there were other equally pressing concerns. And time was of the essence.

Chapter 10

BY the time I reached my room, my head was full of questions. I understood Joe's involvement but why had he selected Emily and Nick? What made them special? Why did he trust them? What hold did he have over them? Or they over him?

But more to the point: how on earth was I supposed to investigate police corruption without speaking to the police? It was the sort of story I'd have loved as a journalist, but now? On some days I'm extremely annoyed with myself for falling off the rails in a moment of greed. On all of the others, I'm livid.

I opened the envelope and flicked through the contents. There were witness statements, photographs, technical-looking documents, even a couple of newspaper clippings. Someone had been busy at the photocopier.

Aware of time pressures, I made myself comfortable on the bed, then went back to the start, my notepad poised for anything that merited further investigation.

Thankfully, there was a summary of the key members of the police team, presented like a cast list in a TV drama. There were twenty-six of them: one Detective Chief Inspector as the senior investigating officer, two Detective Inspectors, four Detective Sergeants, eighteen Detective Constables and one uniformed Police Constable – all supported by four civilian members of staff. In a separate section there were details of the pathologist, the coroner, and several others who had had an input in one form or another.

Any one of them could have deliberately sabotaged the investigation. I started to make a list of the main team members:

Senior Investigating Officer: DCI Brian Dalton.
Detective Inspectors: DI Dougie Compton, DI Graham March.

I stopped there. Case solved. Graham March. My nemesis. The most loathsome, corrupt, hideous, sexist, homophobic mess of a man, and yet he plagued me at every turn. For a time, he'd been suspended thanks to the evidence I'd uncovered in my final investigation at the newspaper. And yet he'd resurfaced in Germany, protesting his innocence, and somehow managed to befriend a gangster from Frankfurt who – bizarrely – I found myself owing a favour to. And the favour he'd requested was that I babysit Graham at some unspecified future juncture, keeping him out of mischief so he could execute some as-yet-unspecified plan. Quite possibly with the emphasis on execute. And now here we all were, with Graham safely back on the Force as a DCI, and me looking into a dodgy eight-year-old murder case that had his name all over it. I wasn't sure who was least happy about the situation: me for having to consider being nice to the bent bastard, or Graham who appeared to despise me in equal measure by return.

Was that the real reason Joe had asked me to help? Because he knew I was already wise to Graham's way of working? Was it merely a case of finding the evidence that proved his guilt, so there'd be ever more on his charge sheet come the day of the disciplinary?

Possibly, but there was a problem. This was a case from 1985. My investigation into Graham had uncovered all sorts of corruption, but it had all been since he'd been promoted to DCI in 1991. What if it *wasn't* Graham? I couldn't allow my contempt for the man blind me to the possibility that this one was actually the work of someone else.

I continued to make a list.

Detective Sergeants: DS Trevor Covington, DS Neil Fearon, DS Kenny Mason, DS Alex Ward.

No women. No ethnic minorities. Welcome to 1985.

I stopped again. Was it wise to prioritise the most senior members? I noted Nick's name on the list of DCs, but with eighteen of those to choose from, I was in a world of trouble if I had to consider them all. Rationally, the most senior people were most likely to be targeted for a cover-up by outside parties, and would have the best opportunity to hide evidence. If I started looking at the DCs, I'd also have to look at the extended team. That could take weeks, and it was time I simply didn't have.

I left the list there, and started to read the report in detail. I didn't need to write down all of the things that were stacked against me.

It was immediately clear that I'd only been given the briefest of snapshots, and that the full investigation would have comprised many thousands, perhaps tens of thousands of documents. In the event that the team had failed to spot the significance of something, it would almost certainly be a tiny detail, buried deep within a box file, somewhere in a dark corner of the New Scotland Yard archives. But I didn't have access to the archives. I had a carefully curated summary. Who had prepared it? Joe? Emily? Nick? Or someone involved in the cover-up, which guaranteed that my reading would be frustratingly pointless?

Nevertheless, it was all I had to work on. The more I read, the more it became clear that Joe had taken a huge risk in passing me the information. Some of it was highly classified, and would almost certainly be career-ending if the wrong person discovered it had been shown to a member of the public, let alone me. I had to repay that level of trust by treating it with the utmost discretion and care.

The original investigation had been predictably thorough. After background information about the victim, his career, relationships and business associates, the documentary timeline started with a transcript of the initial 999 call, made by a sound engineer, Tim Atkinson, as he left work for the evening. He'd called from the radio station reception and sounded as shocked and horrified as any normal person would be.

Was he the killer? Possibly. But the police didn't think so. He'd been on shift, and several colleagues provided an alibi for him at the pathologist's estimated time of death.

The lack of forensic evidence and absence of eyewitnesses were both serious problems. The only prints on the knife were Rex Dexter's own – presumably from where he'd grabbed it in an attempt to remove it, prior to losing consciousness. Could it have been suicide? Unlikely. The police had found no evidence of a motive, and it would have been a highly unusual method if so.

There were statements from Rex Dexter's colleagues at Sound Of London FM, along with other people who had been close to the area at around the same time. There were dozens of interview transcripts, but nobody had seen anything. Nobody knew of any specific threats.

The police were struck by the brutal efficiency of the killing. It was a single knife wound to the left side of the chest that had penetrated his heart, delivered with almost clinical precision. Had the killer been lucky, or was he – or she – an expert? The day had been warm and Rex Dexter hadn't been wearing a jacket. That made the killer's job easier, but was it merely good fortune – if that's the word – or all part of his or her plan? How much of it was premeditated? How much was spontaneous? Without a chief suspect and clear motive to hang the investigation around, it was impossible to know.

Curiously, the angle of the blade suggested the assailant was left-handed. Rex was five foot ten. The knife had entered below the ribs, pointing upwards. I tried to replicate the knife action on myself with a pen, to see if it gave any clue to the height of the attacker, but achieved little more than a blue ink spot on the front of my shirt. It was possible the killer had been crouching slightly, or might have been slightly shorter than Rex, but a lot depended on arm length and how far apart they were standing.

That said, unlike a gunshot, by definition, killing with a knife means standing no more than an arm's length away. Yet there were no signs of a struggle. No obvious attempt at self-defence. Who could jump out, take someone by surprise, and then stab them with laser accuracy, all before the victim had time to react? That implied it was someone he knew, or at least someone he didn't perceive to be a threat.

Or, possibly, a highly skilled hitman. But who would have organised that and why? And would a professional assassin really use a common kitchen knife rather than a gun fitted with a noise suppressor?

The suspects that Nick told me about had been questioned, and in some cases put under surveillance. But as he said, they all had alibis. I made a note of them all anyway:

Alfie Pattison, the rival DJ who lost his job after an on-air spat – apparently broadcasting live in Nottingham, which was about 130 miles away.

Sophie Harper, the former business partner who lost a fortune when their property investments collapsed.

Gemma Dexter, his estranged wife, with whom he was undergoing an acrimonious divorce.

Federico Sanchez, the jealous boyfriend of the woman he'd been most recently dating. The woman herself, Carly Holmes.

Christopher Bell, the journalist who had been ridiculed on air after Rex Dexter took exception to his charity comments.

All of them had been categorically ruled out. I still wanted to double-check on Alfie Pattison, though, just on the merest off-chance that his supposedly live radio show had been pre-recorded.

Had Rex upset anyone else? Once he'd been the kind of DJ who just played records, but in his later years he'd started to speak out, becoming increasingly opinionated and cantankerous.

Could it have been mistaken identity? The longer the investigation went on, the more the police had begun to consider the possibility of a stalker, another unknown lover, or an obsessive fan. But there was no evidence to support any of the theories, so that's how they remained: random suggestions of possible explanations, none of which were impossible, but equally, none of which had any obvious merit. Eventually, as the months passed, activity wound down, and although the case had remained open, there had been no new developments in the last five years. Until now.

By the time I'd finished the first read-through, it was nearly 6pm. Having skipped lunch I was feeling increasingly hungry, but decided to wait until Emily arrived to see if she fancied getting something together. I just about had time to freshen up before there was a knock at the door.

"Coming," I shouted, in the final throes of making sure I looked presentable. A moment later, I opened the door, and very nearly died.

Chapter 11

IT was the shock that nearly killed me. It was definitely Emily, but she looked so different. The navy trouser suit had been replaced by black jeans and a black leather jacket. Her hair was down, and looked hugely more flattering. She was wearing make-up that accentuated her green eyes, no longer hidden behind the tortoiseshell glasses. Though whether she'd opted for contacts or decided I'd look better blurry wasn't immediately obvious.

"Wow," I said, before I could stop myself. "You look amazing."

"Thank you. And likewise."

I doubted that. I was wearing the same outfit I'd been in all day, just now with an ink dot on the front of the increasingly crumpled white shirt. I gestured for her to come in, then offered to take her jacket. Underneath, she was wearing a dark lilac mohair jumper that looked deliciously soft and cosy. I hung the jacket on the back of the door while she took the armchair at the side of the desk.

"I didn't mention it earlier, but I love your ring," she said. "It must have cost a fortune." Immediately she blushed. "Sorry, that was rude. I've got no right to comment on the price."

"That's okay, but thank you." I nearly added that crime pays, but thought better of it. The ring had been expensive, but it was worth every penny. It had a bigger Ceylon sapphire and better quality diamonds than the one I'd lost in my final days of being a journalist, but the new version was nevertheless both a reward and a reminder to stay humble. A symbolic link to my past.

"How's it going?" she asked, nodding to the sheets of paper that were spread across the bed.

"If you want the honest answer, it's slow," I said, with a frown, taking the desk chair. "I've gone through everything once, but nothing immediately jumps out at me. It all looks very thorough."

"We'll go through it again together, and see if that makes a difference."

Immediately I fancied a cigarette, because it'd been ages since the last one, but again I was conscious that she might not approve. I don't know why that bothered me. Perhaps it was because I felt an immediate sense of respect, and didn't want to appear antisocial.

"I don't mind if you smoke," she said, with alarming clairvoyance.

"Really? Do you want one?"

She shook her head.

"No, but seriously, I work in an office with a bunch of detectives. If anything it'd make me feel more at home." She grinned. "Feel free, honestly."

I still felt bad, but when she pushed the ashtray in my direction, I decided one wouldn't do any harm. In one sense, at least.

Emily accepted my suggestion of ordering dinner on room service, so we opted for a couple of pizzas, together with a bottle of wine. While we waited for them to arrive, I gathered the documents together and started to go through them, pointing out the things I'd written in my notepad.

She'd heard about Graham March, which came as no surprise, but I added details that were not yet in the public domain. Then I mentioned the possibility of Alfie Pattison's radio show being recorded, and my theory about the height of the attacker.

When the food arrived, however, it was time to find out more about my guest.

"How did you become a detective?" I asked, as we started to tuck in.

"My dad was one, back in the old days," she said. "So I'm a chip off the old block, I suppose."

"Wow. He must be very proud of you."

"I don't know about that really. I was always closer to my mum, and when they got divorced I lived with her. I never had much to do with my dad."

"Oh, sorry to hear that."

She shrugged and wrinkled her nose. It was quite fetching.

"I say divorced. They were never actually married but they were together a long time so it was kind of similar. Anyway, enough about him."

I took a sip of the wine, which was better than I'd expected. It was time to dispel the crush theory.

"Are you married? Or do you have a boyfriend?"

She laughed.

"In my job? God, nobody would have me."

"I find that hard to believe."

There was a hint of a blush again.

"Well, there is someone, kind of."

"Ooh, exciting. Tell me more."

This time the laugh was more of a giggle.

"Just somebody at work. A DS. But it's more of a good friendship with the occasional benefits. I'm aware that I haven't exactly cast the net far and wide, but we get on and we both understand what it's like."

"You mean in terms of the hours?"

"The hours, the stress of it sometimes. But it's like I said, I've not even been doing this long. Give it a few more years and I'll be as bitter and cynical as the rest of them."

You want to try being a journalist, I thought, but didn't say it out loud.

"So do you live on your own? Or still with your mum?"

"On my own. I rent a flat in Camberwell."

That explained the change of outfit. Camberwell was also in south London, not far from Dulwich, so she'd have had the chance to go home and get changed before coming out to see me.

"Does that bother you?" I continued. "When you get home and you're on your own, late at night, especially after some of the things you've seen during the day."

She shrugged again.

"You get used to it," she said. "I like to think I'm reasonably tough. Ask me again in a year or two and it might be different, but it's okay for now. Anyway, you must have been the same when you lived here. Going home at night, looking over your shoulder."

"Sort of." I tried to think back. There'd been the odd dicey moment, but I'd never felt seriously in danger. In any case I lived in an apartment block in the Docklands with private parking and a concierge, so there was always someone around. "I suppose I wasn't continually exposed to the dark side, as such, though. I mainly investigated corrupt politicians and businesses."

"And police?"

"Well, Graham, but he was a special case. I probably shouldn't admit this but I secretly enjoy the animosity."

She raised her glass and chinked mine.

"Cheers to the pervy old rascal," she said, which cracked me up. "But you were kind of a detective, though, in your own way?"

"Not really. Real police have to follow the rules because you've got to stick to the Police and Criminal Evidence Act so it all stands up in court. Newspaper editors want a story but all they want to know is that you've got enough proof so they don't get sued. It's not anywhere near as stringent, and you can be a bit more creative with how you get there."

"I suppose."

We both took a sip of the wine. It wouldn't be long before we needed a refill.

"So where do you live now?" she asked.

Was she checking me out? No, it sounded genuine, and a friendly enquiry.

"I can't really tell you that," I said. "Anyway, it varies. I've been in Germany for a while but I'm going to be moving on soon, I think. In fact I was supposed be somewhere else today until Joe called me."

"Presumably you don't want to talk about what you did to end up in trouble, either?"

"Mmmm." I thought for a moment. "Probably best not to. You must have heard the basics, and I guarantee that if I'm ever forced to give my side of the story, there may be a few surprises when you hear it from my perspective. But without going into the details, I know I did wrong. There were reasons why certain things happened and I regret those, but it's not really something I even like to think about any more. It's definitely not something I'm proud of."

"And you can't talk about what you do now?"

"No." It was time to nip this one in the proverbial bud.

"I understand," she said. "It's just the way Joe explained it – you're like some special secret agent, mixed with an assassin."

"Haha, definitely not the assassin."

She looked a bit guilty.

"Sorry, I shouldn't ask you any more. But I think it's fascinating, off the record, obviously."

It was definitely time to change the subject.

"What is it with you and numbers?"

"I don't know. I just like numbers. They represent an eternal truth. Two plus two equals four. There's no argument. Nobody saying no comment. No lawyers trying to disprove it."

"That's a fair point."

"Funnily enough, I didn't like maths at school. All the sines, cosines, logarithms, differentiation and integration. I couldn't see the point of it. But give me real world numbers and they actually mean something."

"That must help in the job. Seeing patterns and analysing things."

"I suppose so. But–" she leaned forward and dropped her voice "–between you and me, I do it to show off more than anything. I think it winds people up, so it makes me laugh."

I couldn't help but chuckle.

"That's so mischievous."

"I know. Isn't it? It's terrible really, but it's funny. It seems to really annoy some of them and that makes me do it all the more, so now it's become second nature."

And so the conversation continued, long after the food was finished. She accepted a second glass of wine, after announcing that she'd get a taxi home, then we went off at all sorts of tangents: her favourite music, films, books; what she liked to get up to in her spare time; even her childhood crush on most of Spandau Ballet, but not the one with the saxophone. She announced that she'd definitely be able to beat me in an arm wrestle, but I quickly created a space on the desk and emphatically disproved that one. I didn't mention that I'd done very little for the last eight months other than extensive gym and fitness training. It was perhaps a bit unfair, but I had a reputation to uphold.

Work was almost forgotten. It was only when she looked at her watch and was shocked to notice it was nearly 11pm that we both realised how time had got away with us. But it had been such a wonderful evening that I didn't really mind, and in truth, I doubted there was much she could add anyway. I had a call booked with Joe the following morning, and lots more reading to do in preparation, but I was confident that I wouldn't miss anything major.

Emily left shortly after, though this time with a hug rather than a handshake, and she reiterated the offer to help if there was anything I needed her to look into, albeit with a reminder that her time was likely to be tight.

After that, I had another cigarette, finished the wine and got ready for bed, then continued reading until the early hours. I still couldn't spot any holes in the investigation, and yet, by definition, something had been missed. It must have been. Was it accidental, or deliberate neglect? Again, I only had the information I'd been given. If there were leads that hadn't been followed, they'd either been deliberately omitted from my summary or viewed as insignificant and therefore lost somewhere deep within the archives.

Somebody knew something. But as Joe had said, there wasn't a single mention of Eddie Whitfield, or – as far as I could tell – anyone connected to him. It was a mystery. It was hopeless. It was intensely frustrating.

By 4am I decided there was nothing more to be gained. I was going to look like a sleep-deprived zombie in the morning. I set an alarm, glad that Joe was only phoning me at 7am, rather than turning up in person. How little I knew.

Chapter 12

Wednesday, October 27th, 1993

I DECIDED to brave the hotel restaurant before having a shower and speaking to Joe. I couldn't face breakfast – partly due to the effects of the wine and partly due to tiredness – but coffee was definitely on the agenda. I wasn't sure how I was going to break it to him that I wasn't optimistic. So at 6.45am, after less than three hours' sleep, I headed downstairs.

Unfortunately, he was at a table, waiting for me. I looked a disaster, with no make-up, my hair a mess, and no doubt big black circles under my eyes. I nearly ran back upstairs, hoping he hadn't seen me, but he beckoned me over to join him.

"You look tired," he said.

"I am tired. I think I'm actually sleepwalking at the moment."

"Big night?"

"Not so much a big night as a late night. I only went to bed less than three hours ago. I've been reading through the documents."

"And?"

He could tell from my expression that it wasn't good news.

"It's difficult," I said.

"In what way?"

"I suppose I'm just conflicted." He waited for me to elaborate, but I paused to order coffee. First things first.

"I've been through everything three times," I continued. "And it's frustrating. Really frustrating."

"In what way?"

Maybe it was the lack of sleep. Maybe it was the fact that I felt I was letting him down. Or maybe it was a combination of everything I'd been through over the last year – but suddenly I had an overwhelming urge to cry. I managed to fight it, but still could feel my eyes water.

"Are you okay?" he asked, his voice softening, as he reached out to squeeze my hand.

I nodded, not trusting myself to speak. It wasn't just this case. That was just the latest manifestation.

"Are you sure?" he continued. Then, to his credit, he gave me a moment to compose myself. I dabbed my eyes with a napkin before looking up at him, aware that if I was a mess before, I'd just made it ten times worse.

"I'm tired, Joe. That's all," I said.

He smiled in a fatherly fashion.

"Tell me," he said. "What's the matter?"

I didn't want to say anything. But before I could stop myself, it all came tumbling out.

"It gets me down. All of it. Not this, specifically, but my whole situation. And I know what you're going to say: I've only got myself to blame, and you're absolutely right, and I've got to live with it, and you're right, and I am trying to do that. I've got a new job, of sorts, and in many ways it's brilliant and exciting, and a chance to redeem myself, and I get all of that as well, but it's not the point, really." I paused, looking around. "It's like this. Having to meet in secret. Watching out who's behind me all the time. I know I can't undo the things I did, but sometimes I think I should just hand myself in, take the pain, and be done with it."

He squeezed my hand again. I looked down, trying to hide my emotions before I made the situation even worse.

"Even though you'd be locked up for years?" he said, his voice barely audible, even though there was nobody near who could overhear.

"That's obviously the downside. But maybe I deserve it."

"You definitely deserve it."

I nearly smiled, but it would have been a hollow one.

"You're not supposed to agree with me," I said. "I genuinely think I can be more use to society not being locked up. I'm fundamentally a good person. I really believe that."

"There are several people who would argue otherwise. If they weren't dead."

"Yes, but most of them were really bad."

"*Most* of them?"

That was a bit naive of me.

"All of them," I continued. "So in the greater scheme of things, I think I'm better repaying my debt to society if I'm left to do it in my own way."

"That's not really how justice works."

"I know, but I'm not dangerous."

"You really are."

"Only to bad people. But equally, part of me wants to say to you: take me in, charge me with whatever, and let's hope the judge is lenient. And at least then I'd be able to come out a few years later and meet you for coffee without feeling paranoid."

"Even if you had a lenient judge, I suspect I'd be dead by then."

He really wasn't helping.

"Don't say that. I'd be looking at what? A few years, halved for good behaviour. I could be out before you even retire."

"And equally you could be looking at life and then throwing away the key."

I sighed, a deep, depressed sigh.

"Let's agree this conversation didn't happen," I said.

"We can pretend, but for what it's worth it's painful for me too. I was very fond of the old Clare. I am *so* pissed off with you."

"I know."

"And I'm always going to be pissed off with you, because you had something brilliant and you threw it away."

"I know that as well."

"But I don't judge you for it. As long as you don't ever do it again. If you do, then just so you know, I'm washing my hands of you. And that would nearly kill me, but I'm giving you a chance here. The benefit of the doubt. It's a once-only opportunity because I believe you when you say you regret it, even though I know that's probably stupid of me. Let me down again, though, and there's no going back."

His words were affecting me in ways I couldn't articulate, so I just said "I know" again, and tried to move on. Thankfully the coffee had arrived. I took a sip, but it just emphasised the fact that I really needed to go back to bed for a few hours. Artificial stimulants weren't going to do it.

I mentioned that Emily had come round and that I'd gone through all the documentation in detail.

"What did you make of it all?" asked Joe.

"Do you want the honest answer?"

"Are you ever anything other than honest?"

"Very funny. Okay, in summary, the obvious candidate if we're looking at corruption is Graham March."

"I thought you'd enjoy seeing his name crop up. But I knew Graham back then. Believe it or not, he was a good copper. He only went off the rails when he got promoted to DCI."

"As far as you know."

"As far as I know. But I don't think we can just assume it's him."

I'd pretty much come to the same conclusion.

"Granted," I said. "I never like to assume anything. But if it isn't him, we're looking at a needle in a haystack, if you both forgive the cliché and allow for a very small needle, and a haystack the size of an ocean liner."

"You're saying you need longer?"

"And again, very funny. Who compiled the document?"

"That was Nick, but even the act of doing that was a risk. If he'd been caught at the photocopier I'd have had a struggle to save his career."

That was interesting. Something about Nick bothered me. He'd worked on the original case and he clearly didn't like the thought of me looking into things. Was he worried I might uncover something that made him look incompetent? I decided to keep that to myself for now.

"This must mean a lot to you then. To all three of you," I said instead.

"It does."

"But why? Just because there's the possibility of corruption? Or do you have another agenda?"

"I'd say both. I don't like mysteries. That's what got me interested in being a detective in the first place. But primarily the former. I'm not saying it's definitely a cover-up, but if it isn't, I don't understand the rush to accept Eddie Whitfield's confession."

"Quite." I paused to take a sip of the coffee. It still wasn't really helping, but it gave me something to do.

"But why involve Nick and Emily? What made you choose them to help?"

"Emily is a rising star. She's a brilliant analyst, fantastic with numbers–"

"I noticed."

"Exactly. She's worked on a couple of cases recently that came under my remit and I was extremely impressed. Originally I was just going to ask her to take a look, but then I thought of Nick. He worked on the original investigation and clearly doesn't buy the Whitfield angle either. And then I thought of you, and decided to add a bit of chaos into the mix."

That made me laugh, despite everything.

"So we go back to the starting point," I said. "Why did Eddie Whitfield confess? Who put him up to it and why? And why did he agree?"

Joe nodded.

"It's a shame we can't ask him personally. I don't suppose there's any chance of a miracle moment of lucidity?"

"He died in the night," said Joe.

Ah. This really wasn't going well. But I knew things had a habit of getting far worse.

Chapter 13

I WAS tempted to at least have a croissant to settle my stomach, but decided not to risk it. It could well have had the reverse effect.

"There are a few things I need," I said.

"I'm not getting you a gun."

"Why would I want a gun?"

"You're not a stranger to guns."

"Joe, I've said it before: I've occasionally done things in self-defence but I don't make a habit of shooting people."

I decided not to mention that I'd brought a SIG-Sauer P228 with me from Germany, just in case things got tricky.

"How many is it now?"

"How many is what now?"

"People you've shot?"

"At this precise moment? One fewer than it will be shortly, if you don't stop picking on me. Do you want to hear what it was that I actually wanted?"

"Personally, no."

"What?" I hadn't seen that coming. "Cheers for your help, then."

"Only because that's the whole point of giving you Nick and Emily. Keep me informed if you find out anything, but it's better that I keep a healthy distance."

I suppose that made sense.

"Who's most likely to be able to get things?"

"I'd say Nick. He's more senior. Emily is a brilliant analyst and razor sharp, but she won't be able to open as many doors. She's always worth a try, though, if Nick's hard to get hold of."

I was worried he'd say something like that.

"Can you at least give me some background on the original investigation team while you're here?" I said.

"I can try."

I didn't have my list with me, but I could remember the names.

"Okay. DCI Brian Dalton."

"Now retired," said Joe. "This was one of his last cases. I've not seen him in years."

"Could he have arranged a cover-up?"

"No."

"Because?"

"Brian was straight. Exemplary career, highly commended. Could have gone higher but he enjoyed being involved day-to-day. But more than that, I was with him that night."

Joe told me about the dinner they'd been to, to mark a commendation for another officer who'd solved a particularly difficult case.

"Just because he was with you that night doesn't mean he wasn't involved," I said.

"He wasn't. I'll tell you this about him, though."

"What?"

"He was absolutely devastated he didn't get a result on Dexter. I went to his retirement do, and I could see it was still rankling. Trust me, he wouldn't have been involved in a cover-up, and he definitely had an alibi for that night. You can forget about him."

I sat back, still unconvinced.

"But are you really, really sure? Isn't that the art of a good cover-up – to make it look like it's the very last thing you'd be involved in? Maybe I'm a cynic, but that'd put him at the top of the list for me."

"You're a cynic. Trust me."

"Okay, I just want to be thorough. DI Dougie Compton?"

"Now a DCI. Currently SIO on Nick's murder case."

"That's good. What's he like?"

Now it was Joe's turn to sit back and take a sip of coffee.

"He's only a little fella, but he's a hard bastard. You don't want to go anywhere near him."

"Because?"

"Because he'd lock you up without a moment's hesitation. He's a bit old school. Misses the days when you could crack heads to get a confession, and God help you if you're on his team and you get on his wrong side."

"Potentially dodgy?"

"I can't see it, despite that."

"Okay. I'll have a word with Nick, though. Graham March we know all about." There was no need to recap. Going over Graham's catalogue of sins would have taken most of the morning. "What about Trevor Covington?"

"He went on long-term sick leave and took early retirement," said Joe.

"Can I get in touch with him?"

"With difficulty. He's living in Spain."

"I've got a passport."

"I'm sure you've got several, but trust me, I know Trevor like a brother. He's not involved. He's kind of the opposite to Compton. One of the nicest guys you could ever meet. Actually, he was with us that night as well. Stick him on the Brian Dalton list, and forget about him."

I didn't like the way this was going.

"That makes me nervous," I said. "I've read Agatha Christie books. It's always the one you least expect."

Joe shook his head

"Nobody wants to get to the bottom of this more than me, and believe me, if there was even a one in a million chance Trevor Covington was involved, I'd tell you to look into him. But I can absolutely guarantee he's clean."

"Don't blame me, then. Neil Fearon?"

"Missed out on promotion to DI so left to set up his own security company. He's doing very well, as far as I can tell."

"What kind of security?"

"The personal protection kind, from bodyguards to nightclub door staff."

That sounded more like it.

"Bouncers?"

He nodded.

"Well, that's a red flag," I said. "It might be an urban myth, but they're notorious for being dodgy. Want drugs? Befriend a bouncer."

"I think that probably is an urban myth," said Joe. "He's got staff at big London clubs like Suadela."

"I'm out of touch. I've never heard of it."

"It's just off Leicester Square. The name comes from the Roman god of seductive persuasion. It's classy, you'd fit in."

I checked his expression to see if he was taking the piss, but he was doing his expert poker player impression.

"You say the kindest things, Joe. I'll check it out. Next, Kenny Mason?"

"Sadly passed away."

"Sorry to hear that. What happened?"

"I hate to say it, but it was his own fault. Went out to celebrate another case, drank too much, got behind the wheel, narrowly avoided an oncoming car and ended up wrapped round a lamppost. Actually I think it was a sign post but the result was the same."

"That's horrible."

"What can I say? Don't drink and drive. Of all people, he should have known better, but it's still a tragedy."

We were getting to the end of the list.

"Okay, and finally Alex Ward?"

"Now a DI. He's working with Emily on the missing child case. I believe he's her senior investigating officer. Decent copper, not particularly imaginative, but solid."

"Potentially corrupt?"

"No. And again, with me that night. Emily could tell you more, but I've never heard a squeak."

"What about the DCs? Any of those worth a look?"

I couldn't remember all of those, but I expected Joe was familiar with them anyway.

"Nobody jumped out at me, sorry," he said. "Some have gone now. Some have been promoted. Alan Beattie is now a DS. He's working on Nick's team with Dougie Compton at the moment, too. But no. No known troublemakers as far as I can see."

I leaned back, looked at the ceiling and let out a deep breath.

"So to recap," I said, when I returned my attention to Joe, "we've got Graham, then Dougie Compton who I can't go anywhere near, and Neil Fearon who sounds the most likely and therefore by the Agatha Christie rule is obviously innocent. I'll check him out, though. Anything I've missed?"

"Not that I can think of. It's not easy, I appreciate that. If it was, we wouldn't be where we are. And stop with the Agatha Christie thing. This is 1993, not 1923. Reality, not fiction. And it wasn't the butler in the drawing room with a mysterious poison."

"Have you ever read an Agatha Christie book?"

"In my youth."

"Well, to save you from embarrassing yourself further, the butler never does it, unless it's someone else disguised as a butler. It's rule eleven of S.S. Van Dine's *Twenty Rules for Writing Detective Stories*: 'A servant must not be chosen by the author as the culprit'."

"Thanks for clearing that up."

"You're welcome."

"Have you finished?"

"No. If you want a guilty butler you'd be better off with Mary Roberts Rinehart. Anyway, what about on the other Eddie Whitfield case, the security vault heist? Presumably if there was one of you working undercover in his gang, they'd be well versed in deception. And there's got to be a link there somewhere."

"That's more difficult."

More difficult?

"Because?" I said, trying not to show my increasing sense of futility.

"I looked into that. The undercover officer was called Jason Shelley."

"And?"

"It was an alias, and Jason Shelley no longer exists."

"So he could be anyone?"

"He could. All I know is that he was redeployed, back into normal service, if there's such a thing as normal service."

"Can you get me a picture of him?"

"Obviously not if I don't know who he is."

I wasn't sure, but he appeared to be getting irritated by me.

"You're not being very helpful, Joe," I said, in exasperation. "You're the bloody detective. I'm just the poor sod who you've tasked with an impossible challenge. Presumably there are records relating to the original Eddie Whitfield burglary case. I'm sure I could just breeze into wherever they're kept without arousing the merest hint of suspicion, and probably not be locked up immediately, but just on the off-chance, could you do it for me? If there's a picture of your man when he was Jason Shelley, that would be perfect. If not, then any other information at all. Age, height, background. Presumably he needed to provide evidence at a court case. Somebody must have seen him."

"All right, Mrs Stroppy. I'll see what I can do."

"Thank you."

Sod it.

"I'll be back in a moment," I said. It was time to get a croissant from the buffet. Kill or cure. Also, a couple of minutes away from Joe would give me time to collect my thoughts. I thought about going for the fruit salad for the sake of having something healthy, but the acid really wasn't going to help.

Joe was on the phone when I got back, but he quickly ended the call, then checked his watch. I knew my time was nearly up.

"Why are you looking at me like that?" he said, pocketing his phone.

"I'm not looking at you like anything."

"You're looking at me like you want to know who I was speaking to."

"Am I?" If I was, it was accidental. Or maybe paranoia.

"It was Nick, okay? Not that it's any of your business. I'm meeting the pair of them for a quick coffee brainstorm before work. Hence being here at seven."

I held out my hands in protest.

"Honestly, Joe, I wasn't giving you a look," I said, taking a first bite of the pastry, and wishing it wasn't so dry. "Anyway, back to the point. Anyone else on the Eddie Whitfield team?"

"The DCI was Terry Handley but he's now a Detective Chief Superintendent," he said.

"Same rank as you?"

"One above."

"Of course, sorry." My mind was a mess.

"Please do not go anywhere near him, and for God's sake if

you do, don't mention me," said Joe, before taking a final sip of his coffee.

"Why not? I'm just one person who did bad things. The chances are, in a city the size of London, he probably hasn't even heard of me."

He laughed, and quickly had to grab a napkin to stop making a coffee-flavoured mess.

"What's funny?"

"You haven't got a clue, have you?"

"Obviously not."

"Dear oh dear oh dear." It took him a moment to regain his composure. "Terry is still overseeing the investigation into you. He's got a picture of you on the wall of his office, and he's been applying for more funding to broaden the investigation because he doesn't believe that story about how you died in a helicopter crash for an instant."

"Oh." That wasn't good. I'd spent a lot of time and money arranging that particular stunt, so I could start a new life, free of the danger of being pursued. We live and learn.

"The danger to you is very, very real. The danger to me in talking to you is unprecedented in my career."

"Couldn't you just arrange some sort of immunity to prosecution? That's a thing, isn't it? Queen's evidence?"

"If you're an accomplice in a major crime. Not if you're working on your own."

"So you're saying I've got to do a bad thing as part of a gang, just so I can get off from the things I've done already?"

"No." He stood up and started to put on his jacket, then leaned down towards me and spoke in a near whisper. "I'm saying you'd better keep your nose clean, head down, and not get caught."

"But you could work on the amnesty thing, long-term?"

He ignored that.

"I'll be in touch," he said. "Just take care, please, for all our sakes."

I finished the croissant, and poured another cup of coffee, but decided not to drink it. What I really needed was at least another six hours of sleep, but that wasn't going to happen. A shower would have to deputise.

I returned to my room, opened the door, then stopped, my pulse rate suddenly quickening. Something felt different. I couldn't say what, but every instinct told me the room wasn't quite as I'd left it. Was it a scent? Perhaps an aftershave, lingering in the air? I closed the door behind me, then checked the wardrobe, the bathroom, and under the bed, but found nothing. My bags were still there. The paperwork was there. My clothes were there. Yet something didn't feel right.

Quickly, I checked where I'd hidden the SIG. That was there too, and still loaded. I kept it with me while I went to my bag of equipment, unlocked it, and quickly swept the room for bugs.

Nothing. Was I just being paranoid? Alarms were going off in my head, but I couldn't pinpoint exactly why.

After locking the door, and moving the desk in front of it, for added peace of mind, I had a final look around the room, and behind the curtains, before getting undressed and heading to the shower. The very last thing we needed was an Alfred Hitchcock moment. I made sure the gun was within reach all of the time I was in there.

Chapter 14

ONCE I was dry, I phoned Nick with about as much enthusiasm as I'd normally phone a dentist.

"Nick, it's me," I said, not wanting to give my name on the off-chance someone else had picked up his phone. "Is it a good time?"

He hesitated before replying.

"It's not a great time, but probably no worse than any other. I'm just about to meet Joe for coffee."

"Okay, I'll keep it brief. I need to discuss a few things with you. Are you free at all? Maybe lunchtime?"

"Are you suggesting meeting for lunch?"

"I wasn't but we could if you'd like to." Top marks to me for being civil and not holding a grudge.

"That's the last thing I want to do," he said, rather destroying the moment.

"Oh. Sorry."

"I can't risk being seen with you, for obvious reasons. I thought you realised that."

"Fair point." I gave him the address of an abandoned

warehouse I knew, which was adjacent to a piece of waste ground, and suggested meeting there instead, hoping that it hadn't been redeveloped in the last year or so.

"What time?" he asked.

"Whenever's good for you."

"Earlier's better. Probably 12."

"Perfect, I'll see you there. And bring a sandwich so we can at least pretend."

He ended the call without any further acknowledgement. Project Smile was going to be a bigger challenge than Rex Dexter.

I wasn't sure what to wear for a meeting with Nick, nor what I might face as the day progressed, but my options were limited, so I opted for pretty much the same as the day before, just substituting the white shirt for a pale blue one. Then I lay on the bed for a moment, trying to stop my head from spinning, desperately fighting the urge to go back to sleep. I set an alarm anyway, just in case.

The sound of my phone brought me back to consciousness. It was Emily.

"How did you get on after I left?" she asked.

"I stayed up far too late, but it was worth it," I said, checking my watch. I'd had an hour. That would have to do. "It was a fun night."

"Do you think you'll be able to work it out?"

"In truth, I think there's more chance of Dexter emerging from his coffin, apologising for looking a bit pale. But there are some avenues to explore, which is a start."

"Keep me informed and if you need anything, let me know."

"Shall do. Actually, there is one thing. Alex Ward."

"My SIO?"

"That's the one. As you know, he worked on the original Rex Dexter case. Joe thinks he's decent but I'd like to rule him out properly. Do you know anything about him?"

I heard the sound of a police siren on the far end of the line.

"Joe mentioned that this morning," said Emily, once it had passed. "I've only known Alex a few months, but he seems okay to me. I'll do some digging and let you know. Some of the others will know him far better than I do."

"Perfect, thank you." I lit my first cigarette of the morning, finally confident that I wouldn't fall asleep with it and burn the place down. "How did it go with Joe?"

"This morning? It was just a quick coffee. Nick was running late, and Joe couldn't stay long either. I think he just wanted to touch base."

I bristled at the Americanism. I liked Emily, but there was no excuse for that. I kept the thought to myself, though.

"There's one other thing, for you, while I think of it," she continued.

I waited for her to say what it was, but eventually decided it would be quicker to prompt her.

"Go on."

"It's just ... I know you're going to be super busy, but if you're at a loose end and want to meet for dinner again one night, I'd love to take you out somewhere, my treat."

"You don't worry about being seen with me?"

She laughed.

"It's more if you'd be happy to risk going out. But I'd promise to find somewhere obscure, or we could do the room service thing again. I know it's probably an imposition, and I've got to admit there's a large degree of self-interest because I think I could learn a lot from you, but if you fancy it, I'd really appreciate it."

"I'd love to, if there's time. And we could argue about who was paying the bill, before mutually agreeing that I was. Just so you know."

"We'll see about that." I could hear the smile in her voice as she ended the call.

I made my final preparations to meet Nick, with about as

much enthusiasm as I'd normally have when I'd already made a call to the dentist and was now on the way to have a filling.

———

Detective Chief Superintendent Terry Handley heard the knock at his office door, looked up, and then waved his visitor forward while he finished his phone call. She remained standing until he replaced the receiver and offered her a seat.

"So, DC North," he said. "What gives?"

Emily crossed her legs, trying to look more relaxed than she felt.

"So far, everything you thought might happen has happened," she said.

"Go on."

"I've met her. Twice now. Once yesterday morning and again last night. And I have to say, if I didn't already know what I know, I'd find it all a bit hard to believe."

"In what way?"

Emily glanced at the picture of Clare that took centre place on the DCS's office wall.

"You look at her there," she said, nodding in its direction, "and you can believe that she killed people, but maybe it's because we've been looking at that image too much, or maybe it's because we associate it with the reports of things we know she did. Yet when you actually meet her, she doesn't come across that way at all. She seems almost, I don't know, *friendly*. Like she wants to do good. Her appearance has changed. She's got dark hair now, and if it wasn't for the hazel eyes I'd have thought she was a different person."

"Hmmm." Terry steepled his hands and then leaned forward and rested his chin on them. "That's the thing, though. She's clever. She's charming when she wants to be. That's what makes her dangerous. She can turn in an instant, and when she does, she's ruthless."

"I've got no doubt about that." Emily recrossed her legs. The senior officer had a habit of making her feel nervous, even though she knew they were on the same side. "I've asked her about meeting for dinner, and she seemed up for that. She's going to let me know."

Terry sat back and nodded, contemplating the situation.

"Don't rush things," he said after a moment. "We don't want to make her suspicious by looking too enthusiastic. It's one thing to know where she is, but what you need to find out is what she's up to. What she's planning. Who she's working with. What hold she's got over Joe Leyland."

"And, of course, if she finds out anything about Rex Dexter."

"Exactly. When the moment comes, we'll bring her in. Worst case we'll leave it till Saturday, but let's see where she takes us in the interim."

Emily nodded, her expression serious.

"Is there anything else you need specifically at the moment?" she asked.

"No, just stay close. Actually, there's one thing. Did you see any indication she had a weapon?"

"Last night?" Emily shook her head. "There was a limit to how much I could look around. I wouldn't rule it out, but I certainly didn't see anything."

"Be careful. I wouldn't put it past her."

"I will."

"And if you get even the merest hint that she's seen through you, call for backup immediately. If you're worried at all, let me know and we can pull you out in a heartbeat."

"No, I'm good at the moment. So far I think she likes me."

Terry's phone rang again. It was the cue to end the meeting.

"Keep up the good work," he said, before picking up the handset. "You're doing a great job."

As he answered the call, Emily stood up, mouthed a farewell, and turned towards the door, making sure that nobody spotted her leaving.

Chapter 15

"I DIDN'T want to say this in front of Joe and Emily," I said, once Nick was in the passenger seat of my car, parked up alongside the warehouse in the middle of nowhere, "but I get the impression you don't really like me."

"I'm not paid to have opinions," he said. "I'm paid on the basis of facts."

Short of tickling the man, I didn't think I'd ever make him smile.

"That's not actually a denial, is it?"

"Look, the facts are the facts, and no offence, but I deal with criminal lowlife every day who are either in denial or think they've got a justification for their actions. So it's not a question of whether or not I like you as a person. I don't know you. You might be a laugh a minute and kind to old ladies, but I'm struggling to see beyond what you are and what you represent because those are things that I particularly struggle with."

At least he was acknowledging that I *might* be funny.

"I get that," I said. "But what can I say? I'm sorry you feel that way, and I'm truly sorry for the things I did, but I can't go back and undo them. The facts might be the facts, but the past is also the past."

"But if it's within you, it's there. I struggle to believe that you could possibly change. Not really. You know what they say about leopards."

"That they're not as good as tigers?" No, still nothing. To be fair, It wasn't one of my best. "My final word on the subject, then: thank you for giving me a chance. I would say thank you for not judging me, but it sounds like you have – so thank you for giving me the benefit of the doubt, for the moment at least. And I know that that's more than a single final word, but without Emily to count them, we'll just have to let it go. Should we move on?"

"Please."

"Okay."

I consulted my notepad.

"Joe tells me that Dougie Compton is now your SIO."

"Yes, he was a DI back then, but he's a DCI now."

"What do you know about him. Is he straight?"

"You want the truth?"

"There seems little point in anything else."

"Okay. I don't like the bloke. I'm not saying he's bent, but he's a throwback to a different era. Do I think he's corrupt? No. Anybody could be, but he's not the sort of guy you question openly if you value your career."

"But I don't have to worry about my career, so I could look into him."

"Good luck with that." He hesitated. "For the avoidance of doubt, do not go and talk to Dougie Compton."

In truth I was no further forward in working out how to do it anyway, so I returned to my list.

"Graham March I know all about," I said. "What about Neil Fearon? Joe tells me he runs a security company. Do you know what it's called or where they're based?"

"I don't know the address but the company's called No Fear

Security or No Fear Protection. Something like that. Safeguarding, I think. I could find out for you but you might be quicker calling directory enquiries. They're in London somewhere."

"Okay. Much appreciated."

"Again, you're not going to go and see him, are you?"

I sighed in exasperation.

"I might have to. It's already Wednesday. There's quite a time pressure here. I've set myself a challenge of not going home till I've found out the truth, but much as I'm enjoying your company, I'd prefer to get a move on."

"It's your funeral."

I hate it when people come out with unimaginative phrases, yet seem to think they're being clever or incisive. *Between every rock and a hard place there's an elephant in the room, singing from the same hymn sheet until the fat lady joins in. And so on and so forth.* Dear oh dear.

"Joe told me about Kenny Mason and Trevor Covington," I said. "I've asked Emily about Alex Ward. What about the other people involved in the investigation? Alan Beattie's still working with you apparently."

"Yeah. Big Al's a mate. We came through the ranks together. He's sound. Seriously, though, the more I think about this, I'm not sure what the point of you is."

"Charming."

"What? No, I mean, you can't start looking at serving detectives. They'd lock you up in a blink, especially if one of them had something to hide and thought you were a danger to them. I did say this to Joe."

"Let me worry about all that. In the meantime, I want a recording of Rex Dexter's last radio show. I'm working on the basis that there must be one in the archive somewhere. It should have been requested as part of the original investigation. If not, that's a failing already."

"In case he said anything that hinted at what was to come?"

"Precisely. So can you see if there's a tape in the archive?"

"I'll try. Anything else?"

"Yes." I consulted my list again, for what it was worth. There were only a couple of things that Nick might be even vaguely helpful for. "Alfie Pattison."

"What about him?"

"I want to meet him."

"Why?"

"Because according to his alibi he was on air at the time, in Nottingham. But radio shows can be pre-recorded, and as well as that, I want to get a feel for Rex. Alfie knew him."

"Okay. I'll see if I can get contact details. Is that it?"

"No. Eddie Whitfield died in the night."

"So I heard."

"I need to speak to people who knew him. Family members. People he was inside with. Members of his crew."

Nick let out a low whistle

"That's going to be hard as well."

"Why?"

"Most of his immediate family are already inside, and not wanting to put too fine a point on it, if you go inside a prison, you might not get out."

That was a valid observation.

"Okay, so can you do those?" I asked.

Nick snorted. It was nearly a laugh, although not a funny one.

"And ask them what?"

"If they think there's any grain of truth in the confession."

"I can tell you already, they were all as shocked as I was. Listen, I'm on a bloody difficult murder case at the moment, on top of everything else I'm working on. Seriously, don't rely on me having a vast amount of time here."

I was midway through starting to nod when my attention was

suddenly grabbed by the sight of someone walking across the wasteland towards us.

Surely not. For heaven's sake. My blood ran cold.

"You need to go," I said to Nick, my voice urgent.

"What?"

"Now!"

He looked up and saw what I'd seen, and couldn't get away quickly enough.

Chapter 16

ECIDING I might as well tackle this head on, I got out of the car.

"Hello, Graham," I said, as he made his way towards me with a sickeningly smug grin. "I knew I was in a rough part of town, but I didn't realise it was this much of a gutter."

It didn't faze him. Instead, he cast his eyes in the direction of Nick's retreating Ford.

"Who was your friend? Or should I say client?"

I lit a cigarette, primarily so I could annoy him by looking all relaxed and nonchalant, while trying to conjure up an insult so final he'd accept defeat and leave me alone forever.

"What do you want?" I said instead, when nothing new would come.

"I heard you were back in London, so I thought I'd come to find you and make sure you're okay, now we're colleagues."

I shook my head, fighting the urge to punch him, just to assess how much he wobbled.

"Graham, we are not colleagues. I've been asked to babysit you on an unknown project because your inherent twattery means you'll mess it up. But I'm doing that as a favour to Florian Straub and getting paid for the ... I almost said privilege, but it's far from that."

"So what are you doing back in London? Aside from turning tricks out here."

It was a conundrum. The last person I wanted to ask about the Rex Dexter case was DCI Graham March, but equally there was still a significant chance he was the corrupt policeman at the heart of the thing.

"Helping a friend," I said. " And trying to avoid you."

"You do realise you're driving a great big bright red car with German plates. It's not the most subtle approach to staying under what I like to call the radar."

"But on the upside it's red, so if I accidentally smash it into you, hopefully the stains won't show."

I was quite pleased with that one.

"Very good," said Graham. "Although I think that adds a charge of threatening behaviour to your rap sheet."

"*Rap* sheet? What's a rap sheet in English? Have you been watching too many American crime dramas? Do you fancy yourself as Ironside? Because I'd happily put you in a wheelchair."

"You're so scary. Excuse me while I piss myself in fear. All over your passenger seat."

I pressed the button on the fob to lock the doors.

"You're not getting into my car."

"You know what? I've gone off the idea. It'd be full of your bodily odours, and whatever fluids your client just left behind. Christ."

I leaned back against the car, and took a deep drag on the cigarette, before trying again.

"Going back to the original point, why are you here?"

"Purely to remind you to be nice to me," he said. "One word in the appropriate lughole and you're inside faster than you'd drop your knickers at the first sign of a fiver. Terry Handley, isn't it? I've heard he's still looking for you."

"Have you finished?"

He clutched his ample stomach.

"Ooooh," he groaned. "I'm suddenly not feeling very well. I think it was the thought of your knickers. Crustier than a scotch roll, and far less fragrant. I'd better go before I'm sick. I'll see you around."

"You won't."

"Oh, I think I will."

"You really won't."

"I'll make it my mission."

He finished with the groaning charade and then leaned against the front wing of my car and started playing with the windscreen wiper, as though he was going to snap it off. If he did, I'd definitely hit him.

"You should come to the shelter and have a look at some of the work I've been doing for the homeless," he continued while I eyed him nervously. "Actually, perhaps you could help out! The toilets get filthy, so you'd be right at home scrubbing those, and it'd be good practice for when you're slopping out your cell."

Thankfully he let the wiper snap back into place.

"Now have you finished?" I said, taking one last drag of the cigarette before crushing it under the toe of my boot.

"I've hardly started, my dear."

"In that case can you let me into a secret?" Perhaps I could question him about the case in a roundabout way.

"I don't have secrets. You know me. What you see is what you get, which is what the ladies seem to find so appealing."

"Okay, not a secret then, but more a clarification. When did you start being a corrupt bastard?"

"I think you'll find that's yet to happen. When did you start being a cheap whore giving random strangers blow jobs in your

Mercedes? Actually, don't answer, because that's another challenging mental image."

One day I was supposed to be looking after the man. God help me.

"Back at the start," I continued, ignoring him, "presumably you were a lowly PC, wearing the uniform, and possibly even passed a fitness test, though God knows how. Were you on the take right back then?"

"Obviously not."

"Then at some stage you became a DC, then a sergeant, then an inspector. What did they see in you? Presumably it wasn't talent."

"My record speaks for itself."

"Precisely my point. Which makes the promotions all the more baffling. How did you manage it?"

He grabbed the lapel of my trench coat, which was annoying, because now I'd want to wash it, then pulled me close. I thought he was either going to hit me or spit in my face, but instead, he just stared at me for a few seconds before finally letting me go with a shove.

"You're not worth it," he said, not realising how close he'd come to a knee in the nuts.

I took a deep breath before continuing, deciding on a different approach.

"Listen," I said, "being serious for a minute, I know we don't always see eye to eye, but your friend in Frankfurt seems to think we should be nice to each other. Maybe we should try to do that, for his sake."

That took him by surprise, which was the general plan.

"Oh God. I knew this was going to happen," he said. "I've told you a hundred times, you're not my type. If you were the last woman on earth, I'd happily turn gay."

"Grow up, Graham. I was talking about being mature adults. I'm going to be in London for a few days. Maybe we should have a drink, and you can tell me all about your homeless work, and fill me in on some of the famous cases you worked on. Maybe try to change my mind. Show me what I've missed. And by that I don't mean your nether regions. I like to think I've got a strong stomach, but there's a limit."

"You're clearly up to something."

"I'm clearly trying to do the right thing by Florian. No other agenda."

Well, not that I was going to admit to.

"You're weird," he said, after appearing to consider it. "You know that?"

"I'm really not."

"No, but you are. You insult me. You cast doubts on my professional standing. You commit the most heinous of crimes. And then you expect me to go for a drink with you, but don't expect me to question what you're really up to. I'd classify that as industrial-scale weirdness."

"Well, give it some thought. You've got my number. And in the meantime, much as I've enjoyed our little chat, I really do have to be elsewhere."

"I'll see you later," he said, taking a step back, away from my car. I wasn't sure whether that was in relation to my invitation or a thinly-veiled threat.

Chapter 17

IT took me about five minutes of phone calls to ascertain the address of No Fear Safeguarding, and then a further ten to find somewhere to buy a London A-Z street atlas to work out how to get there. It was about half an hour away, in an anonymous-looking industrial unit on the outskirts of Edgware. With the time approaching 2pm, I pulled up far enough away that they wouldn't be able to see my car and take a note of the registration. Now I just needed Neil Fearon to incriminate himself.

After pressing a bell on the intercom, I was buzzed through to reception, from where a middle-aged woman in a fleece No Fear jacket watched me approach. I wondered if the similarly-named American lifestyle clothing brand would have an opinion on the quality of the embroidery.

"Hi, sorry to call unannounced but I wondered if Neil was in?" I said, by way of introduction.

"Who's calling?" she asked in a Welsh accent.

"My name's Charlotte. Charlotte Sadler." The name had served me well, so why mess with a winning formula? One day I should come up with a new one.

"And what's it regarding?"

"I was looking to speak to him about a security issue."

"I can see if Hugo's available. He looks after new clients."

"Ah. It was recommended that I speak to Neil directly. It was a personal referral."

She looked me up and down, as though assessing me, possibly trying to work out how much revenue I represented. Perhaps I should have worn a nicer shirt.

"I'll see if he's available," she said eventually. "Take a seat."

There were three cheap, fabric-covered chairs in front of the window. I opted for the one closest to the table, as it had the fewest coffee stains, and then spent the next few minutes flicking through issues of Autocar and Esquire, as though I was in a particularly manly doctor's.

Eventually a door opened.

"Charlotte? Neil Fearon," said the man who emerged, walking towards me, arm extended.

I rose and accepted the handshake. Neil was not as I imagined. I'm not sure why, but I was expecting someone young and fit, built like a bodybuilder, perhaps with long, flowing, leonine hair. But instead he was, if anything, a little bit weedy, middle-aged, greying, and almost unremarkable apart from his red-framed spectacles that were at least a decade out of date.

He showed me through to his office and offered coffee, which I refused. The last thing I needed was to leave fingerprints on porcelain.

The office was as bland as the reception. Another door in the far corner led, I thought, to a meeting room. There were security grilles over the tinted, steel-framed windows, which I supposed were more for show than any real concerns about a break-in. The air was tinged with stale cigarette smoke.

I took a seat, putting my bag on the one adjacent, while Neil returned to his desk.

"How can I help you?" he asked.

It was time to deliver the line I'd mentally prepared on the way over.

"I'm an actor's agent and I have a reasonably A-list client coming into town in the next few weeks. I was told that you could do the whole security package. Meet them at the airport, make sure they're not bothered by the public, all that kind of thing."

He nodded, looking interested.

"Yes, that's all possible. Does he or she have a name?"

"I'd rather not say that at the moment, but he's very well-known."

"Okay, and just out of interest, how did you hear about us?"

"It was a friend of a friend who has a connection with Suadela. I used to work more on the author side of the agency and writers tend not to get recognised. I suppose they're fundamentally less interesting. This is the first time I've had to deal with the excesses of Hollywood."

So far so good.

"We can certainly meet him at the airport and get him to the hotel in one piece," said Neil. "Have you already made a hotel booking?"

"His US agent insisted on the Savoy. I assume they're used to high-profile guests."

He nodded. It really was another world to me.

"Do you then offer a kind of babysitting service?" I asked.

"How do you mean?"

"I'm thinking that I need to protect him from fans and autograph hunters and all that kind of thing, but he's also got a certain, how should I put this, reputation."

"Do you mean as a Hollywood hellraiser?"

Neil laughed and I smiled, hopefully coquettishly.

"Kind of. The thing is, it's a fine line, isn't it? On the one hand, my job is to make sure he arrives safely, leaves safely, and doesn't get in any trouble in the meantime. But at the same time,

I want to make sure he enjoys his visit, if you know what I mean."

He nodded, then took a packet of cigarettes off his desk and offered me one. I'm not normally a Marlboro girl, but free is free so I accepted.

"We can certainly be on hand to provide transport, make sure of reservations in decent restaurants, all that kind of thing," he said, passing me his lighter. "In terms of nightclubs, we know of a few with discreet VIP areas. I don't think you'd have any worries there."

"That sounds excellent. It sounds like you've done this sort of thing before."

"Lots of times." He pushed an ashtray in my direction. I was remembering why I wasn't a Marlboro girl as I felt the smoke burn my throat. I needed to up the ante.

"He's going to want to party, but it's a question of balance," I said. "I don't want to stop him having a good time, but at the same time, I need to keep it out of the tabloids."

"Of course. When's he coming?"

"At the end of November." The cigarette made me cough. Then I realised I had a bigger problem. Could you get fingerprints from a cigarette butt? I wasn't positive, but equally thought it might look a bit odd if I stubbed it out and pocketed it. I'm my own worst enemy at times. I parked that one for now as I still wasn't finished with trying to get Neil into trouble. "So if he does want to party we need to ensure it's discreet, if you know what I mean."

"I do."

"I mean, not wanting to put too fine a point on it, I don't want him phoning some escort agency and ending up in a kiss and tell situation, or going hunting for certain substances in the backrooms of east end pubs."

"I think you could leave all of those details with me. We have experience with the peccadillos of the rich and famous."

"So you could help him get hold of things that he was looking for, without making a fuss?"

Suddenly, his expression changed. The frown was ominous, as though he'd had a moment of clarity, and not in a good way.

"Sorry, what did you say your name was again?" he said.

"Charlotte."

"Charlotte who?"

"Charlotte Sadler." In retrospect, it was probably an error not to have changed it sooner.

"You look familiar," he said, staring at me in a way that was quite disconcerting.

"Really?"

He didn't nod, or speak, but just kept looking at me until appearing to come to a decision of sorts. He stood up.

"Okay," he said. "I'll tell you what I'll do. Wait here one moment and I'll see if one of my colleagues can come and join us. He has a bit more experience in these areas."

"Perfect," I said, thinking it was anything but.

Even more ominously, he picked up his keys, then made his way past me to the door to reception. Which he then locked behind him.

Fuck.

The windows were barred like a prison. The door was locked, but I moved to it and soon wished I hadn't. Through the small glass panel I could see Neil talking to the receptionist, and then heard him asking her to phone the police and tell them to make it urgent. I tried the handle anyway, but the door was big and heavy and wasn't going anywhere.

I was trapped. The cigarette butt was the least of my worries.

Chapter 18

I STUBBED out the cigarette and pocketed the butt in my trench coat, aware that it would make it smell horribly, but I already needed to take it to the dry cleaners after Graham's greasy fingers had touched the lapel.

It was a small gesture to take attention away from the bigger panic. If my cover was blown I was in a world of trouble. I tried the door again. It was futile. The glass panel was far too small to squeeze through, even assuming I could smash it.

The receptionist was on the phone, in a fluster, looking in my direction.

I'd had training for moments like this. I'd faced mock abductions and interrogations, but they were designed to help me if I was ever caught by a bunch of gangsters in some far-flung country. Not the police, who would simply slap on the handcuffs and take me away.

There was only one glimmer of hope. If there were big burly security staff on the premises, a couple could have come in and attempted to pin me down, but the fact they hadn't implied this was more of an admin office and the thugs were based elsewhere.

Although perhaps there was no need for muscle if Neil knew there was no way of escaping.

The only option was the other door, but if that led to a meeting room, I'd be trapped anyway. I could try to hide in the suspended ceiling, but it would hardly be difficult to check, and I very much doubted the aluminium grid would be able to hold my weight.

I tried the other door anyway. It was also locked.

Double fuck.

I wasn't even sure where it led. There was another glass panel, but it was dark on the far side, and from the faint light coming in from my side it didn't even look like a meeting room. It was more of a storage cupboard and that was even worse.

I did, however, have my bag with me. And in my bag was the SIG-Sauer P228.

If Joe heard about this, I was dead. But better dead than locked up for twenty-five years.

I ran back to the door to reception, and checked nobody was standing directly outside. There was nothing else for it. I racked the slide and fired directly at the lock. Twice. The receptionist screamed. The third bullet did the trick. The splintered wood gave way enough for me to push it open so I could make a dash for the main entrance.

I'd underestimated the number of big burly security men. Suddenly I was crashing to the floor with one attached to my back. The gun went skittering away, across the tiles, and under the chairs with the coffee stains.

I hadn't seen the man who'd brought me down, but I was pretty sure it wasn't Neil. He was huge and heavy, and his arm was across the back of my neck, his knee pinning my arm to the floor. His free hand grabbed hold of my hair, taking a firm grip of a handful, before pulling my head back until I thought my neck was going to snap.

Nobody messes with my hair.

With an almighty effort and the risk of whiplash, I did the rest of his job for him, and snapped my head back in one dramatic movement. I felt the crunch as it connected with his face.

It was enough to make him loosen his grip. That was all I needed. I reached behind, grabbed him, rolled away then smashed my elbow into his face, all in one fluid movement.

He yelled, though whether in pain or shock I wasn't going to wait to find out. But as I managed to get back to my feet, he was getting up. And worse still, Neil was closing in on my gun.

I've never played rugby, but I've seen it on TV. Even if my tackle wasn't legal, it was certainly effective. It brought Neil crashing to the floor, his shoulder smashing into the table on the way down. But the security man was nearly back on top of me. The receptionist screamed again.

I tried the old knee-to-the-groin routine, but he was wise to it and grabbed my leg, twisted it, and threw me off balance, causing me to fall to the ground. Sharp pain shot up my leg where he landed on my ankle.

But the benefit of being on the floor was that the SIG was back in reach. I didn't want to fire it. Guns can be dangerous. Instead, I grabbed it and swept my arm up so it smashed into his temple, knocking him momentarily off balance.

That was enough. He fell backwards, giving me a chance to take aim. The receptionist fell down behind her desk, having seen enough. Neil made one last attempt to grab me, but the heel of my boot made a strange snapping noise as it stamped down on his fingers.

"On second thoughts," I said, as I stood up and brushed myself down, "I might get a second quote from somewhere else, if it's all the same with you."

Then I ran back to my car, despite the pain from my ankle, and fired the engine, passing police cars heading in the opposite direction as I calmly drove out of the industrial estate.

So, first impressions of Neil Fearon? It was difficult to tell. More research would be required.

The bigger issue was that there was an added sense of urgency. Now the whole of the Metropolitan Police would be on red alert and looking for me. I couldn't rely on Nick Brooks to do things in a hurry. There was an alternative, but it wasn't going to be easy.

Actually, the more I thought about it, it was madness. But sometimes a little bit of insanity goes a long way.

I drove back into central London, navigated my way to a familiar car park, left the car on the deserted top floor and headed to one of my favourite old pubs to make a phone call.

Chapter 19

I KNEW the *Daily Echo* number off by heart. I'd worked there for years.

"Derek Hughes, please," I said, when the woman on the switchboard answered.

"Who shall I say is calling?"

"It's a personal call." I hoped that would be enough. It was.

Derek Hughes was a sub-editor. While I was a journalist, I'd always worked hard to nurture relationships with the subs. They bestowed the gift of column inches, wrote the headlines, and added the polish that won the awards. But of all of them, Derek was my favourite. He was there for life, set in his ways, but brilliant, and the closest I had to a work friend apart from my young protégé Danny Churchill. It was still far too soon to call Danny. I wanted to make things up to him properly, because I knew how much trouble I'd caused for him last spring. That left Derek as my only hope.

"Derek, don't say my name out loud whatever you do," I said as soon as he answered.

"Who is this?"

"It's Clare."

"Cl–"

"Shhh for heaven's sake! Call me Charlotte."

"Okay. Hey, Charlotte, howyadoin? I thought you were dead."

"If so, I think you're about the only one left. No offence."

Yes, this was madness. But I knew Derek well and I thought I could trust him.

"But what? I don't understand," he said. "What are you doing? Why are you calling me? Don't get me wrong, it's great to hear from you, and especially because it means you're *not* dead, but given the way you left this place, I didn't think I'd ever hear from you ever again."

"No, but you can't keep a good girl down. And I'm sorry about all that. It wasn't ideal, and I'd love to tell you all about it one day, seriously. But listen, I need a favour. Can you meet me? Kind of now-ish?"

"What kind of favour?"

"I'll tell you when you get here."

"Where are you?"

"In the Cheese."

Despite the unusual name, Ye Olde Cheshire Cheese was one of the most historic pubs in London, and had served patrons including Samuel Johnson, Charles Dickens, G.K. Chesterton and Mark Twain – as well as countless Fleet Street hacks. It had been rebuilt in 1667 after the Great Fire of London and had enough nooks and crannies to make a clandestine meeting feasible, even if considerably high risk.

"I could look out of the window and wave at you," said Derek.

"Please don't do that. Utmost discretion."

"I'm not going to get in trouble, am I?"

"For meeting a former colleague for a drink? I wouldn't have thought so."

"Conspiracy for whatever?"

"Shhh."

"I've got a wife and children to support."

"You'll be fine. Just don't tell anyone where you're going. I won't need long."

Ten minutes later, I stepped out from the shadows to take Derek by the arm and lead him deep into the labyrinth, via the bar where I ordered him a pint of Samuel Smith Old Brewery Bitter alongside a Diet Coke for me.

"I didn't recognise you," he said, when we reached a table outside the earshot of anyone who might be a threat. In fairness, my hair had changed several times in the interim.

"You don't know how happy I am to hear you say that," I said, thinking it was an immensely timely observation.

"So what happened?" He started rolling a cigarette with expert precision. I was still suffering from the Marlboro so didn't join in, but casually managed to lose the butt from my coat pocket.

"Do you want the full story or the one I concocted to make it sound less awful?"

"The full one."

So I told him. About my frustration working on the newspaper, dealing with office politics, and writing about people who ran various scams and schemes but got caught because they weren't very clever and I was able to expose them. But how, in a moment of madness, I'd concocted a plan of my own, which involved selling fake artwork to shady collectors, who would be prepared to believe me out of sheer greed and one-upmanship. And finally, how I'd left a trail of clues for Danny last February, so he could write the story and make his name, while I faked my death in a helicopter crash and then began a new life somewhere else entirely.

In retrospect, it was all a catastrophic misjudgement, and hadn't even been particularly successful. I'd made lots of money but I'd lost everything I really cared about. I nearly got arrested in

Cologne, than almost got abducted by one of my victims who was intent on revenge, until being rescued by a man called Matt who worked for the mysterious Blood Angel organisation, and who I held strong suspicions about, until a final bloody shoot-out in Paris revealed the devastating truth.

In a nutshell.

"And now?"

"I'm still working in Germany for the moment, but I'm back in London for a few days."

"Writing for a newspaper?"

"No, not as such. I've been learning German but I'm not good enough to write it yet with any conviction. More a kind of freelance investigator. Kind of."

He nodded, knowing when it was better not to ask.

"And the favour?"

It was deep breath time.

"I need to get into the *Echo* archive, to look up some old issues and research some stories on the computer," I said.

At least he didn't immediately make a run for it.

"Because?" he said, instead.

"Because I'm interested in Rex Dexter. You remember, the DJ who got murdered?"

He nodded.

"I need to look at some old coverage," I continued. "But I need to do it without anyone seeing me. Or at least, knowing who I am. Is Mike Walker still the editor?"

"He is."

"I definitely need to avoid him, and everybody else in editorial. Especially Danny."

"I thought Danny was your friend."

"He is. And I will make things right with him, but now wouldn't be a good time. I've got plans to make it up to Danny."

In truth, I was still working on those. They could best be described as "formative" where "formative" is defined as "pretty much non-existent because whatever I try is just not good enough".

"And what exactly do you need me to do?" asked Derek, making short work of the pint.

"Swipe me in. That's it. I know my way from there. Once I'm in the library, it's big enough that I can find a quiet corner."

"I won't ask why. But they won't just let you into the library."

"Okay, come with me to that as well, but once I'm there you can leave me to it."

"And when do you want to do this?"

I looked at my watch. It was just past 4pm. The day shift wouldn't be leaving for another three hours. It'd be far safer to go when it was comparatively deserted. But some things were worth taking a risk for and sometimes it's better to hide in a crowd.

"Sort of now," I said.

"Are you mad?"

"Quite possibly, but look, it's on a separate floor. All I need is a bit of help getting past reception."

"And what if the security staff recognise you?"

"You didn't."

"But I'm not security, am I? I'm a short-sighted sub."

He had a point.

"I've dyed my hair since I was last in the office and I've brought a pair of sunglasses. I'll take my chances. I won't make eye contact. All I need to do is sign the visitor's book and get a pass, and I can do that, but I need to go in with you because it's not like they can phone upstairs and tell someone I'm coming to see them."

He reached across and squeezed my hand.

"Clare, it's great to see you. It really is. You've made my day. Honestly, I can't tell you how happy I am to know you're okay."

I put my other hand on top of his. He was looking at my ring, and suddenly I felt very self-conscious about it. And at the same time, it all came flooding down on top of me. All of the things I'd done wrong. All of the good people I'd lost. I tried to speak, but my throat had tightened, and I could feel the tears not far away.

"Okay," he said, and for a moment it didn't sink in. Then he let go of my hand. "Let's get going."

"You're the best, Derek," I said, overwhelmingly grateful.

"I'm as mad as you are."

Chapter 20

GRAHAM March opened the door of the homeless shelter and stepped out on the street to greet his guest.

"Dougie, you old bastard, great to see you," he said.

They shook hands. Neither was the type to exchange an embrace.

"So this is it then?"

"Indeed it is. Come inside and I'll show you round."

DCI Dougie Compton wrinkled his nose as he crossed the threshold.

"Cheer up," said Graham. "We give them access to showers."

After a quick guided tour, he led the way through to an office towards the back of the ground floor. It was sparsely furnished, with painted breeze block walls, and the unflattering glow of a pair of fluorescent strip tubes. On one wall was a map of London, showing the separate boroughs, dotted with pins in various colours. On another was a noticeboard with pictures of young people in happier times.

"These are the ones we keep an eye out for," explained Graham. "Their parents send in snaps, hoping they'll turn up here eventually and we can put their minds at rest." He pointed to a colour picture of a stunningly beautiful young blonde girl, standing on a beach and smiling at the camera, seemingly without a care in the world. "I'm particularly looking forward to getting this one."

Dougie took a chair.

"You don't change, do you?" he said with a grin, accompanied by a head shake.

"I'm joking. Although some of them clean up nicely and who am I to argue if they ask to be shown a bit of affection for once in their lives." He sat down on the opposite side of a cheap melamine desk. "No, but seriously. We do good work. Get them off the streets. Give them a hot meal, shelter, help them sort their lives out."

"And you run this place, do you?"

"Me? No. I just help out occasionally, one or two afternoons a week. Doing my bit. I'm a charitable man, although obviously if it crops up at my disciplinary, I'd like to think the panel would see it as evidence of what I like to call my outstanding good character. Cup of tea?"

"I'd rather not, if it's all the same to you," said Dougie, casting a glance at a filthy kettle that was standing next to a selection of chipped and stained mugs.

"Don't blame you, in fairness," said Graham. "I normally bring a flask." He sat back, and put his feet up on the desk, crossing his legs. "Anyway, tell me, what's the latest on Rex Dexter and Eddie Whitfield."

Dougie gave a summary, mentioning Whitfield's death and the imminent press conference.

"It'll hit the news tomorrow night and be in the papers Friday," he said in conclusion.

"And they're still happy to go along with it? They're not looking for anyone else?"

"No, very much all done and dusted."

"Excellent work." Graham paused, and called out to someone who was walking past in the corridor. After a brief discussion of the forthcoming night's expected occupancy rate, his attention returned to Dougie. "Talking of old cases, any luck finding Clare Woodbrook?"

"Personal interest in that one, have we?"

"You know how it is, Dougie. I just heard a rumour she might be back in London."

"Really? And who did you hear that from? Some tart in a massage parlour?"

"What is it with everyone? You shouldn't believe everything you've heard about me."

"You're forgetting that I actually worked with you."

"Yeah, well, I can't be responsible for the way that you misinterpret things. Probably why I made DCI before you, no offence."

"You're a cheeky bastard."

Graham took his legs off the table, and sat up straight, then dropped his voice.

"Going back to Clare Woodbrook, though. I'm not in a position to do anything about it personally, but I'd like to think that if I happened to come across information that led to her being taken off the streets, it might be also taken into consideration come the day, if you catch my drift."

"You reckon?" said Dougie.

"A bit of the old mutual back-scratching could presumably be on the agenda?"

Dougie leaned forward.

"Listen, Graham, let me tell you this. You want my opinion? You could find Shergar, Lord Lucan and Jack the Ripper and I doubt it'd make any difference to your disciplinary, given what I read in the papers."

"Interesting."

"I'm only telling it like it is."

"No, I mean it's interesting that you believe scurrilous tabloid press stories rather than your old mate Graham. But being serious for a minute. If I did get word of her whereabouts, could I rely on you to, at the very least, make it deeply uncomfortable for her?" He was aware of Dougie studying his expression.

"What have you heard? You're hinting at something."

"Me? Nothing concrete, Dougie. I just heard a rumour from an associate in Germany. Well, I say an associate. He's not really my kind of chap. He's a bit on the naughty side. But he seems to know her and he thinks there's a possibility she might be rearing the old ugly head back on home turf."

"You cannot accuse Clare Woodbrook of having an ugly head. Half the lads at the station only want to catch her because they're smitten."

"They're obviously all in need of counselling, then. Let's just say, she's not my type."

"And what's your type then? Homeless waifs?"

"I resent the implication. It's not my fault if some of them develop feelings."

Dougie snorted.

"Yeah right. Anyway, your friend in Germany?"

"Hardly a friend," said Graham.

"Associate then."

"Not even that, really. I don't know why I said that. He's just some bloke I came across."

"I really don't want the mental image of you coming across a bloke, if it's all the same."

"I don't mean like that, you pervert. The point is, he said if I found her, he'd appreciate me not doing anything about it, because he's got plans of his own – but you know how it is. If I get a better offer, we could certainly have a conversation. Assuming, you know, I heard anything."

"You are aware that withholding evidence is an offence?"

"I think you've already got all the evidence. I'm just offering to supply a bit of intelligence, on the off-chance I come across any. In a bit of a mutual benefit scenario."

Dougie looked momentarily lost in thought. Finally he spoke.

"I'll give you a bit of advice."

"Go on."

"On the off-chance, and all that bullshit, let me know and I'll take it to Terry Handley. It's his case, and I'm sure he'd be grateful. But in the meantime, you can do something for me."

"Go on."

"DSI Joe Leyland."

"That old twat. What about him?"

"He's making me nervous. He's been hovering round like he's up to something. I caught him chatting to one of my sergeants. If you hear anything on your grapevine, be sure to bring it straight to me. All right?"

"Of course. You think it might be related to this Clare Woodbrook rumour?"

"For the moment, all options are open."

Dougie stood up. Graham followed him to the door and then back out onto the street. He'd had quite enough of being charitable for one afternoon. And there was still no sign of the blonde girl.

Chapter 21

ALTHOUGH the sunglasses in October made me look like a cross between a pretentious fashion victim and a third-rate spy, both of which were actually valid accusations in any case, they served the job of getting me past reception, with considerable assistance from Derek. But that was when my problems started.

As we approached the lift, the doors opened and Simon Oakley, the news editor, emerged. I'd never seen eye to eye with Simon. It was more than just a rivalry between news and features. I fundamentally didn't like or trust the man, and he'd rarely had a good word to say about me in the morning editorial conferences. I managed to turn away as soon as he approached, but it was enough to make my heart start pounding. To make matters worse, he then started talking to Derek about the progress of a story, and while the two of them chatted, I had to wander away, taking an unnatural interest in a potted plant, with my back to them. Time appeared to be standing still.

Eventually, however, Derek gave a low whistle to say the coast was clear and I followed him into the lift, thinking this was perhaps the worst idea I'd ever had. Until, a split second later, I remembered the art fraud. The stairs would have been an option, but they were often used as an informal meeting place when conversations needed to be had away from the desk. The library was on the fourth floor, one above editorial. I consoled myself by calculating the likelihood of the lift stopping on the way. It was low.

I was wrong. And as the doors opened on the third floor, giving me a clear view of my former workplace, I held my breath as though that would help, catching a glimpse of Danny in our old office in the far corner, and having terrible pangs akin to homesickness. Part of me wanted to run up to him and say hello. The sensible part knew that I'd sacrificed that kind of freedom the minute I'd attempted the perfect crime.

Thankfully I didn't recognise the woman who got into the lift and then rode up with us to the fourth, and she didn't seem to recognise me either. The stress was almost unbearable, though. What if it had been Danny himself? Or Mike Walker? Or anyone else that I'd grown close to throughout my career?

Derek, again, was magnificent in helping me get past the door to the library. It was a huge space, full of filing cabinets, rows and rows of shelving, and desks that either served as temporary workspaces or held computers that were attached to the network.

He led me to a quiet corner, and then turned to leave.

"Good luck, Charlotte," he said with a wink. "I hope you find what you're looking for."

"Thank you," I said. "I really, really appreciate this. And it's been fantastic to see you."

He paused for a moment.

"You look like you want to say something," he said.

"I kind of do, because I've just thought of something, but it's another favour and I've asked enough already."

"I can't promise, but what is it?"

"Have you heard of Alfie Pattison?"

He looked blank, as though trying to place the name but failing. Eventually he shook his head.

"He was a radio DJ. Used to work with Rex Dexter but got fired and ended up in Nottingham. He was one of the suspects."

Derek clicked his fingers.

"I remember. What about him?"

"I need to speak to him. You wouldn't be able to get a contact number for me?"

He laughed.

"Just like that?"

"I've asked a friend in the police to help track him down but I thought you might be quicker."

"Aren't you trying to avoid the police?"

"I'm trying to avoid everyone but it's a bit complicated."

He said he'd see what he could do. I gave him a card with an email address and a phone number.

"Do you have email?" I asked.

"Within the building."

"But not on the internet?"

He gave me a blank look.

"Not sure. I've worked on stories about it, but I don't think I've got it."

"You'd know if you had. Do you have a computer at home?"

"We've got an Amstrad PCW. Would that have it?"

"Don't worry. Use the phone number instead."

I gave him a hug, and suddenly I was on my own.

Around thirty people worked in the library at peak time, marking, cutting and filing as many as 1,600 articles each day. This was both good and bad. It increased the possibility of being identified, but equally, it meant there were enough people milling around that one more wouldn't really make a difference.

When I first started working at the *Daily Echo*, late afternoon was traditionally peak time as deadlines approached. The phones were red hot with journalists shouting through requests for information that saw the staff frantically running around. By the time I left, however, we all had our own ATEX terminals and access to online media archives through systems like the Datasolve World Reporter service. It was a fantastic resource, containing digitised archives from hundreds of publications including our own newspaper, the *Guardian*, *Financial Times* and even *TASS* from the Soviet Union – although searching came at a cost per line of content downloaded.

On top of that, just before I left, we gained access to the new Fleet Street Data Exchange, in which an increasing number of national newspapers uploaded a full electronic version of their day's stories so that they could be accessed by all of us. It was a rare example of co-operation, and useful for recent coverage. Older stories were going to take a bit more work.

I took a space at one of the terminals on the far side of the library, with my back to the rest of the room, and removed the sunglasses.

Typing keywords brought up vast amounts of information. From there I could either read it online, or make a list of cuttings to search for in the cabinets. In the end, though, I decided to look at full copies of the newspaper to see exactly how the Rex Dexter story had been reported in context.

I started with Saturday, July 27th, 1985, the morning after the body was discovered. It was the front page splash, but aside from a rudimentary report of the murder, the *Echo* news desk clearly hadn't had time to pull together any additional background information. I was struck by how old-fashioned it all looked. It was just before I joined, and within a year we'd started using colour images. The pace of technological change was relentless.

Over the next few days the story dominated the front page, with further profile pieces inside. Theories were put forward, and the journalists clearly had their eyes on several potential suspects

– including his new girlfriend's ex-partner. I sensed the frustration as the early contenders fell away.

By August 7th, Rex was almost forgotten about – eclipsed by the discovery of five bodies at White House Farm in Essex, in a suspected murder-suicide. Over the following weeks he barely merited a mention, apart from an occasional finger being pointed at the police for a lack of progress.

Eddie Whitfield's failed security vault heist, meanwhile, wasn't big enough to make the front page, but there were a couple of articles on the inside news pages.

It was all very frustrating. Aside from jogging my memory about the events themselves, I hadn't learned anything new.

I made notes of the names of the journalists that covered the story. I recognised some of them, but many were unfamiliar.

I did, however, spot an article about the death of DS Kenny Mason. As Joe had said, he'd been killed in a car accident – hitting a signpost after a night celebrating the successful completion of another case. It was a minor scandal that a policeman, of all people, should be guilty of drink driving. The coverage was not particularly sympathetic, which seemed wrong to me, despite a testimonial from a colleague. Yes, he'd done a bad thing, but he'd left behind a grieving widow and a young child who would no longer have a father.

My concentration was broken by the vibration of my phone. I quickly answered it, trying not to draw to much attention, but I didn't recognise the voice at first.

"Clare?" The sexy accent was vaguely familiar, but so much had happened since I'd last heard it. And then it came to me.

"Iglika! Hi. Sorry." I glanced around to make sure nobody had noticed. "How are things?"

"Fine, but you sound tired. Everything is okay in London?"

"Everything's good," I lied, trying to keep my voice low.

"You are sure?"

"Yes, just a couple of late nights."

"You are still okay to come to Sofia on Monday?"

"Of course."

"Excellent. I have lots of things lined up. It is going to be busy."

"I'm very much looking forward to it."

I made a couple of minutes of small talk but ended the call as soon as I could without appearing impolite. I was keen to get back to my research.

Once I finished with the newspapers, I moved across to the photographic archive. It was similarly comprehensive, but slightly easier to navigate, given that sections were organised by surname. There was a picture of Rex Dexter that hadn't previously been published. A note, attached with a paperclip, suggested it was to be used with a profile piece, but that the story had been cancelled. Was it a separate feature that had been planned before his death?

Finally, I returned to the computer, searching for anything I could find on Alfie Pattison, Neil Fearon, Dougie Compton and all of the others that I could remember from Nick's summary of the case. Alfie got the occasional mention, but there was very little about the others, apart from one or two references in relation to a different investigation or court case. None of it was at all controversial, on first glance at least.

Aware that I'd been there for several hours, and every passing minute increased the likelihood of being disturbed, I packed up, leaving no evidence that I'd ever been there. And then, with a deep breath, I took the stairs back down to reception before heading out into the night.

It had been a long day, on not much sleep, and by the time I reached my hotel, I was tired, hungry, and frustrated that I hadn't achieved much apart from having a fight with Neil Fearon and his colleague that had potentially blown my cover.

The receptionist called me over as she saw me enter the lobby.

"Miss Mäkinen," she said. "We've got some post for you."

I waited while she retrieved a padded envelope from a pigeonhole.

"Did it come in the mail?" I asked.

"No, it was delivered by hand."

"Did you see who by?"

She shook her head.

"It was a bike courier, that's all I know."

"Ah, okay, thank you."

Excellent news, I thought. That'd be Nick, hopefully with a tape of Rex Dexter's last radio show. Good work. She handed it over.

"Is it too late for a dinner reservation?" I asked, looking at my watch, shocked to discover it was nearly 9pm.

"No, it's okay," she said. "Do you want to go through now?"

"Can I say ten minutes?"

"Of course."

I took the envelope back to my room, and took off my boots, lay back on the bed and closed my eyes. I was exhausted. I didn't have the energy to sweep my room for bugs. In any case, my paranoia was slightly eased by knowing that if things had moved, it was probably the chambermaid while she'd been making the bed.

It was no good. If I stayed there, I'd miss dinner entirely. With an almighty effort, I stood back up, checked myself in the mirror, and decided I'd do. Just about. As long as there was nobody there who knew me.

I selected different shoes, then picked up the envelope and headed to the restaurant. It was quiet, and within a couple of minutes I'd managed to place an order for pumpkin and walnut ravioli, together with a large glass of sauvignon blanc.

The wine arrived. While I waited for the food, I opened the envelope.

But it wasn't from Nick.

It was a typed note wrapped around a nine-millimetre bullet.

You are not welcome here. Go home or prepare to die.

Chapter 22

I WAS still looking at the bullet when my phone rang. It was Nick.

"I've got you a cassette of the radio show," he said, without any pleasantries. "Do you have a tape machine?"

"Yes, in the car."

"Perfect. I'm getting grief but Emily will drop it off in the morning. Probably about 8am if you'll be up by then."

"Uh-huh." I put the bullet back in the envelope and focused my attention on the note. Nick picked up on my distraction.

"Are you okay?" he asked.

"Yes, just something a bit annoying."

"Anything to do with the case?"

"No, a personal thing."

"Something I can help with?"

"Not really."

"Okay then."

I was less surprised by his lack of concern than the fact he'd offered to help in the first place.

"I'm going to have to go in a second," I said. "I'm in a

restaurant and the waiter is heading over. But any luck with Eddie Whitfield's family?"

"I told you. I'll look into it if there's time. So no."

"Okay. And what about tracking down Alfie?"

The sigh was louder than strictly necessary, presumably for effect.

"I called the radio station in Nottingham," said Nick. "He left five years ago. They don't know where he's working now."

"Can you check the electoral roll?"

"I can, when I get a chance."

"You might not need to worry about it. I've asked a friend to help me."

Perhaps that was an error.

"What do you mean you've asked a friend? Christ." He sounded angry. "You do know this is top secret? Who?"

"Relax, nobody you know and someone I trust. But don't worry, they know better than to ask questions why."

———

After dinner, I took the envelope back to my bedroom. A normal person would have been intimidated but Graham March didn't scare me. It was hardly his most subtle work. I phoned him.

"I got your note," I said. "Very good. It was even all spelt correctly."

"What note?" he asked.

"You know what note."

"You're losing the plot, my dear. I haven't written you a note."

"Do we really have to go through this charade? What is it you're actually trying to achieve?"

"By not writing you a note?"

"For fuck's sake, Graham."

"That's no language for a nice lady. Although no surprise coming from you."

I lit a cigarette, and lay back on the bed.

"For the avoidance of doubt, I am, of course, going to ignore it," I said.

"Ignore what? Your own appalling language?"

"No. Your ridiculous message."

"Ignore away. Although feel free to advise me of the contents so I've got the first clue in hell of what you're blathering on about."

"I'm impressed that you know where I'm staying."

"Rest assured I have no idea where you're staying, and even I did, I'd make sure I didn't go anywhere near it."

"How did you find me today, by the way?"

"Ah, that would be telling. But you're not as clever as you think you are. Actually, let me rephrase that. You're not very clever."

I wasn't in the mood.

"Goodnight Graham," I said. "Don't have nightmares."

I ended the call, then looked at the note again.

Of course it was from Graham. It was exactly the sort of thing he'd do to try to wind me up.

It had to be.

If it was somebody else, I was in trouble.

Chapter 23

Thursday, October 28th, 1993

SHORTLY before 8am I answered a call from Emily.

"Could you pop down to meet me?" she asked. "I've got the Rex Dexter tape for you, but I haven't really got time to come up."

I quickly threw on some clothes, and then took the lift to the ground floor. As I exited the revolving door, Emily climbed out from the passenger's side of a Ford Mondeo.

"Thanks for coming down," she said, with a warm smile, passing me a cassette tape. "Sorry I couldn't come up, but we're heading to a briefing."

I could see a man in the driver's seat. It was difficult to guess his age but I thought late thirties at least. In fact, it was hard to spot anything apart from his ginger hair and pronounced cheek dimples. He waved when he caught me looking, so I waved back.

"Who's that?" I asked, curious.

"That's Jonathan," she said. "He's a colleague."

"He's a what?" Immediately I wanted to run and hide.

"Don't worry, he doesn't know who you are but we're out

working together. I couldn't get away on my own. It's all right, he thinks you're a friend of my mum."

That made me feel old.

"Not that I'm saying you're old," she continued, a bit too late.

Something clicked.

"Ooh, is that the one you said you had the occasional kiss and cuddle with?"

I could tell by the way she started blushing that it was.

"Let's just say he's a very good friend," she said with a grin.

Even so, I was keen to get out of his line of sight as quickly as possible, so I started to walk in the direction of my car, beckoning for Emily to follow.

"Thanks for this," I said, holding up the tape.

"My pleasure. Word to the wise, though. I heard rumours about a kerfuffle at the No Fear office."

The use of kerfuffle made me smile.

"In a bad way?" I asked.

"Let's just say not in a good way. You might want to keep a low profile. There was a lot of chat about it yesterday afternoon, although the good news is that they didn't seem to have any clue where to start looking for you."

"Until your friend Jonathan puts two and two together."

She shook her head.

"He won't. Honestly. I'll keep him distracted." The wink was back.

"I wanted to talk to you about the dinner suggestion, actually," I said, as we turned the corner. "You might not want to do it now, but if you did, I could be free tonight, I think. Though I appreciate that's short notice."

"I'd love to but I'm not going to get off till long gone 10pm. Sorry. Tomorrow?"

I thought about it for a moment. Who knew what would happen?

"It's a possibility. I'll do my very best. It'd be fun. I'll call you."

"Perfect. We'll confirm tomorrow."

Suddenly, though, dinner was the furthest thing from my mind. There was something seriously wrong with my car.

Emily noticed my change of expression, then followed me as I ran towards it.

It was a mess.

Someone had poured bleach, or paint stripper, or something similar, over the bright red paintwork of the bonnet, and carved the word *SLUT* into the passenger side door. Brilliant. I walked round to the driver's side, and discovered the same there.

As if it wasn't already distinctive enough.

"Shit," said Emily. "Do you want me to report it? Seriously, the kids round here. They see a nice car and they can't cope. It's pathetic. I'm so sorry. I should have thought."

I ran my hand through my hair then shook my head. I doubted it was a random attack by local hooligans. This looked planned. And deeply personal. The top of the U on the driver's door had been closed off so it looked vaguely like a bullet, as though to remove any doubt that this was linked to last night's package.

"The last thing we can do is report it," I said. "I'll find somewhere and get it fixed."

"But that's going to cost a fortune."

Again, the cost was the furthest thing from my mind.

"Can I ask you a question," I said, while I checked for tyre damage and made sure the door locks hadn't been compromised. They were all fine, which was something at least. "I understand you might not be able to answer, but if you can't, I'd prefer it if you just said that, rather than making something up."

"I'll give you an honest answer, of course," said Emily.

"Thanks, I appreciate it. Who else knows I'm here?"

"How do you mean? In this specific location, or in London generally?"

"Specifically here. And maybe London generally before the kerfuffle thing. You, Nick, Joe. Anyone else you're aware of?"

"Nobody as far as I know." Her expression looked truthful and I was prepared to believe her.

"And none of you mentioned it to anyone?"

"I know I haven't. I can't speak for the other two but I wouldn't have thought so. We all know what's at stake." She nodded at the car. "Do you think this is related to the case?"

It was still too early to mention the bullet.

"The thing is, I bumped into someone I know yesterday," I said. "I say bumped in, but it was as though he knew exactly where I'd be. I'm a bit concerned he might be following me, but more specifically because that'd mean he knew where to start from." I glanced back at the hotel.

"Who?"

"Graham March."

"Shit. You don't think this was him?"

I shrugged.

"Let's just say we don't get on, but it's a new low for him if it is."

"And you're sure you don't want me to report it."

"It's not worth the risk." I checked my watch. This had taken far longer than it should have done and I was aware that Jonathan was still waiting for her. "You get going and I'll call if I need you. I'm going to try to track down Alfie Pattison, if I can. Thank you again for the tape."

"No problem at all. It's not the full show – it's just the links with all the records cut out. That should save you a bit of time."

I gave her a quick hug then watched her turn the corner before starting to think about my next move.

Of course I could ring Graham, and he'd deny it. But what if it wasn't him? It wasn't exactly his style. I looked around with an increasing sense of paranoia. If someone knew I was there, they could be here now, watching me.

I thought of the note. *Go home or prepare to die.*

Of course I wasn't going to go home, but that didn't mean I couldn't make it appear that way. And it didn't mean I had to hang around like a sitting target. It was time to up my game.

Chapter 24

I RETURNED to my room and quickly phoned around a few local car body shops until I found one that could fit me in at short notice, could get hold of red Mercedes paint, and – crucially – who could give me a courtesy car. The more I thought about it, this could actually work to my advantage. If I could leave my car somewhere secure for a couple of days, and drive around in something bland and anonymous, it could only be a benefit.

After that, it was time to make a very visible exit. I packed my bags, checked I'd left nothing behind, then went to reception and explained that my plans had changed and I had to check out because I'd been summoned to go home. Once that was done, I made a show of loading my bags into the car. If someone was watching, they'd at least start to think that I might be taking them seriously. And if they enquired at reception, there was an outside chance they might believe I'd actually gone back to Germany.

That, however, presented other problems. First I had to leave the hotel in such a way that nobody could follow me, but the bigger challenge was finding somewhere new to stay. I'd been trained in anti-surveillance techniques so the first part was easy enough.

For the second, I called Anders. I didn't dare think about the eye-watering expense of making an international mobile call. The standard rate was fearsome enough. Thankfully, all that was taken care of, although I'd yet to work out who paid the bill. If there was a central Blood Angel support office that handled the mundanity of admin, I'd yet to come across it.

"Everything okay?" he asked when I explained the situation.

"Yes, I just need to be careful, that's all. I had a threat so I'm moving out of the hotel."

"What kind of threat?"

"Nothing I need to take too seriously. It's just Graham March being an idiot, but I don't like the thought of him knowing where I am in case he decides to make things awkward for me. What about the safe house in Enfield that I stayed at with Matt?"

"I can do better, I think," said Anders. He was good.

"Ideally I'd need somewhere to park a car too. Like a lock-up."

"A lock-up?"

"Sorry, I mean a garage, or something like that. If not, street parking would do. I'm swapping cars but it would be good to have somewhere to leave the new one."

"I'll call you back."

Two minutes later, my phone rang. But it wasn't Anders. It was Derek from the *Echo*.

"I've got a number and possible location for Alfie Pattison," he said.

"Excellent work. You're a superstar. Thank you."

"I'll warn you, though, I don't know how good it'll be."

"Is he still in Nottingham?"

"No, the good news is that he's back in London, or at least he was the last we heard. But by all accounts he's gone downhill. Spends most of his days between the pub and the bookies."

"Do you know the pub?"

"I'm not a magician. How would I know the pub?"

"Sorry, I was getting carried away. I suppose I thought whoever told you might have mentioned it."

"I'm teasing. It's the Horse and Groom, somewhere near Shepherd's Bush station. I don't have an address for it but I'm sure you'll find it."

"Derek, you're a gem."

I ended the call, feeling like I might actually be getting somewhere.

A moment later, Anders called back with the address of a house in Farringdon, not far from Fleet Street and even closer to the offices of the *Guardian*. I knew the area well.

"What's this one?" I asked.

"It's just another property you can treat as your own. It's been empty for a while, although it gets looked after so it should be clean."

"That sounds perfect, thank you. How do I get hold of the key? Assuming there's a key."

"There's a garage at the back with a padlock. Write this down: press 2 and 4 simultaneously, then 3, then H, then 1. That opens the padlock. Once you're in the garage, the house keys are hidden in a hollowed-out section of a wooden beam towards the back."

"That is amazing. I won't ask how you do it, but I'm hugely grateful."

"Don't mention it. But please, don't tell anyone where you are. At least not until you know who it is who wants you out of the way."

"I'm pretty sure it's Graham."

He hesitated for a moment.

"We have to hope so. We have enough to worry about already."

I didn't like the sound of that, but it wasn't the time to delve deeper.

With my car safely dropped off, and a replacement Vauxhall Astra provided, I set off for Farringdon. Luckily the Astra also had a tape player, so I listened to the radio show as I drove, all the while keeping alert to the possibility of being followed.

Most of the chat was the inane sort of DJ banter you'd expect, and my attention wandered. The weekend was looming. Rex discussed his plans, which hardly sounded like the act of someone about to commit suicide, and invited listeners to call to identify a mystery voice, with the chance to win an ever-growing jackpot that now stood at £400. After records by Queen and Ultravox he made reference to the giant Live Aid concert at Wembley less than a couple of weeks before, then had a rant about Depeche Mode and how they weren't there and possibly hadn't been invited.

He discussed his ex-wife before playing the Simple Minds record *Don't You Forget About Me*, which was either creepy or romantic, depending on how you looked at it. I decided on creepy, as he then went on to discuss his new girlfriend before launching into Stephen "Tin Tin" Duffy's *Kiss Me*. By the end of the recording I was no further forward. It was actually frustrating that the records had been cut out. I liked a bit of Ultravox and Tin Tin back in the day.

I rewound the tape and pressed play again. Five minutes later I slammed on the brakes.

I hadn't spotted it the first time, perhaps because I wasn't attuned to the way he used records to highlight his personal agenda. Second time round it hit me.

After George Michael's *Careless Whisper*, he said: *"I'm playing that for a couple of people I met at lunchtime today, who certainly seem to have some exciting plans together, and we all need a bit of excitement in our lives. Don't worry guys, this one's for you also."* It was followed by Go West's *We Close Our Eyes*.

I skipped back and played it again, analysing every syllable.

A couple of people he met at lunchtime – "guys". So men perhaps? Who were they? What were their exciting plans? Why *careless whisper*? Perhaps more importantly, why *we close our eyes*?

How had I missed it? It couldn't have been any more obvious. Immediately I had a theory. He'd overhead something. He was letting them know. He was suggesting he'd keep it a secret. Implying he'd like to get involved. But this was a man who was happy to discuss his private life in public, so that was a risk they were not willing to take. There was the motive, right there. But who were they? I didn't even know where he'd been.

I got the report from my bag and skimmed through to the pages that mentioned his movements on his final day. Details were minimal as it wasn't deemed to be important, but it referred to a meeting in the Seven Crowns pub in Islington with a journalist called Michael Steward.

Journalist, singular. Guys, plural. Either the journalist brought someone with him or he was referring to someone else.

Potentially it was a red hot lead. My thoughts returned to the picture in the *Echo* photo library. Had the meeting been for a profile piece? The name Michael Steward didn't mean anything to me, but he could have been a freelancer. I couldn't see us publishing a profile article in the daily version, but for the Sunday edition, or one of the supplements, it was a possibility, and they employed endless amounts of freelance writers.

It was a lot to think about, but I was nearly in Farringdon, so I decided to head to the house before settling on a plan. It was in the middle of a residential terrace, within walking distance of Exmouth Market. Once I'd retrieved the keys, I undid a mortice lock and then a Yale lock above it, and even then had to give the door a shove, as it was stuck slightly in its frame.

The house was clean, bland and reasonably well-equipped. I could have done without the Ikea prints decorating the uniformly magnolia walls, but I was grateful for the fresh tube of toothpaste in the bathroom cabinet. It wasn't the Schloss, but as an emergency central London bolthole it was perfect.

I called Alfie's number. Predictably, it had been disconnected, but I could try the pub and hopefully find him there. Before setting off, though, I had a question for Nick.

"Good time?" I asked when he answered.

"Not really," he said, true to form. "What is it?" Given that I was in London, unpaid, specifically to help him, his lack of gratitude was beginning to grate. Actually, correct that. It had been grating since the first night when he met me at the hotel. Now it was beginning to seriously piss me off, but I tried to rise above it.

"I'll be quick," I said. "The day he died, Rex Dexter met a journalist in a pub in Islington. Michael Steward. What do you know about him? And what do you know about who else was there?"

"Personally? Nothing. It'll be in the report."

"You don't have any other insight? You didn't interview him?"

"It was a big team. So no. Is that it? I've got to go."

"It's fine. You go. I'll call you when I've solved it."

He disconnected the call. Which was fortunate because I then added "you miserable twat" and stuck two fingers up at the handset.

I'd had enough of Nick. It was time to get to work, and head west to Shepherd's Bush.

Chapter 25

NICK ended the call. It could hardly have come at a worse time.

"Who the hell was that?" shouted DCI Dougie Compton.

He took a deep breath and turned to face his boss, who was leaning on the door frame of his office.

"It was nothing," Nick called back. "Just someone checking an old case."

"Have you got time to waste on nothing? Get yourself in here."

DS Alan Beattie raised eyebrows and mouthed "good luck".

"Don't arrest me if I murder the bastard," Nick whispered back, as he set off for another bollocking.

"Shut the door," said Dougie, returning to his desk, once Nick was in the room. "And don't even think about sitting down."

Nick closed the door, and then awaited the dressing-down. So far the script was running true to form.

"What have you got to tell me?" asked Dougie.

"Regarding?"

"The case? What the hell you're playing at? I don't know.

Anything you think I should know about."

"I can give you an update on the case, but it's pretty much the same as I gave at the briefing twenty minutes ago." Nick shrugged. He doubted that was the correct answer.

"Okay, fuck the case. We'll try again," said Dougie. "Explain to me why I think you're up to something."

"In what way?"

"In what way? Do I need to spell it out, son? You've been seen chatting to DSI Joe Leyland. You've been seen chatting to DC Emily North. Are either of those involved in your investigations? No. But a billion times worse than that is that you've lied to me."

"How have I lied to you?" Nick's mouth felt dry. He had a sick, hollow feeling in his stomach.

"You're going to pretend you don't know? Tuesday, when I asked where you'd been, when you rolled in late. Remind me what you said."

"That I was chasing up a lead."

"Ah yes. Chasing up a lead. What a load of utter shite."

"I was." This was only going to get worse.

"You bloody weren't. Because I checked. Show me your pocket book."

Nick passed it across, opened to the relevant page, feeling like a schoolchild handing in his homework.

"There," he said, pointing to a phone number.

"Ah yes. Some old bastard. And if I ring him now, he'll verify it for me, will he?"

"He would."

"And that's his number, is it?"

Nick nodded. He'd be okay as long as Dougie didn't dial it. He felt a bead of sweat forming on his forehead.

"Okay, let's put it to the test."

Dougie punched the number into his desk phone with enough force to threaten the well-being of the keypad, then hit another button to put the call onto the speaker.

It rang for about twenty seconds before being diverted to a generic voice mail.

"That's convenient," he snarled, before prodding the button to end the call. "So I'll ask you again. What have you been discussing with Joe Leyland?"

Nick was trying not to show his relief that Clare hadn't answered.

"Nothing dramatic," he said. "He was telling me about the Rex Dexter case. We finally got a result."

"And why was he telling you about that?"

"Because I worked on the case. As did you."

"Exactly. I'm the most senior surviving member of that team. He hasn't spoken to me about it."

"I imagine he thinks you'd already know, or that you're too busy."

"And you're not too busy?" Dougie's voice was getting louder. "He's aware you're investigating a murder? Where did this conversation take place?"

Nick thought back to Tuesday's rant. What had Dougie said?

"On the stairs," he said, remembering. "It was a two-minute chat."

"On the stairs?"

"Yeah."

"And when was that?"

"I can't remember exactly. A few days ago. You said you'd seen us, so whenever that was."

"And you haven't spoken about it since?"

"No."

"You see, that's interesting."

Dougie turned over a piece of paper that had been lying on his desk and thrust it in Nick's direction. It was a photograph of Nick, Emily and Joe in a coffee shop.

"Who's that in the picture?" asked Dougie, with menacing calmness.

"It's me."

"With?"

There was no point denying it.

"DSI Joe Leyland and DC Emily North."

"That doesn't look like a stairwell."

"It's not."

"Damn right it's not." Dougie's temper was beginning to show in his voice again. "And it wasn't a few days ago either. This was yesterday morning."

"Who took the picture?" asked Nick, fighting hard to stem his own rising fury. It wasn't so much that he'd been caught as the thought someone was spying on him.

"It doesn't matter who took the picture," shouted Dougie. "The point is, what the picture shows."

"Of course it matters. If someone's checking up on me, they should at least have the decency to tell me."

"Ha! And that's what you'd do on a surveillance op, is it? Tell the person?"

"No, of course not, but that's not what I meant. Why am I under surveillance?"

"You weren't. Somebody else in the shop was. You just happened to be there and I had to explain to a senior detective running an undercover team what one of my boys was doing in the place, potentially fucking things up. So I'll ask you again, for the final time. What the fuck were you talking about?"

Nick took a deep breath, trying to regain his composure.

"I met Emily for coffee. She's a new detective and she was asking my advice. Joe happened to be there. He popped over and said hello. I introduced him to Emily. It's not what it looks like."

Dougie laughed, then stood up and leaned over his desk, before stabbing his finger in Nick's direction.

"I'll tell you what it looks like. Either you're brown-nosing to the brass or you're up to something. Or more specifically Joe Leyland is up to something. I'm a detective, son. I'm not stupid. I see evidence and I come to conclusions. Is it about Clare Woodbrook?"

"*What?*" Nick immediately felt another bead of sweat forming.

"Don't pretend you don't know who I mean. I've heard a rumour she might be back."

"Wasn't she killed in a helicopter crash?"

"Obviously you don't believe that shite."

"What have you heard?"

"It's none of your business what I've heard. Let me tell you the way this works, son: you report to me. Not the other way round. Understood? So for the final fucking time before I fire you, is that what you were talking to Joe Leyland about?"

Nick shook his head.

"Clare Woodbrook wasn't Joe's case, was she? Wasn't DCS Terry Handley more interested in that one?"

"Don't try to be funny, son, and answer the question."

"No, hand on heart." Nick put the palm of his hand on his chest to emphasise the point. "I can absolutely promise you, on my mother's life or anything else you want me to promise on, we were not discussing the possibility of Clare Woodbrook coming back. He wasn't telling us to keep an eye out for her. There was no mention of her getting arrested. Happy?"

"Okay." Dougie's voice dropped, and he sat down again. "Well, a word to the wise, or in your case, the terminally inept. There's a possibility she might resurface. If you do hear anything, on your travels, you bring it to me, all right?"

"Not DCS Handley?"

"Are you taking the piss? You bring it to me, I'll take it to Handley. If there's any glory to be had, I'll make sure some of it heads in your direction, but you come to me first. Understood?"

Nick nodded. He was waiting for the worst enemy speech, but it didn't come.

"Now fuck off and find me a murderer," his boss said instead.

Chapter 26

MY phone rang, but I didn't answer it. The incoming number was the Metropolitan Police switchboard. If someone was checking Nick or Emily's call records, the last thing I was going to do was hang us all.

Instead, I set out in the Astra in the direction of Shepherd's Bush. It wasn't my favourite part of London. Despite the huge BBC Television Centre nearby, with all the attendant glamour and theoretical steady flow of celebrities, the area appeared rough and grimy. That might have been an unfair assessment, as I'd never spent significant time there, but there was something about the prevalence of concrete and how the Underground trains were no longer underground that gave it an air of being a backwater. It was busy, though, full of cars, buses, taxis, vans and more, along with small, bustling independent shops, and non-chain takeaways.

The Horse and Groom was every bit as grim as I'd expected. I'd opted for a skirt, boots and trench coat again, and it was far from appropriate dress. Not to worry. I'd long mastered the art of feeling uncomfortable.

The bar was largely deserted, but there was a grey mist of

cigarette smoke and an aroma of stale beer to complement the dark wood and aura of decay. Two old customers sat in the corner, playing dominoes. Actually they might not have been old, but regularly hitting the hard stuff before noon can have a cumulative effect on the complexion.

The only picture I'd seen of Alfie Pattison was one in the *Echo* library that had been taken at least eight years ago, and he hadn't looked in peak condition then. But I was confident that neither of the customers was him.

"Can I help you, love?" asked a tired-looking barmaid, who was perhaps in her late fifties, as she picked up a glass and started polishing it on a filthy-looking tea towel. It didn't look like the kind of place where the glasses got polished regularly, so I suspected her motivation was to keep one close at hand in case she wanted to smash it into my face.

It was tricky. The last thing I wanted was to have a drink in the place, but equally, I didn't want to appear rude or to give the impression that I felt superior.

"I was looking for someone," I said, once I'd ordered a Diet Coke with no ice to minimise the risk of cholera.

"Oh yeah?" said the barmaid, squirting a vaguely brown, vaguely fizzy liquid into a half pint glass.

"I don't think he's here, though," I continued, looking around again.

"Do you have a name?"

In for a penny.

"Alfie. Alfie Pattison."

"I meant your name. You don't look like an Alfie."

"Oh, I see what you mean. I'm, er, Lottie. Lottie Sadler."

Variation on a theme. I really did need to come up with something new altogether.

She sniffed.

"You're looking for Alfie, then. Come to arrest him?"

"What? No! Just about the opposite. I'm not the police. Anything but. Is he due in, do you know?"

She shrugged and shouted across the bar.

"Anyone seen Alfie?"

The hardened drinkers were slow to react, but eventually one looked up and shook his head before returning to the serious business of daytime intoxication.

"Any idea where he might be?" I asked.

"What's it worth, darlin'?"

She passed me the glass of something that really wasn't Diet Coke, and I gave her a couple of pound coins in exchange. I didn't expect change, and none was forthcoming.

"Why does everyone think I've got money?" I said. "How about, if I find him I'll bring him in here and buy us both a drink, and if you're really lucky I'll go for a bag of dry roasted peanuts."

"If you're going to be like that, I've not seen him. Fact is, the name doesn't ring a bell. I think you got the wrong boozer."

I sighed.

"Okay, I'm sorry," I said. "I didn't mean that to come across the way it probably did. But the fact is, I'm looking for Alfie as much for his own benefit as mine. It's nothing to worry about, and I'm not being paid by anyone to do it, so I don't have a budget for information. If I can't find him, so be it. I'll go back home and not bother you again. But a friend of a friend suggested I might find him here, so if you do know, that would be hugely appreciated. And I very much will bring him here and probably end up buying several."

She looked at me as though coming to a decision, then looked at the clock on the wall.

"Depends on the fixtures, I suspect. If he's on a roll you'll find him in the bookies two doors up. If not, he'll be back in to nurse his losses any minute."

That gave me a decision. And it meant I could avoid drinking the non-Diet Coke.

"I'll go and have a look, and drag him back," I said, giving her a smile. "That's a huge help."

"Think nothin' of it, darlin'," she said. "Mine's a double Gordon's when you get here."

I found the bookmakers. I found Alfie. And I was right, he hadn't aged well. He wasn't difficult to spot, given that the only other person in the betting shop was behind a perspex screen. He didn't seem to notice me enter, his eyes fixed on one of the colour television monitors suspended from the ceiling, showing a horse race from God-knows-where. Judging by his language at the finishing line, I suspected things hadn't gone well.

"Not your day?" I asked as I approached. He looked up, regarding me through bloodshot eyes, though whether it was the heartbreak of losing or general ill health, I wasn't sure.

"You look like a man who knows what you're doing," I continued. "I've never done this before, but I've been given a tenner to stick on a race. Could you help me? If it comes in, I'll buy you a drink with the winnings."

He grunted something, took the ten pound note and filled out a betting slip for me. A few minutes later, the horse lost.

"Okay, better still, why don't we go and drown our sorrows?" I said, as he screwed up the slip and threw it on the floor. "My treat."

Not wanting to blow my own trumpet, but I like to think I'm reasonably presentable when I'm dressed nicely, and it was probably the best offer he'd had in years. But still he looked uncertain.

"You're up to something, mate," he said, in a voice scarred by nicotine and alcohol.

"Not really," I said. "But are you Alfie?"

Immediately he was on guard, his eyes darting past me, showing a mixture of confusion and uncertainty.

"Don't worry, I'm not here to cause anyone trouble."

"Are you the police?"

"No."

"Journalist?"

"No."

"What then?"

"I suppose you could say freelance investigator, but it's not my main job. I've just got an inquisitive mind, that's all."

The lure of free alcohol cleared any lingering doubts, and within ten minutes we were back at the Horse and Groom. Alfie wasted no time in attacking his pint.

"It's about Rex Dexter," I said.

"What about him?"

"Someone just confessed to his murder."

His expression grew more confused still.

"I haven't read anything about it," he said.

"It hasn't been announced yet." I dared to take a sip of my second glass of fake Diet Coke, but it was a tiny one and I was in no rush to ever have another. "I'm trying to find out a bit of the background. You knew him well, didn't you?"

"Rex Dexter?" He shrugged. "Yeah, we were mates, back in the day."

It was time to take a risk.

"Didn't he once get you fired?" I asked, aware that it could go one of two ways: either he'd have a rant or he'd shut up completely. In the event, he took an unexpected third option and laughed.

"God no. I was done anyway. They were already getting rid of me."

"But I thought he said something about you on air?"

"Of course he did. He used to do that all the time, and I did the same to him. It was a running joke, ask anyone. It was all banter."

The pint was already nearly finished. I headed back to the bar.

"Another pint of whatever that was and another Gordon's for yourself," I said to the barmaid.

"Double?"

"Rude not to."

This time she did give me change, but I didn't risk offending her by counting it.

"So you weren't enemies then?" I said, returning to Alfie, and putting the new drink in front of him.

"No, far from it. He was a mate if anything. I couldn't believe it when he died. It was the end of an era. We were the last of the old guard. The last to actually care about the music." He looked wistful, as though lost in thoughts of happier times. "But that was the industry as a whole. I kind of lost the will after that. By the time I packed it in, it was all manufactured Stock Aitken Waterman shit, then house and rap, and boy bands and Christ-what-have-you. And now all the talk is this new bloody Britpop. What a load of wank. I thought I'd come back to London, perhaps use some of my contacts, and set up as a promoter, putting on real bands for real people, but nobody's interested. Our time is done."

I had to admit, he had a point. When I was young, growing up in the '70s and '80s, I never thought I'd lose the love of music, and the excitement of watching my favourite bands climb the Top 40. But now I had no idea who was number one.

"Was he in trouble before he died?" I asked.

The question brought Alfie back to the present.

"Rex? He was always in trouble, mate."

"How do you mean?"

"He was a relentless skirt chaser. You must have heard of his reputation?"

"I heard about his ex-wife and his new girlfriend."

"And the others. He was always like that, though. He loved the glamour of it. The glamour. Ha."

He looked around the pub, as if to emphasise the point.

"Did you talk to him often?"

"Once I'd gone to Nottingham? Not every day but every so often, if you know what I mean."

I didn't, but I let it pass.

"You don't know anything about a journalist he met the day he died?"

"Haha, that."

That sounded a bit more optimistic.

"What happened?" I asked.

"Nothing happened, as far as I know, but it was one of a long list. The thing you need to know about Rex, God bless his soul, was that he was trying to persuade someone to write his autobiography for him. A ghostwriter. He had this thing about it making him seem legit. Thought people would be interested in the warts-and-all lifestyle."

"You don't think they would be?"

"I didn't see anyone wanting to buy a book about it. He'd been in the tabloids plenty of times. I wasn't sure there was anything left to add."

Aware that the barmaid was watching us, I picked up my drink, and pretended to almost take a sip before putting it down again.

"The journalist he met was called Michael Steward," I said, returning to Alfie. "You don't know anything about him?"

"Nah, mate. Like I said, just the latest in a long line of hacks who were going to turn him down, I suspect. Although circumstances spared him the need to say it."

"Did you have any theories on who killed him?"

"Rex? Presumably your geezer who's confessed to it."

The second pint was diminishing rapidly. Aside from anything else, I was impressed at his bladder control.

"But if it wasn't him," I said. "Did you have any theories at the time?"

"Me? Nah. I mean, it was a shock, but some of the conspiracy theories I read about it were obviously a complete bag of shit."

"Which ones?"

"All of them. He wasn't an angel but the thought he'd annoy someone enough to kill him is just ... I don't know. I found it hard to believe then. Still find it hard to believe now."

"Does the name Eddie Whitfield mean anything to you?"

In fairness to Alfie, he at least seemed to consider it.

"Nope," he said, shaking his head, and looking longingly at the near-empty glass. Surely he'd need to offload some soon. "Who's he when he's at home?"

"Just a bloke whose name got mentioned. He's died now, so I can't speak to him personally."

"Well, he doesn't ring any bells with me."

It was time to wind things up, but I bought him a third pint anyway.

"So what are you up to now?" I asked when I returned.

"Me? I just soldier on, don't I? You've got to hope it's all cyclical and that things'll come back into fashion. Believe it when I see it, though. I'm waiting for real bands and real music, and then I'll stage my comeback, haha. I mean look at the charts this year. Look at the bloody number ones. Shaggy, 2 Unlimited, Take That, Culture fucking Beat. Christ help us."

Again, he had a point. I left Alfie to ponder the demise of civilisation and returned to my car. My overriding impression was that his heart was in the right place. True, I only had one side of the story, but every instinct told me he wasn't a murderer.

And that left me ever more needing to track down Michael Steward and still trying to find a link to Eddie Whitfield. There had to be something, but whatever it was defied any logic. It was time to make another call.

Alfie stood up, belched, and then popped to the gents. On his way back, he bought a pack of seventeen cigarettes from the vending machine, and took them to the payphone at the end of the bar.

Propping himself up on a stool, he took a piece of paper from his jacket pocket, and carefully dialled the number he'd been given.

"She's just been in," he said. "Called herself Lottie something. No. I didn't tell her anything new, as far as I know. All right, mate. Pleasure doing business with you." He ended the call and ordered another drink.

Chapter 27

THE phone was answered on the third ring.

"Derek," I said. "Charlotte."

He laughed.

"I'm struggling with Charlotte. Charlotte's a nice name. I couldn't imagine a Charlotte doing the same kind of things a Cla–"

"Shhh. Heaven's sake."

"It's okay, nobody can overhear. Howyadoin? Tell me you don't want another favour. If you do, I assume you're trying to get me fired."

"No, no more favours, I'm still hugely in your debt for the last one."

"The last several."

"That as well. And I definitely don't want to get you fired. You're one of the few people in this world I think I can trust."

"That sounds like you're about to ask me another favour."

"Me? Haha. Far from it."

I was, but I was building up to it. I sat back in the seat of the Astra, glad I'd found a parking space that was reasonably discreet.

"Are you going to tell me what's going on?" asked Derek.

"I'd be very happy to, if I knew," I said.

"There's clearly something."

It was time to trust my instincts.

"Look, you're going to hear about this any minute anyway. Remember I mentioned Rex Dexter, the DJ."

"Of course."

"Someone's confessed to his murder. There's going to be a press conference."

"Wow. Okay."

"But personally I don't think the person who confessed actually did it, so I'm checking out some of the background."

"Can't you ask the person who confessed? Suggest it to the police. You get on well with them." He started to laugh.

"Good one. No, he's dead. It was a video confession as he was on his deathbed. So that makes it harder."

"And what is it to you?"

"Call it the pursuit of justice. You know I've always been a big fan."

"Hmmm."

"Within reason, and as long as it doesn't mean I get arrested, but that goes without saying."

I found a mint in the pocket of my trench coat and started to suck it, hoping it'd take away the lingering aftertaste of whatever the brown stuff had been.

"I imagine it's not easy for you to investigate, though, especially given your circumstances," said Derek, sounding thoughtful.

"Believe me, it's hopeless. But I'm resourceful. I've just spoken to Alfie Pattison."

"Do you think he was the real killer?"

"No, I really don't think so."

"And so this new favour?"

"Ah, Derek, as if. No, I was just wondering if you'd ever come across a journalist called Michael Steward? Steward with a d."

He paused. Was he thinking or trying to come up with a way of avoiding the question?

"I've heard the name," he said at last. "I'm just trying to think of where."

"He's a freelancer, or at least I think he was."

"And you want his phone number?"

"I mean, if you're offering I wouldn't turn you down, as that could be extremely useful, but you definitely just offered that. I didn't ask."

I couldn't stop a chuckle.

"You didn't need to," he said.

"You're an absolute diamond."

"I'm an absolute idiot, I'll give you that. Wait there and I'll find out and call you back."

I had a better plan.

"What are you doing tonight?" I asked.

"Oh God."

"It's nothing bad. I wondered if you'd be happy to meet me for dinner, my treat. Catch up on the old days."

"That makes me very suspicious."

"It's a genuine offer, with no other agenda, I promise. I owe you."

"I'd have to check indoors."

"Do that. It'd be lovely to see you and talk about things properly."

"Leave it with me. I'll call you back."

While Derek consulted with his wife, I called Nick. And when he didn't answer, I tried Emily.

"Hiya, how's it going?" she asked.

"Interesting meeting with Alfie," I said. "I'd like to chat to you though. Bring you up to speed and discuss some ideas. Is this a good time?"

Judging by the hesitation, I suspected it wasn't.

"I'm about to go into a meeting and it's going to be a late night tonight, but I could pop out for a little while. Could you get to the South Bank around six?"

I looked at my watch. There'd just about be time to do that before meeting Derek, assuming he said yes. Which I hoped he would.

"Perfect," I said. We agreed a meeting place and then ended the call.

A moment later, Derek rang back and confirmed his availability. It was exactly the kind of boost I needed. It would be lovely to catch up. I suggested a restaurant I knew in Covent Garden, then drove back to Farringdon with a lot on my mind.

"Was that her?" asked DCS Terry Handley.

"It was." Emily was pleased they were meeting in the underground car park. If anyone noticed, it would look far more like a casual conversation between two colleagues, albeit of vastly different rank. "She's been busy. She said yes to the South Bank, though."

"Excellent. I'll get someone down with a camera. Keep doing what you're doing. Let me know what she says."

Emily was waiting for me, leaning on the metal railings opposite the National Theatre, with her back towards the Thames. When she saw me, she waved, and then fell in step as we walked along the bank of the river, dodging joggers, skateboarders, and tourists taking pictures, despite the darkness.

"So, a successful day?" she said.

"Not really. It's Thursday already. So far all I've managed to do is get in trouble with Neil Fearon, get my car wrecked, and have a drink with Alfie Pattison. And none of that has got me much further forward. Any luck with Alex Ward?"

"I've asked around. Nobody has a bad word to say about him."

"Are you sure?"

"More than that, he actually has commendations for arresting a couple of police officers who were on the take."

"He could still be corrupt, though."

She shook her head.

"Everyone I asked said the same. Everyone thinks he's brilliant, which is incredibly rare in our place."

That was frustrating, but it tallied with what Joe had said. I thought about rehashing the Agatha Christie theory, but I didn't want to spend the remaining days getting sidetracked if he was as innocent as everyone said. On their heads be it.

"How was Pattison?" asked Emily.

"He was okay. Surprisingly lucid for someone who seems to spend most of the day getting pissed."

"Did he tell you anything you didn't know?"

I shook my head, then paused while we walked past one of those street artists who dress in a silver outfit and pretend to be a statue.

"He claims he was big mates with Rex Dexter," I continued once we were safely out of earshot. "I'm inclined to believe him. Thanks for the tape, by the way. That was useful."

I decided to keep my theory about the overheard conversation in the Seven Crowns to myself for now, until I'd tracked down Michael Steward and asked him if he could remember anything about it.

"Is there anything you need from me?" asked Emily.

"A miracle?" I laughed. "Actually, I asked Nick if he could speak to some of Eddie Whitfield's family for me, but I get the impression it's the last thing he's going to find time for."

"Okay. Do you want me to do it? I can't promise either but I can check to see if he's done it and if not I'll do my best. What would you need to ask them?"

"I'm still looking for a link between him and Rex Dexter. Even if it's not a direct one, there's got to be something. Did he have a particular fascination with the Dexter case? Had he ever talked about it? Did he know anybody who knew anybody who might be involved?"

"I'll do my best but it won't be till tomorrow at the earliest."

"Don't worry if you can't. Nick says they were as shocked as anyone, and I've got no reason to doubt that. Better still, if you can get me names and addresses, I'll do it. They might be happier to talk to me than to the police. Possibly not, but I'm working on the basis that they don't want their dad, uncle, whatever, remembered for a crime he didn't commit."

When we reached the Oxo Tower we turned round and started heading back towards Waterloo Bridge. That was the closest to Covent Garden. I opted against telling Emily about Derek.

"Have you managed to get your car sorted?" she asked.

"I have. It's going to be a rush job but hopefully they'll have it finished by Saturday. If not I'm going to have a long walk home."

"When are you heading back?"

"Sunday, I hope. Although that only gives me two more days here and I think I'd need two years to get to the bottom of this."

I didn't tell her about the relocation to Farringdon. Anders had warned me not to tell anyone, and although I trusted Emily, there was no reason to mention the move.

We had to wait while a couple of young lovers took pictures of each other with the river in the background, not that they'd see the water in the finished result. Their flash wouldn't travel that far, but I didn't want to disillusion them.

"Everything else all right with you?" I asked.

"I'm struggling with the case. Missing children are the worst."

"I can understand that. If I was a parent I couldn't imagine anything more terrifying."

"Have you never thought about having children?"

"Haha, me? What sort of mother would I make?"

She laughed.

"A good one, I think."

"Right. Can you imagine the bit where they're at school and they have to write an essay about their parents' occupation? Anyway, I'm not a doctor but I think it'd be biologically impossible without some input from someone male, and there's very little chance of that."

"Have you not got a boyfriend?"

Sometimes her naivety was touching. How to even begin explaining that one?

"No," I said instead. "Although I think Nick quite likes me."

Hopefully she realised I was being ironic.

By the time we reached the bridge, Emily said she had to go. I gave her a hug, told her I'd call her tomorrow to confirm dinner arrangements, and then watched as she walked towards Waterloo Station. I was ready to have a couple of hours off, and was very much looking forward to seeing Derek. I made my way up to the bridge, started walking across, and only a couple of times thought about jumping off.

It was several years since DCI Dougie Compton had last worked on a case with DCS Terry Handley, but the two knew each other well enough that Dougie's invitation to meet in the canteen for a cup of tea had been accepted without too many questions as to the reasons why.

Once they'd caught up on job-related small talk, Dougie sensed it was time to get to the point.

"I've heard a little rumour Clare Woodbrook might be back in the vicinity," he said.

"Interesting," said Terry. "And where did that particular nugget come from?"

Dougie didn't want to mention Graham March by name. That would blow any sense of credibility, and this was all about potentially scoring points with the top brass.

"Just a rumour on the street. Nothing guaranteed but I've asked some of my boys to keep an ear out. Obviously, if I hear anything I'll bring it to you."

"That'd be appreciated. Any more details than that? Where she is? What she's up to?"

"Nothing at the moment. Although I've got a possibly-related suspicion."

Dougie looked around to make sure he couldn't be overheard, then leaned forward and lowered his voice anyway.

"Joe Leyland is up to something," he said. "He always got on well with her, didn't he?"

"I really wouldn't know," said Terry. "My job is to find her, not find out who her friends are."

"Understood. But he's been hovering round, meeting with one of my sergeants and a DC. Emily North. Do you know her?"

Terry shook his head.

"I lose track. There are so many of them."

"That's understandable as well. But listen, I spoke to my sergeant and he gave me some shite about it being a chat about the Rex Dexter case. You've heard about the confession?"

"Of course."

"I think it's bullshit, but I'm going to check it out," Dougie said. "Get to the bottom of it, and if it is about that, then I'll find out what the hell they're playing at. But it's all a bit of a coincidence and I don't like coincidences. Suddenly Joe Leyland is having secret meetings at the same time that Woodbrook is rumoured to be back. Something about it doesn't smell right."

"You think Leyland's meeting up with her?"

"I think she could wrap the old bastard round her finger if she wanted to. Like I say, it's just a suspicion, but I'm going to keep an eye on it. I'll keep digging, and if I come across anything about that – or even if it is just about Rex Dexter – I'll let you know."

"Intriguing." Terry finished his cup of tea and placed the Styrofoam cup back on the table. "You do that, Dougie. It'd be appreciated."

"Pleasure, sir," said Dougie. "Leave it to me. I'll be back in touch."

Chapter 28

WE were halfway through the main course before Derek confessed to his marital problems.

"I'm sorry to hear that," I said. "God. Are you okay?"

"Yeah, kind of." He didn't look okay. He looked on the verge of tears. "Don't breathe a word of this to anyone. I haven't mentioned anything at work, and I've got no intention of doing so."

"Of course. Not that I'm actually on speaking terms with anyone apart from you."

"I appreciate that." He looked wistful. I have to admit, it killed the mood a bit.

"I don't want to pry," I said, "but if you'd like to talk about it, I'm happy to provide a sympathetic ear. God knows I'm not best qualified, but sometimes it's good to get things off your chest. And you know I'm going to take your side, whatever happens."

Derek took a big slug of wine.

"In one sense I'd like to talk about it, but in another I'm still in denial, you know?" He took a mouthful of pasta. "It's like tonight. You invited me out and I gave you some rubbish about needing to check with my wife. There was nobody to check with. She moved out three weeks ago."

I immediately wanted to give him a hug.

"That's awful," I said, instead.

"We were married twenty-two years. As far as I knew we were happy. Then one day she announced she'd had enough and wanted different things and that was it. Next thing I knew, she was literally packing her bags."

"But why? Is there someone else?" Immediately I wished I hadn't asked that as it was probably the last thing Derek wanted to think about. Thankfully he seemed unfazed.

"That's the thing. I could understand if there was. But no, she's gone to stay with her sister in Scarborough. I think that's what hurts the most. I could understand if she'd found someone else, but it seems like having nobody is better than having me."

"Oh, Derek." Definite hug territory. "You can't think like that. People are strange. They do strange things. Look at me if you want evidence of that. I suspect once she's had a bit of time to clear her head, she'll come running back."

I hoped I was being reassuring, but instead he shook his head.

"No. She rang last night. Wasn't on long, but long enough to say she wanted a divorce."

"Did she say why?"

"Only that she felt we'd grown apart, and she wanted to do new things with her life. So now I'm here, aged fifty-three, facing up to the fact that I've got to start all over again. Living in a city with eight million other people, but utterly convinced I'll never meet anyone."

"Oh, you will, if that's what you want. But there's no rush, is there? You'd be a huge catch for someone, and I'm sure they'll come along eventually, but in the meantime take some time out for yourself. Try new things. Most important of all, though, don't listen to a word that I say, as I'm hardly a shining beacon of rationality."

That made him smile, which was a start.

"Don't take this the wrong way," he said, "but that's why I'm conflicted."

"How do you mean conflicted?"

"About you. I mean, this is lovely, and I can't tell you how happy I was to hear from you, but I'm also pissed off that you went away in the first place, because I think back to the start of this year, and everything was happy. You were in the office, and we were good friends, and I'd go home, and I thought I was happily married. And I'm not for one minute suggesting that you disappearing had anything to do with Angela moving out, but it just adds to the sense of loss. Does that make sense?"

I reached out and held his hand, giving it a squeeze, before letting go and taking an equally big slug of wine.

"I feel awful," I said.

"You shouldn't. It's not your fault. And yet, yes you should, because that bit was. I want to wind the clock back to 1992 and start this year all over again."

"You and me both, Derek."

He shrugged.

"Sorry if that annoys you," he said.

The earnest look on his face nearly broke me.

"Of course it doesn't annoy me," I said, softening my voice. "I deserve everything I get. I let everyone down. You, me, everyone. I keep thinking I should just turn myself in and be done with it, and yet I'm scared of what would happen. I don't want to go to prison." I paused to check nobody was listening in. Thankfully. none of the other diners was paying us any attention. "But sometimes I think I should. Get it over with, because until I do I'm always going to have it hanging over me. I'd love to think that one day I could walk down the street without looking over my shoulder, but then I think: is that me being selfish again?"

"How do you mean?"

"I don't really know what I mean. I suppose that I feel I want to put things right. I didn't for one minute think of the hurt I'd cause other people until that night in Geneva when Danny and Anna found me. I thought I was being ever so clever, but then I looked into their faces and realised the scale of the disaster I'd just created. And I hate to think I hurt you, of all people, because you really are one of the good guys. But how do I put it right? By being a good person? The truth is, I don't ever really think I can."

"We're as bad as each other."

"Oh, Derek, don't for one minute think that. I've got an unassailable lead in the badness race."

He smiled, just slightly.

"I meant in terms of emotions. I always think of you as this incredibly strong person, but I suppose we all have our weaknesses."

The food was finished and he'd started to roll a cigarette. I offered him a Silk Cut but he declined so I took one for myself, but waited till he was ready before lighting it.

"I've definitely got weaknesses," I said, blowing smoke at the ceiling and then focusing my attention on the cigarette. "More than you'd ever be able to count." That made me think of Emily, for a moment, and the strong likelihood that she'd be able to give me a definitive number off the top of her head. "I don't know what the answer is. Sometimes I'm not even sure I understand the question."

We both decided it was time to change the subject. Over dessert he told me that the Eddie Whitfield confession story had broken and would be the lead the following morning. Then he gave me the latest office gossip, and when the bill arrived he tried to pay, but I absolutely wasn't having any of it.

"Thank you for tonight," he said, as we stood on the street, waiting for cabs to take us in our own separate directions. "It really was good to see you. And it was good to talk, even though it's a painful process."

"It's my absolute pleasure," I said, giving him a farewell hug.

"You have my number. I really mean it. Call me any time. If there's no answer or the number gets disconnected for any reason, you've got my email address too. And if none of that works, I am going to patch things up with Danny, if I can. Either way, we absolutely have to stay in touch."

"We will, I'm sure."

I knew I'd worry about Derek far more than he'd ever realise. I spent the taxi ride back to Farringdon desperately trying to think of something I could do to help him, but I was still no further forward.

I replayed the conversation in my head. Not all of it, but the highlights. Something was nagging at me, but I couldn't place it. And no matter how deeply I searched the inner recess of my mind, it remained tantalisingly out of reach. Maybe I'd imagined it.

All I wanted to do was curl up in bed and sleep forever, but I couldn't. I had a nightclub to visit.

Chapter 29

PERHAPS it was madness and I should have stayed well clear, but I still had strong suspicions about Neil Fearon. And while I couldn't exactly turn up at his office again and say "sorry about the last time, let's start afresh", I could, at least, try to find out more by watching his door staff in action, looking for evidence of drug dealing or anything else that would cast doubt on his credibility.

I'd never been to Suadela, but reminded myself of Joe's words. *It's classy, you'd fit in.*

I didn't feel classy. I felt tired, emotional, and a physical mess. And on top of everything, I had nobody to go with. That wasn't a problem in one sense – I didn't have any fear about going out on my own – but, frustratingly, we live in a world where a woman going to a bar or club by herself is going to attract unwelcome attention in myriad different ways.

My outfit choices were limited, so I opted for a black dress, sheer black tights, black suede heels and my trench coat. If I was going to look like a prostitute, I might as well also look like a flasher.

I didn't expect that Neil himself would be there, but

nevertheless fixed my hair to look as different as possible to the day before, and added a pair of clear lens glasses for at least a token element of disguise.

Since I'd already had several glasses of wine, the car had to stay at home, so I hailed a cab and ten minutes later I was in a side street just off Leicester Square. Even though it was nearly 11pm, the place was still buzzing, with hundreds of people milling round, fresh from the cinema or a restaurant, or heading out for a night on the town. It's not true to say that London never sleeps. It's not New York. But at 11pm, Leicester Square was a long way off contemplating bedtime.

The unwelcome attention started as soon as I left the safe confines of the taxi. I ignored the leering of a group of drunk young men, even though I was tempted to punch the lot of them, and instead made my way to the club. There was a queue of hopefuls outside, but the door staff were being selective in that irritatingly elitist way in which people are judged on their appearance and outfit rather than personality and character.

That said, I didn't fancy queuing, so I took my chance by turning up at the front and was waved straight through. Thank God for make-up.

The club was vast, with room for perhaps a thousand people. Pulsing electronic dance music assaulted my ears. Huge lighting rigs spun, flashed and swirled over the stage and main dance floor, with ultraviolet strips causing anything white to glow through the haze of cigarette smoke and lingering dry ice. There were perhaps half a dozen bars at ground floor level, while several staircases led to upper gallery floors that looked down upon the main action. All around, darkened alcoves offered sanctuary for those needing a break from dancing, Or just for a smooch. I wouldn't be needing those.

It was already busy, but the steady flow of new arrivals meant it was getting more crowded by the minute. I made my way to one of the bars, narrowly avoiding the gyrating bodies of the young and glamorous, and ordered a double vodka and lemonade. I don't know why. I don't like vodka, and it wasn't wise to mix drinks, but the half-dressed girl behind the bar didn't look like a competent sommelier. No disrespect to her.

With the drink in hand, I set out to explore, looking for evidence of any bouncer-sanctioned drug dealing. But if there was any, they were discreet about it. The security staff were generally keeping a low profile, hovering in the shadows, with dark suits and earpieces, casting a glance on proceedings and alert to trouble should any arise. But it wasn't that kind of crowd. I suspected most were tourists, not yet used to the currency and therefore oblivious to the extortionate prices. They all seemed to be having a good time.

The upper floors were much the same. The building had clearly been a theatre in a former life. The gallery levels gave a fantastic view of the main stage and dance floor, and it was fascinating on a technical level to look down on the spinning lighting rigs, wondering just how much carnage there would be if one of the wires snapped.

There was a wall at the front, just above waist height. I stood for a while, leaning against it, trying to take everything in. And then a man approached me.

I say man. He couldn't have been more than eighteen or nineteen. He was wafer-thin, and smoking a cigarette and trying to look cool with it. His floppy hair, eyeliner and black nail varnish were joined by a white shirt, undone to the waist.

"Hi," he shouted, just about audibly over the thump of the music. "You don't look very happy."

"Me?" That took me aback. "I'm fine. I'm having a whale of a time."

"Are you sure?"

I nodded and turned away.

"Would you like a drink?" He was persistent, if nothing else.

I held up my glass to show him it was still half full but was shocked to discover I'd finished it, so that backfired.

"What are you having?"

I couldn't place his accent. It was vaguely northern, possibly Manchester. I shook my head and waved my hand over the top in a "no thanks" gesture.

"Are you sure?"

"Positive."

"I can't hear you. Do you want to go somewhere quieter? What's your name?"

The grin told me he'd heard every word quite clearly, but if he thought I was going to head off into the darkness with a man-boy he was very badly mistaken. I was more likely to push him over the wall.

I turned and walked away, momentarily considered going to the bar myself, then headed back to the ground floor, past a corded-off VIP area. I tried to look inside, as you do, but a big security man gave me a stern look and then waved me away.

The whole operation was too slick, too glossy and too professional to openly take any risks with illegal sidelines. If there was anything going on, it would be out of sight. I checked the toilets, and stood for a while, reapplying lipstick and adjusting my hair, all the while listening for any evidence of dealing, but there was absolutely nothing.

In the end, I decided the direct approach was the only option. The trouble was, my experience with drugs was minimal and I'd certainly never bought any. Not that I actually wanted to now – I just wanted to see if they were supplying them. I didn't even know what I was supposed to ask for. Cocaine? Charlie? Colombian marching powder? Some other code word that I wasn't aware of? Or maybe ecstasy, or MDMA. Was that the sort of thing you'd get in a night club or was it all uppers, downers and magic mushrooms? Were they even still a thing in 1993?

I thought about heading back upstairs to find the man-boy. He looked like the type who would know, but I didn't want to start giving the wrong impression. But just as I was considering the possible outcomes, I saw him heading down the staircase, arm in arm with a gorgeous young blonde. He noticed me looking then gave a momentary shrug as if to say "your loss". The arrogant shit. Even then, though, he kept looking in my direction as they walked towards the dance floor.

Logic suggested that if there was any action anywhere, it would probably be back in the VIP area. Which I'd already been waved away from. It was worth a second attempt, though, so I headed back and approached the bouncer, rubbing my chin with my right hand so he couldn't possibly miss the ring.

His immediate headshake wasn't encouraging.

"I don't want to come in," I shouted. "I'm looking for something."

He obviously didn't hear me, but at least he leaned down to bring his head closer for a second attempt. I felt like pulling the earpiece out for the sake of mischief, but instead just repeated the words.

"What are you looking for?" he shouted back in a big deep voice. He was everything the man-boy wasn't.

"Something to help me dance the night away," I shouted, with a wink and a smile, hoping he'd take the hint. Instead his face darkened.

"I'll pretend I didn't hear that," he shouted back, standing back up until he was towering over me, despite my heels. I suddenly realised it was time to get out of there.

With as much haste as possible, I made my way back to the cloakroom, and retrieved my trench coat. What a waste of a night. Well, maybe not a complete waste. I hadn't proved anything, but at least I'd seen the set-up. And there was one last opportunity. I still had to walk past the door staff.

The cold night air was a welcome change, but my ears were still ringing from the music, and it took a moment to assess my options. I paused at the door to light a cigarette, but then pretended my lighter was broken, so stepped towards the friendliest-looking bouncer.

"Excuse me," I said, "you don't happen to have a light, do you?"

He tapped a colleague on the shoulder, and when the man turned, performed a hand gesture that simulated sparking a flame and nodded in my direction. His colleague reached into his jacket pocket and passed me an orange Bic, waited until I'd finished, then took it back off me and turned back to face the queue.

"It's busy in there," I said to the first one, as I let out a stream of smoke. He might have looked friendly, but he wasn't particularly conversational. There was the hint of a grunt but nothing more.

"I'm heading home," I continued. "Although I think I could do with something to give me some energy." Admittedly, it probably wasn't the strongest line I'd ever delivered. He definitely heard me, though, because suddenly I felt like I was being scrutinised. And then I realised things were about to go very badly indeed. He had two fingers over his earpiece, blocking the ambient sound, and was clearly listening hard to some instruction that quite possibly indicated my disguise hadn't really done its job.

I didn't hang around to find out if I was just being paranoid. Instead I darted past him, narrowly avoiding his arm which had reached out to grab me. I wasn't in the shoes to run, and he was twice my size. But just as I thought I was really in trouble, his attention was taken by a scuffle in the queue.

I seized my chance, and ran as best I could, away from the club and back down the deserted side street where I'd been dropped off by the taxi. But relief was short-lived. A second later, a man in a balaclava jumped out of the shadows to confront me.

"We told you to go home," he snarled.

This wasn't a bouncer. This was someone else. And it was not his wisest move. I'm not sure he was aware I'd recently spent many months in intense physical combat training with a beast of a former East German athlete.

Before he knew what was happening, my fist had connected with his face, causing a sickening crunch as his nose collapsed. A second blow to the stomach winded him. I was lining up for a third when he decided I wasn't in the mood to be trifled with, and fled using whatever breath he had left.

Interesting, I thought.

A cab was approaching, displaying its yellow light of hope. Once inside, I asked the driver to take me back to Farringdon, by the most illogical route possible.

When I was sure we weren't being followed, I asked to be dropped off, and made the final approach home on foot.

Once indoors, I washed my hand, slightly concerned that I'd broken the skin on my knuckles. They were sore but they'd mend. I poured a glass of water and took it through to the living room, and curled up on the sofa.

Whoever was in the balaclava, it wasn't Graham. It was someone much fitter, about six feet tall. I couldn't tell much by the voice as it sounded like a fake cockney accent. Was that important? Would I have recognised it if he'd spoken normally?

So maybe it wasn't Graham behind the bullet and the vandalism of my car. But if not, then who? I wasn't short of people I'd upset, but which of them would be well-informed enough to know I was in London, let alone the address of my hotel?

I parked those thoughts for now and reassessed the case.

Alfie was innocent. I was fairly sure of that. So far there was no suggestion that Neil Fearon was anything other than a legitimate businessman. Of the original suspects, Rex Dexter's business partner, former wife, new girlfriend and her ex-partner had been conclusively ruled out. So what was I left with? Dougie Compton, who Joe had told me not to approach because he'd lock me up in a heartbeat. Emily's SIO, Alex Ward, who everyone spoke highly of. "Jason Shelley", the mysterious undercover agent who had infiltrated Eddie Whitfield's gang, but who had shed the fake ID and now nobody knew who he was. And DCS Terry Handley, who'd locked up Eddie Whitfield and who now wanted to do the same with me.

That left everything hanging on the mysterious conversation that Rex Dexter had possibly overheard in a pub. But that was eight years ago, and in any case it was only my theory that it had ever happened, based on a spoken link between two records that I could have quite possibly misconstrued.

My last remaining hope was to speak to Michael Steward, assuming I could find him and he was still alive and willing to talk to me.

And in among it all, someone was out to get me. Well, bloody well join a very long queue.

Before heading upstairs, I put Eddie Whitfield's taped confession into the VCR and watched it twice. Something about it didn't add up, but it was time for bed. Maybe a new day would bring some answers.

I hadn't liked the edge of tension when I'd spoken to Anders, but he'd assured me that the house was safe. Nevertheless I took the SIG to bed with me, just in case things were about to get far worse.

Chapter 30

Friday, October 29th, 1993

"WHAT the hell happened to you?"

DS Alan Beattie looked horrified, and Nick understood why. He knew he was a mess. It wasn't so much that his nose needed straightening as the two black eyes which had developed overnight.

"It's a football injury," he said, wincing as he sat down at his desk.

"I didn't know you played football."

"It was the first time in years. I remember why I don't, now." He laughed, and a sharp pain shot across his face. "It was a mate's five-a-side team. They were a player short so they asked me. Stupidly, I agreed."

"And what happened? Did you get run over by the team coach?"

"Haha." Nick winced again. "No, it was a fifty-fifty with a lad called Big Colin. The clue's in the name. I won the ball, though."

"Well, that's something." Alan laughed and shook his head. "Can I get you anything? Paracetamol? Ibuprofen? A new face?"

"No, you're all right," said Nick. "I put ice on it when I got home and had painkillers this morning."

Alan raised a finger to stop Nick talking and then jerked his head in the direction of their boss's office. Nick turned to see what he was looking at.

"Fuck me," said DCI Dougie Compton. "Look at the state of you. Your missus been beating you up, son? Tell her I owe her a pint." And then, in a blink, his expression hardened. "Briefing room, five minutes."

"Yes, sir," said Nick, turning back to his desk.

"I think it's actually bleeding again," said Alan.

"Is it? Shit. Back in a minute."

Nick headed to the toilet to check in the mirror. But as soon as he opened the door his phone rang. It was Clare. He didn't have time to get into a conversation, but reluctantly agreed to meet her an hour later, at a coffee shop. Then, as he ended the call, he realised how stupid that would be. But he didn't call her back. She'd just have to have a wasted journey.

<hr>

I phoned Nick and asked to meet him for coffee and a progress report at half past nine, not far from his office, but hopefully far enough that none of his colleagues would arrest me. Surprisingly, he agreed. Perhaps he'd decided to be helpful at last.

On the way, I bought a copy of the *Daily Echo*. As Derek had said, the Eddie Whitfield confession was the lead story on the front page, with further coverage of Rex Dexter's life, career, and untimely death across four pages inside. The resolution of the case was being hailed as a success but for me it felt like a failure.

I ordered a cappuccino, took it to an empty table in a quiet corner towards the back and started to read while I waited. Then, once I'd finished that, I started flicking through the rest of the paper to see if I could spot a Danny Churchill byline. There weren't any. I wondered what he was working on, and had an almost overwhelming urge to call him and clear the air. The only thing that stopped me was the fear that he'd tell me to disappear forever and never bother him again, and that would break my heart.

Nine-thirty came and went. There was no sign of Nick. I gave him half an hour's leeway before deciding to call.

"Where are you?" I asked when he picked up the phone.

"Sorry – things cropped up."

I sighed.

"So you're saying you're running late or not coming at all?" I asked.

"I'm not coming at all. Look, I'm going to have to back off completely. My DCI is watching me and I'm in enough trouble as it is. I'm sorry but I can't help you at the moment."

"Fine." I was aware that men think women say "fine" when it's anything but. Maybe they have a point. "Take care and I'll see you around."

I ended the call. It wasn't a huge loss because he'd been minimal help anyway.

Time to think.

I decided to try Emily to discuss the dinner plan. The way it was going, I wasn't going to have anything else to do.

Emily didn't answer.

I was beginning to wonder why I'd bothered getting up.

Then I thought about phoning Graham. If he wasn't the person who was out to get me then maybe it was worth meeting him for a clear-the-air drink, for the sake of our future working relationship, in whatever limited form that might take. But I was in a bad enough mood already, and couldn't imagine being anything other than utterly hostile towards the idiot, so I put my phone back in my pocket.

Pushing the empty cappuccino cup to one side, I got up, went to the street and hailed a cab back to Chancery Lane and from there, walked through the back streets to Farringdon, making sure I wasn't being followed. Even that whole charade was beginning to get on my nerves. I was missing Germany, missing the freedom of walking round Koblenz without having to constantly look over my shoulder.

As I was approaching the front door, my phone rang. It was Derek.

"Hi Charlotte, howyadoin?" he said with a laugh when I answered. He was learning. "Have you seen the paper?"

"I have. Most importantly, though, how are you feeling?"

"Ah, I'm okay. I think last night did me the power of good, really."

"And likewise." I opened the door, removed my coat and headed to the sofa.

"If I was twenty years younger I'd be asking you out on a proper date," he continued, presumably jokingly.

"Really? Derek, for your own sake, trust me on this. Age doesn't come into it, but I'm a disaster and you can do so much better."

"And you should learn not to put yourself down."

"I'm not. Honestly. Disaster is a massive understatement."

He laughed.

"Anyway," he said, "I've got a number for you. Michael Steward."

"Oh, brilliant. Said it before, will say it again, you're amazing."

I grabbed a pen and wrote down the number as he gave it to me.

"I don't know what he's up to, but best of luck with it," said Derek. "I hope he gives you what you're looking for."

I thanked him again then ended the call with a promise to let him know how it went.

After another quick – and fruitless – attempt to contact Emily,

I tried Michael Steward. And it felt like my luck might be changing.

Yes, he said, he remembered meeting Rex Dexter. Yes, he'd be happy to meet me. And yes, most astonishing of all, he'd be willing to do it at the Seven Crowns in Islington – the very pub where he'd had the fateful meeting with Rex – as soon as it opened. I felt like punching the air in triumph, but resisted as my knuckles were still a bit tender, and knowing my luck, I'd hit a lampshade.

I didn't have long to get ready, sort my head out, and come up with a list of questions. It felt like back to being a journalist again and that was always my happy place.

Chapter 31

PERHAPS it was because we'd shared a career of sorts, or maybe that he also pronounced certain words with a faint north-eastern lilt, but I instantly felt myself warming to Michael. He must have been in his late forties or early 50s, and had slightly shaggy dark hair with only a hint of grey. His grey eyes were alert and his manner was open.

The pub stood in a side road close to Upper Street, and was still quiet at the time we got there. It was a traditional kind of place, yet to succumb to the latest trend that was seeing traditional British drinking establishments gentrified into *gastropubs*.

I bought Michael a drink, then asked about who he'd worked for and how things were going. If he was telling the truth, it was an impressive track record, primarily in magazines, and including stints on prestigious titles in New York. That perhaps explained why his name wasn't familiar. I didn't tend to read American lifestyle magazines aimed primarily at men.

Luckily for me, he'd returned to the UK the previous year, and the bulk of his income now came from ghostwriting celebrity autobiographies. So far so good.

"In fact, that was why Rex Dexter originally got in touch with me," he said.

"Because he wanted you to write a book?"

"His life story. I'd just started doing them."

That tallied with what Alfie had told me.

"Were you tempted?" I asked.

"No, not really. I knew he'd been hawking it round. It would have been work but there was something about the guy I didn't like."

"What sort of thing?"

"There were rumours, you know?"

"About his womanising?"

"You could call it that."

His eyes rolled, ruefully. That sounded intriguing.

"Go on," I said.

Michael took a look around, then reached for a cigarette. I offered him one of mine, but he refused.

"Have you any idea what the music industry was like in 1985?" he asked.

"A vague one but I'd have been twenty-three."

"Precisely my point. A huge part of the pop machine has always been targeted at young teenagers and pre-teens. Just think about it. The entire industry is run by middle-aged men, and it's based on encouraging very young girls to have sexual fantasies about male pop stars in their twenties and thirties, with posters on their walls, and screaming at concerts, and declarations of lifelong love when they're like twelve years old for God's sake. Is it any bloody wonder some of the men took advantage of that?"

"Wow, I'd never thought of it quite like that, but it's a valid point." It took a moment to let that sink in. "Are you saying he was a paedophile?"

"Rex Dexter? Technically not, in his case." He hesitated as though deciding whether or not to continue. Eventually he did. "I'm not going to name names, but there's one specific person who definitely is. A huge household name, who works at the BBC, presents *Top of the Pops* and is on primetime TV making children's dreams come true while puffing on a cigar. Some of the things I've heard make me feel physically ill."

The only person I could think of who fitted that description was Jimmy Savile. I'd heard vague rumours about him myself, but he'd always denied them. If they were true, it'd be an unprecedented national scandal. He'd been knighted by the Queen in 1990 and even received a Papal knighthood.

"In fact," Michael continued, "there's more than one, but as ever it's tricky to prove. I know someone who's digging into it at the moment. It's the sort of thing you'd have got stuck into at the *Echo*, I expect. I'm not religious but I pray it'll all come out one day."

The conversation had definitely taken an unexpected turn. I was feeling nauseous just thinking about it, but Michael had said it with such conviction, I couldn't help but believe every word.

"But how does this relate to Rex Dexter?" I said, taking a much-needed sip of Diet Coke. "You said 'technically'."

"Ah, well that's where he was either clever or devious, depending on your viewpoint. He always had an 'adult' partner, for want of a better word, but he had quite a fetish for the young and impressionable alongside. The rumour, though, was that he liked to keep things legal, in inverted commas, so he only preyed on them if they were at least the age of consent."

"Sixteen?"

"It's actually eighteen if you're in a position of trust, but if not then yes, sixteen. So in Dexter's case, sixteen and no younger. And while nobody had a poster of Rex Dexter on their wall, if you were a young girl and you wanted entry into the world of pop stars, Rex was your man. He could get you backstage to meet your idols, but there might well be a favour expected in return."

"God, that's awful."

How had none of this come up in the original investigation?

Maybe it had, but just not in the sanitised version that was given to me. My mind was racing at the implications.

"And did you ever see evidence of this?" I asked.

"Not personally, but it was more than idle gossip. The whole thing had been going on in the industry for years. Decades even. Sorry to go on, but I feel so passionately about it. I've got a young daughter myself, and, well ..."

"No, don't apologise. I absolutely understand what you're saying."

I had to stop and think for a moment. It was terrifying, but how was it linked to his murder, if at all? It was one thing being appalled about child exploitation, but it didn't necessarily get me any further forward.

"Do you think that's maybe a reason he was killed?" I asked.

Michael thought for a moment then shook his head.

"I really don't know. Don't get me wrong, he was an evil bastard, but I could give you a long list of people in that industry who were just as bad, if not massively worse. So, my gut feeling? Probably not. But all this public sympathy for the loss of a national treasure, albeit with flaws that people knew about? Sorry but the whole thing makes me very uncomfortable. That's why when you called me and said you were looking into it, I was happy to meet up with you."

It was all a lot to take in, but none of it was answering the questions I was here to ask.

"What do you remember of your meeting with him?" I asked. "Was there anything, in retrospect, that you thought was unusual?"

He shook his head again.

"It was what? Eight years ago? At my age I struggle to remember much about yesterday."

I laughed.

"Understandable. But was it lunch or just a drink?"

"It was lunch – pub food, nothing special. I think he chose

this place because it was quiet and he didn't want to be recognised."

"Can you remember anyone else who might have been here? I know it's asking a lot."

"It's strange. Even though I just said I couldn't remember much about yesterday, there are certain bits of that day that are actually etched in my mind."

That sounded more encouraging.

"Normally I wouldn't have given it another thought," he continued. "Can you remember every pub you were in eight years ago and who else might have been there? But because of what happened, some of it has stayed with me and I've thought a lot about it since. It's still vague, though. Sorry."

It was time to start looking for triggers.

"Look around," I said. "Was this the table you were at?"

"No," he said, after a moment. "It was that one." He nodded at a table in a quiet corner, furthest from the bar.

"Okay," I said. "Let's move there. You be you and I'll be Rex."

We carried our drinks over. There was something slightly unsettling about re-enacting the meeting, knowing that my character would be murdered a few hours later. I've never been a fan of coincidences, and was keen to ensure there wouldn't be another one. I couldn't worry about that for now, though. Once Michael confirmed we were in the same positions, I pressed him further.

"Okay," he said. "It was quiet. It was mid-afternoon, after the peak lunch trade, but you can see what it's like now. I don't think it ever gets particularly busy in here."

"How many other people do you think were in here?"

"I've got to say, whatever I think I can remember, it could well be wrong. But as far as I recall, the only others were a couple of blokes over there."

He pointed to a table in the opposite corner, nearest the toilets.

"Can you remember anything about them? Old? Young? Well dressed? Scruffy?"

Michael screwed up his eyes in concentration, as though willing the image to come back to him.

"One was older than the other, I think," he said at last. "The younger one was in a suit, from memory. I couldn't vouch for it. I think he might have been wearing a hat. Like an old school trilby, but don't quote me on that either. I wouldn't be able to recognise him even if you showed me a picture."

"But you might recognise the hat?"

"Like I say, it's a possibility. I couldn't be certain."

"Was it a trilby or a fedora?"

"Christ knows. Aren't they the same thing?"

I shook my head.

"The trilby brim is narrower."

"I don't know. Maybe a fedora then."

I nodded. Details might be important.

"You didn't see what colour hair he had underneath the hat?" I continued.

"How would I do that?"

"Presumably the back of his head."

"No, sorry."

"Not to worry."

It was so frustrating. I felt like I was both agonisingly close and yet still a million miles away.

"Actually, there was one thing a bit strange," Michael said after a moment.

I raised my eyebrows to urge him on.

"They disappeared to the toilet together, the two men. And a minute later, Rex decided he needed to go too. That struck me as odd. They didn't look the type to be having sex in a pub toilet."

"You think they were dealing drugs, then?"

"No. It did cross my mind when Rex went after them, because he might have been into that kind of thing, but then I thought if that's what he was into, there'd be plenty of opportunity in the music business and he wouldn't have to resort to pub toilets. Anyway, they didn't look the type for that either."

He seemed to be running out of steam, so it was time to try a prompt. I unfolded my copy of the *Daily Echo* and placed it on the table between us, then pointed at a picture of Eddie Whitfield.

"Could one of them have been this guy?"

Michael took a pair of reading glasses from his inside pocket, then studied the picture at length.

"I think it actually might have been," he said at last. "But equally I might have just made that up completely. You could ask the barmaid. If they were regulars, she might remember them."

That was a good point.

"Back in a moment," I said. "Same again?"

Michael nodded and I made my way to the bar.

"Could I order another Diet Coke and another pint of whatever that was," I said, nodding in Michael's direction. "Castlemaine, I think."

She nodded and fetched down a couple of glasses.

By the time the drinks were poured, my newspaper was on the bar.

"While I'm here," I continued, "my friend is trying to recall a couple of people he saw chatting in here a few years ago. I know it's a long shot but I wondered if you'd know who they were, if they came in often, that kind of thing."

"I can try, love," she said. "What did they look like?"

"One younger, one older, the younger one wearing a hat."

She laughed.

"You'd have to give me more than that."

I pointed to the picture of Eddie.

"I was wondering if one of them might have been him?"

It didn't take her a moment.

"Oh him. Yeah, he used to come in here. Years back. He got done, didn't he? I always knew he was up to no good."

"He did. So it might have been him. I don't suppose you know who he used to drink with?"

She shook her head.

"Perils of working in a pub, love. The old brain cells get a hammering."

"It's actually the person who he was with that we're trying to think of the name of. He was younger, wearing a suit, wearing a fedora hat. Does that ring a bell?"

"Possibly. There was one a bit like that who came in here a few times around then. I don't think I ever knew his name, though, and I haven't seen him in years."

A thought struck me.

"It couldn't have been a policeman, could it?" I asked.

"In this place? I wouldn't have thought so, love," she said with a laugh.

I took the drinks back to our table.

"Any luck?" asked Michael.

"Maybe. Eddie Whitfield was a regular, apparently. So it could have been him. But we're no further forward on the other one."

We continued to chat for another twenty minutes or so, but it was clear I wasn't going to get any more. In the end, Michael said he had to get back to work, transcribing taped conversations with the manager of a well-known Premier League football club. I thanked him and asked him to call me if anything else occurred.

"Of course," he said, standing up. "I wish I could have been more help."

"You've been a huge help," I said, rising also and then offering him a handshake.

We made our way to the street, and after a careful look in both directions, I set off for the half-hour walk back to Farringdon, trying to make sense of everything I'd learned. The answer was there, I was sure of it. I just needed to know the identity of the man in the hat. It was time to start thinking in earnest.

Chapter 32

SHORTLY after crossing Pentonville Road, south of the Angel tube station, I tried Emily again. There was still no answer. I didn't want to leave a message, but if we were going to meet for dinner we'd need to make arrangements, and time was cracking on.

Furthermore, with Nick out of action, I was very much on my own. I didn't want to bother Joe until I had something concrete, but there were plenty of ideas that I was trying to assemble into a cohesive theory.

I'd established a definite possible link between Rex Dexter and Eddie Whitfield, if that wasn't a contradiction. In some ways it was understandable that it hadn't been picked up in the original investigation. Even if the detectives had tried to identify the men in the Seven Crowns, at that stage it could have been anyone. I had the advantage of having a picture and Eddie Whitfield's confession to work from, neither of which would have been available to the original investigation.

But while it established a link, it still didn't fully explain a motive. I thought back to the radio show. *Careless Whisper*. I'm not an expert in men's toilets, but it wasn't a giant leap of faith to think that Rex had followed them in, possibly accidentally, as a victim of unfortunate timing, and had overheard a conversation that was too top secret to be had in the open space of even a near-empty pub.

Considering this was the week before the security vault heist, it seemed logical that the conversation was related to that. And if so, was the man in the hat Jason Shelley, the undercover policeman? That would make sense too, because if he was still around, and he was somehow implicated in the murder, it would explain why the police were so keen to accept Eddie Whitfield's confession at face value. A cover-up of sorts, designed to protect one of their own.

Thinking it through further, it was logical to deduce that the men had recognised Rex. He was a well-known celebrity. So perhaps, aware that he'd caught them, they listened to his radio show that night. Rex couldn't help showing off, but it was to prove his downfall. They heard his comments and decided he couldn't be trusted to keep quiet, so had to act fast.

As a result, perhaps Eddie went straight round to the radio station, waited for him to finish his show, and then confronted him in the car park. By that stage they were no longer strangers, which would explain why the killer had got so close. I could even imagine the conversation: Eddie saying *what were you referring to?* Rex saying *not to worry, their secret was safe with him*. Eddie deciding he couldn't take the risk, so plunging a knife straight in the heart, before disappearing into the night with nothing at all to link them. In some ways it even explained why it was a common kitchen knife. The whole thing was spur of the moment with no time to plan.

It was all very neat. It explained everything. I wasn't sure that Joe would be happy. He'd asked me to disprove Eddie's confession, yet all I'd managed to do was to show why it could have been genuine.

Unless I was still missing something.

Because if that was all the case, and Jason Shelley was somehow implicated, there was still a police cover-up somewhere along the line. And that would still raise the question of corruption.

Above all else, there still wasn't any tangible evidence. It was all just a theory, and while the theory made sense, if one single part of it was wrong, the whole lot would come tumbling down.

And then it hit me. The single part that potentially disproved it all.

The person who killed Rex Dexter was shorter than him. And left-handed. I didn't know how tall Eddie Whitfield had been, nor which hand he favoured, but if he fell down on either of those it was back to square one. Unless it was his companion who'd done the killing, but if that was the case, Eddie's confession still made no sense. I needed to uncover the identity of the mystery man.

What if it hadn't been Jason Shelley? Shelley was part of the gang, but that didn't mean he'd be having regular meetings in a pub with Eddie Whitfield more than any of the rest of them. What if it was another policeman and they were discussing something completely separate? Perhaps he was offering protection, or on the take in some entirely different scam?

I was brought back to reality by the sound of my phone. It was Emily.

"At last," I said. "I've been trying to call you."

But it wasn't Emily. It was someone else using Emily's phone.

"You're really testing our patience," said a distorted voice. "We've told you to go home."

"Who is this?" I said, my mind trying to make sense of it. "Where's Emily?"

"She's here," said the voice. "And if you're not on the ferry by 8pm, she's going to die."

And with that, the line went dead.

Chapter 33

THERE was no time for second thoughts. I immediately rang Joe.

It went straight to voicemail. A message saying he was in a meeting but would be free by 4pm.

I swore.

I had to call Nick. Shit.

"I've told you I can't talk to you," he snarled when he answered. "Call Emily. Jesus."

"It's about Emily," I shouted, trying to keep any edge of panic out of my voice. "She's been kidnapped."

"She's *what?*"

"I've just had a call from her phone. Some man saying he had her, and if I didn't immediately go back to Germany, he was going to kill her."

"For God's sake. Where are you?"

I couldn't tell him Farringdon, but I could catch a cab to anywhere.

"About fifteen minutes from you," I said.

"How the fuck do you know where I am?"

It was exasperating but there were bigger issues.

"Obviously I don't, but fifteen minutes from your office. Tell me where you are and I can be there instead."

He swore again, and I heard muffled voices, imagining he was covering the mouthpiece.

"Okay," he said at last. "Go back to that coffee shop."

"The one you didn't show up at?"

"Don't take the piss."

"I'm not. I'm bloody clarifying."

"I'm not in the mood for this. Yes, that one. Be there in fifteen minutes. I'll be there as soon as I can. If I'm not, just wait for me. Okay?"

"I'm on the way."

He ended the call and I hailed a cab. As we carved through the early afternoon traffic, I tried to make sense of it all.

The last thing I wanted to do was tell Nick about the bullet, the car, and the attack outside Suadela. But I wasn't going to have an option. Who wanted me to go home and why? Was it linked to the case? Were the stakes rising because I was getting closer to the truth? That made no sense at all, because if anything, all I'd done was prove the case for them.

I hated the thought of Emily being in danger because of me. I could catch the ferry, no problem. Actually, big problem, my car was still at the body shop. I couldn't exactly leave that behind and steal the Astra. Well, I could, if Emily's life depended on it.

But the very fact someone wanted me out of the way was the precise reason why I knew I needed to stay. There was something not right about all of this. Something from the start.

Unless it really was just Graham March, being a monumental twat.

The cab dropped me off. I checked my watch. It had taken fourteen minutes. The coffee shop was largely deserted, so I quickly ordered a drink and made my way to a table at the back.

I knew my heart rate was peaking. I could feel the tension in every pore. I drummed my fingers on the table, impatient for Nick to arrive.

Five minutes passed. Another five. He'd told me to wait for him. I didn't have any other option.

I took a deep breath, trying to calm myself down, but with every sense on high alert.

The door to the coffee shop opened. It wasn't Nick. It was two men. I didn't know who they were, but I instinctively knew exactly *what* they were.

Police. Coming for me.

They saw me. They started running towards me. I had a second to react. It was fight or flight, but there was nowhere to fly to, and that only left one option.

On the opposite side of the street, Nick was watching the drama unfold. He saw the two men enter the coffee shop. They quickly scanned the room, then started running towards a table at the back.

He hadn't expected what happened next.

Even over the noise of the afternoon traffic, he could hear the sounds of shouting. The scream of the barista. A table being overturned, crockery being smashed.

And then the door flew open and Clare emerged onto the street, leapt onto the back platform of a passing bus, and disappeared into the depths of London.

Chapter 34

AS soon as the bus turned a corner, I jumped off, much to the chagrin of the conductor, who shouted something uncomplimentary about fare-dodging bitches.

I didn't have time to argue about either semantics or the need for creativity in an insult. Instead, I ran, until I saw another cab, flagged it down and asked him to take me to Chancery Lane, before sinking down across the rear bench seat, out of sight of the windows.

What the fuck had just happened?

Why did my knuckles hurt again? (I kind of knew that one.)

Where was Nick?

Had he just set me up?

The moment I was dropped off, I called him.

"What the hell happened there?" I shouted. Had he been standing in front of me, I'd have punched him even harder than I just had his two colleagues, and I was fairly sure one of them had a broken jaw.

"Where are you now?" he said.

"It doesn't matter a flying fuck where I am. What I want to know is why you just tried to get me arrested, you two-faced bastard."

"I didn't."

"Oh, really? So what? I just knocked out two innocent businessmen who'd popped in for a quiet cappuccino? Give me some credit, Nick."

"Jesus, no. Listen to me. I saw what happened. I was there. I was about to come in but they were just ahead of me. They must have recognised you. It's not like you're exactly low profile. I swear, it had nothing to do with me."

"Bullshit."

"Seriously, where are you? Come back and we'll try again. Somewhere else. I still need to talk to you about Emily."

I ended the call. If he thought I was that stupid, I'd need to punch him twice.

My phone rang, but I ignored it. There was too much to think about without even considering talking to Nick again. Even if it was a perfect opportunity to vent my least-used but most colourful swear words.

But what now? I couldn't just run. Not if Emily's life depended on it. I couldn't go back to Germany without my car. I couldn't speak to Joe for nearly another hour.

Somebody wanted me out of the way.

Somebody wanted to silence me.

As far as I was aware, the only people who knew I was in London were Joe, Nick and Emily.

Unless, at the risk of repeating myself, it really was Graham March being a monumental pain in the arse.

He wound me up enough when I was in a good mood. I was not in a good mood. Aware my language might not be the best, I phoned him. If nothing else it would be good to let off steam.

"Good afternoon, my dear," he said in his most irritatingly

condescending voice. "Are you calling to discuss arrangements for our drink?"

"Oh, fuck off, Graham."

"Fair play. Although I'm flattered that you've gone to the effort of ringing me to say it in person."

"Where's Emily?"

He hesitated.

"Who's Emily?"

"Don't even start. Where is she?"

"At the risk of another onslaught of foul language, it'd help if you told me who she was. At least then I could help you look for her. Is she a young homeless girl? I'm quite a magnet for those."

"Listen, Graham, you're not funny. Somebody has got Emily. The same person wants me out of the country. Only four people know I'm here. You're one of them and it's not the other three. So I'm going to ask you again nicely, and then if you still don't tell me I'm going to come to wherever you are and shoot you in the eye."

"I thought we were going to try to be nice to each other?"

"Seriously, I'm going to count to three."

I counted to three. He still didn't answer. And then I remembered that the person who attacked me outside Suadela was much younger and fitter than Graham, so it couldn't have been him either. Bugger.

Well, I wasn't going to apologise to the idiot. And in any case, in the unlikely event that Nick was telling the truth, and he had nothing to do with what had just happened, it still raised the possibility that Graham was following me and had tipped them off.

"Did you just try to get me arrested?" I said. "Because if you did, it probably won't surprise you to discover you failed dismally."

"Why would I try to get you arrested? And I still don't know who this Emily girl is."

I took a deep breath and reached for a cigarette, and seriously thought about the logistics of trying to smoke ten simultaneously, even if just to hasten the escape from the inexorable mess of my life.

"I wish I could trust you. I wish I could believe a word you said," I sighed, once I'd decided that one at a time was probably bad enough. "Do I have to ring Florian? Tell him what you're up to?"

"I'm not up to anything, my dear."

I was back to square one. So I thought I might as well end things as I'd started.

"Oh, fuck off, Graham," I said, and disconnected the call.

By the time I returned home, I still had half an hour before I could call Joe. I made a cup of tea almost without thinking about it. My every thought was with Emily. I reopened the original file of documents, to look again at the senior investigating team.

Which of them could it be? Not Kenny Mason as he was dead. Trevor Covington was somewhere on sick leave, and Joe vouched for him. It wasn't the SIO Brian Dalton, because Joe vouched for him as well. Alex Ward? Both Emily and Joe said he was squeaky clean. And Graham I knew all about already.

So that only left two. Neil Fearon and Dougie Compton.

Security people potentially mixed in dark circles. Maybe Neil Fearon had someone keeping a watch on me. Maybe he'd heard I was coming over. Maybe he knew why. If he was the bent cop, then that would explain why he wanted me out of the way. But I'd investigated him and come up blank, and although things hadn't gone well at his office, I'd got the impression he didn't realise who I was when I first turned up. If he'd been onto me from the start, he could have had reinforcements lined up and the police on standby, the moment I arrived.

That left Dougie Compton. What had Joe said about him?

"He's only a little fella, but he's a hard bastard. You don't want to go anywhere near him ... he'd lock you up without a moment's hesitation."

I started to fixate on the first part. "He's only a little fella." By my reckoning, the person who killed Rex Dexter was a little fella ...

Finally, it was 4pm. It was time to call Joe.

Chapter 35

"THANK God," I said, when he answered, my voice full of breathless urgency. "Joe, we've got a major problem. Emily's been kidnapped."

"How do you mean kidnapped?" he asked. "I've just come out of a meeting with her."

"*What?*" My head was spinning. Nothing made sense any more. "Are you sure?"

"Of course I'm sure. I can see her at this moment, on the far side of the office. She's about to get into the lift."

"That's great news." The sense of relief was fighting utter confusion. "But I had a call. She's not been answering her phone, then somebody rang me back from it and said they'd kidnapped Emily and if I didn't go home they'd ... Well, it wouldn't end well."

"I can assure you that was a hoax." His voice was the embodiment of calm. "I couldn't get any answer either, so I went to see her. She's lost her phone but she's very much alive and well. She'll have a new one in a couple of days, but in the meantime feel free to call me if you absolutely have to and can't get hold of Nick."

My heart rate was slowly calming but it was going to take a while.

"I think I've fallen out with Nick," I said, almost hoping Joe wouldn't hear.

He chuckled.

"I daren't ask," he said.

"It's not my fault. He said he couldn't help me anyway, because Dougie Compton was getting suspicious. But he agreed to meet me when I got the news about Emily, and then I nearly got arrested. We've had a difference of opinion."

As I said it, Dougie Compton's name was flashing like a beacon, drawing me in.

"Nick can be difficult, but he's good. You should give him a second chance."

"But he doesn't like me." I appreciated I sounded like a petulant child rather than a thirty-one-year-old woman. "I'll take your word for it. Anyway, there's still something I want to discuss."

"The hoax call, yes." It wasn't that, but I suppose it was understandable why it had caught Joe's attention. "I suppose you've got no idea who it was or what they were playing at?"

"I wish I did. Does Emily have any idea where she lost her phone?"

"She said she left it on her desk."

"And what? It was stolen? Did she call the police?"

He laughed.

"Very funny. What exactly did the caller say to you?"

"That I had to be on a ferry by 8pm or she'd be killed."

"Whoever it was knew you'd arrived on a ferry, then."

"Oh, Joe, whoever it was knows everything about me. They've been following me since day one."

And so I told him about feeling someone had been in my room, the bullet, the damage to my car, the attack outside Suadela.

"Why on earth haven't you told me about any of this before?" asked Joe, sounding exasperated.

"Because I'm responsible for my own problems and I can deal with them. Even more than all that, though, I very nearly just got arrested. I'd arranged to meet Nick, but two police turned up. Nick said that they'd recognised me but it wasn't that at all. I saw them come in. They looked around. They'd been tipped off that I was there – if not by Nick then by somebody else."

Joe sighed.

"I understand if you want to go home," he said. "Seriously. Maybe the call was for your own good."

"If it was, they had a funny way of going about it. Anyway, is it a good time to chat about the case? I've got a couple of things to talk to you about."

"If you're quick."

"I'll try."

Where to start?

"Okay, first of all, any luck with identifying Jason Shelley?"

"Not yet, but I told you, the whole point of being undercover is that you stay under the radar. But it's good timing, actually, because I'm at an event tonight with someone who might have worked with him. I can't promise, but if I find anything out I'll let you know."

"Perfect, that would be a help. It might be important. Meanwhile, I've established a link between Eddie Whitfield and Rex Dexter."

I recapped my conversation with Michael Steward and the theory about the overheard conversation.

"But I still think there's more to it," I said. "And it doesn't explain the urgency of the police accepting the confession at face value, nor take into account Rex Dexter's abuse of girls who, to all intents and purposes, were children. So I still think there's a cover-up somewhere along the line and I'm determined to get to the bottom of it. Especially when people threaten me."

"You are aware it's Friday?"

"Yes."

"And you're going home on Sunday?"

"Also yes, but there are forty-eight hours between now and then, and if I have to stay awake every one of them, I will do. Meanwhile, how tall was Eddie Whitfield? Was he left-handed?"

That took him by surprise.

"I'm not sure exactly, but he was a big bloke," he said. "Is it important?"

"It could be. Looking at the forensics and having tried to re-enact it – don't worry, on myself with a pen, before you ask – I think the knife was in the killer's left hand, and from a reasonably low angle. Actually, you said Dougie Compton was short. Is he left-handed?"

"You know, I actually think he is."

I let that sink in for a moment, my brain fully engaged with the implications.

"Joe ..." I started, but he cut me off, as though he could tell where I was going.

"I can't go around accusing a senior police officer. Not based on a theory and not without evidence. Lots of people are short. Lots of people are left-handed."

"He wouldn't be my first corrupt DCI, though, would he?" I said, thinking of Graham March.

"Clare, no."

"But think about it. It'd be perfect, wouldn't it? He was one of the two DIs along with Graham. If the pair of them are good friends, it stands to reason they're as bent as each other. I don't know how it fits exactly, but imagine this. Dougie was meeting Eddie Whitfield in the pub. They heard the show, Dougie killed Rex. Best of all, he was then on the investigation team, always on hand to push things in other directions, and hide any evidence that pointed to him. And then, because he's also friends with Eddie Whitfield, he persuades Eddie to make a confession, ending this once and for all. Meanwhile, Dougie gets wind of Nick helping you look into things and tries to put a stop to it. Nick said he'd been followed. Maybe Dougie was onto him from the start, and then orchestrated the campaign to get rid of me. Honestly, it all fits. Not least because we've pretty much ruled out all of the others."

"Do you have any evidence for this? Or is everything circumstantial?" said Joe, not sharing my enthusiasm.

"I can find evidence if it's out there."

"By doing what? Taking a picture of Dougie to the pub and asking if they recognise him from a meeting eight years ago? That's never going to stack up in court, even if it was true."

"I'll think of something else then."

He sighed again.

"Just be careful, okay? You've done your best, and I really do appreciate the amount of effort you've put into this. Just don't get into any more trouble."

"I won't."

"I've got to go, but speak to Nick, okay? Patch things up."

"It might have gone beyond that."

"I'll speak to you before you go."

And with that he ended the call.

The tea had long gone cold, and I didn't have the energy to make a new one, so I lay back on the sofa, lit a cigarette and closed my eyes.

Was it Dougie? It fitted. Equally, though, a couple of hours ago I'd been equally convinced it was Jason Shelley, whoever he was now.

And then another possibility struck me. Was it Nick? Oh my word. Had it been in front of me all the time?

Okay, he wasn't short, and I didn't think he was left-handed but had I ever seen him write? The killer didn't *have* to be short. He could have just been crouching. Nick had always been curt with me. I'd instinctively been wary of him. He knew all of my movements. He'd promised Joe he wouldn't arrest me, but that made sense. The last thing he wanted was me in custody, telling everyone what I'd discovered. No, much better that I went home ... Nick could easily have had access to Emily's phone. The person who attacked me outside Suadela was about his height. I'd wondered why the voice was disguised. Whether it was because it was someone I'd recognise?

There were flaws. Joe spoke highly of him, but Joe could be wrong. I'd arranged to meet him and nearly got arrested. He'd denied any involvement in that. Maybe he was telling the truth because he didn't *want* me to be arrested. He wanted me to go home.

I was beginning to think the unthinkable. It was Dougie or Nick. Or possibly Jason Shelley.

Or one of the others, but they'd all been ruled out.

I couldn't get sidetracked. I needed to interview Dougie Compton, whatever it took.

It was time to phone Nick. I'd suggest the Dougie theory and test his reaction.

But that wouldn't work on the phone. I'd have to do it in person so I could see his expression. Project Smile was quickly being replaced by Project Self-incrimination.

There was no way I was going to arrange to meet him and walk into another trap. I'd have to catch him when he least expected it. I stubbed out the cigarette and retrieved my coat. It was time to do a little bit of stalking.

Chapter 36

"DS Brooks. Get your bone idle arse in here."

Nick had seen Dougie Compton lose his temper before, but this was something extra special. His face had turned a worryingly deep shade of purple. With a deep breath, Nick rose from his desk and headed to his boss's office. This time he was going to give as good as he got.

"I've just had a call from the hospital," the DCI snarled.

"Not bad news, I hope, sir?" said Nick, leaning on the door frame, aware he might need to make a swift exit.

"Not bad news? Are you taking the piss, son? Two of our men – of your colleagues – are in A&E. One will be off work for the next six weeks. Do you care to shed any light on a diabolically dark situation?"

"Me?"

"Yes you, you miserable lying fuckwit. And shut the fucking door, and do not fucking sit down. What were you doing out of the office at about 2pm? Meeting another non-existent geriatric witness?"

Nick tried to keep his cool. It was going to be hard.

"At about 2pm, from memory, I went out to a coffee shop. I didn't actually go in as I changed my mind, then came back here."

"Oh, bull-fucking-shit."

"Sorry, sir, but that's exactly what happened."

"All right, I'll ask you another way." Dougie's voice was getting ever louder. Nick could see veins pulsing in his neck. "What were you going to the coffee shop for? And if you say a cappufuckingccino, then God help me I'll put my fist through your face with so much force it'll fill the cavity where your brain should be and make a massive fist-sized hole in the back of your head."

Now probably wasn't the time to caution Dougie for threatening and abusive behaviour, but the thought crossed Nick's mind.

"I was supposed to be meeting a contact, sir," he said instead. "The meeting was called off."

"Oh yeah? Anyone I know? Let me guess: female, former journalist. Wanted for fraud and murder? And I said shut the fucking door, son."

Nick took a couple of steps forward, then swung the door shut with more force than strictly necessary. He didn't respond to the question. He wasn't quite sure how to.

"You know the funny thing?" Dougie continued. "And when I say funny, I mean not very fucking funny at all. A couple of the boys heard you arranging to meet someone and let me know about it, so I suggested they went along in advance, to see who it was. And guess who they found there?"

"You tell me."

"Clare Woodbrook."

Dougie paused, staring at Nick, waiting for a reaction.

"Did they arrest her?" Nick said, in a calm voice. Dougie picked up his empty tea mug and threw it hard in Nick's direction, narrowly missing him. The mug shattered into shards of porcelain as it smashed into the wall behind.

"Did they arrest her, he asks. Good God alive. I don't need to tell you what happened because you already damn well know."

Nick could almost feel the heat radiating from his boss's face as Dougie stepped forward until they were almost touching.

"I think you're taking the piss, son," spat Dougie. "You're chatting to Joe Leyland. You're up to something. You arrange to meet with Clare Woodbrook and yet you lie to me about it as though I'm your fucking mum and you've come home from school stinking of cigarettes. It's my job to sift through bullshit to get to the truth. I expect it from criminal scum, but not from my own shagging team!"

Nick took a half step back.

"If you don't trust me," he said, "then perhaps it'd be better for both of us if I applied for a transfer."

"Oh yeah? To what? Traffic? Fucking lollipop man? You're heading that way anyway, son. Why were you meeting Clare Woodbrook?"

"You want the truth?" Nick's voice was rising. "It might have been Clare. I don't know. I had a call. Didn't leave a name. Maybe it was Clare, and maybe she was wanting to turn herself in. I have no idea. It was an anonymous meet, but your boys beat me to it, which, with all due respect, is your own loss because she ran from them when clearly she wouldn't have run from me, if indeed it was her, because she was the one who requested the meeting."

"You are unbelievable, son." Dougie closed the gap again.

"The point is, if it was her, I could have brought her in. The fact that you don't trust me, the fact that you've got a couple of twats spying on me, means she's still out there roaming free, whereas if you'd just left me to get on with my job, she could well have been behind bars by now. So you, sir, have fucked up. And don't try to pin that on me."

Dougie launched forward, pinning Nick to the wall, one arm rammed into the DS's throat, the other raised into a fist.

Somehow the senior officer managed to stop himself from using it. Instead, he finally loosened his grip then pushed Nick away.

"Get out of my sight, sergeant," he shouted. "Permanently."

Nick opened the door and made his way out, his pulse pumping hard, Behind him, the office door slammed shut so hard, the glass panel rattled in its frame.

"Go well?" asked DS Alan Beattie with a wry smile.

Nick shook his head. Words weren't necessary. He turned off his computer.

"See you tomorrow. Possibly," he said. Then headed to the door.

———

Admittedly, for someone who was doing her best to avoid the police, skulking around in the shadows near the steps leading to the underground police station car park was at best unconventional, and at worst outright madness. But I wanted to catch Nick when he left for the night, to ask him questions, gauge his reaction, and then quite possibly follow him.

Luckily, I didn't have long to wait. I just hadn't expected him to be wearing a full motorbike outfit and carrying a crash helmet.

"Nice leathers," I said, stepping out into the light.

I don't recall Nick ever being exactly pleased to see me, but this time he looked positively livid. He pushed me back into the darkness.

"What the hell are you doing here?" he growled.

"I was missing you. What happened to your face?"

"Jesus, you are something else."

"It's a serious question. Have you been in a fight?"

For a moment I thought he was going to hit me. Which would have been interesting.

"It's a football injury," he said.

"Not an incident outside a nightclub, then?"

"*What?*" He looked more angry than ever. "I don't need this from you, for Christ's sake. I've just had it in the neck from Dougie about the shambles this afternoon."

"Why was he taking it out on you?"

"Because apparently someone overheard me making arrangements for a meeting, so he sent a couple of his detectives ahead to see exactly who it was with. And now they're in hospital, and he's blaming me because he thinks I was meeting you. Funny that."

"That's not good."

He gave a hollow laugh, took a step back and clenched his fist, although I'm not sure whether it was in frustration or he was gearing up to give me one. As it were.

"I'll speak to this Dougie," I said, trying unsuccessfully to defuse the situation. "I need to ask him some questions anyway."

"You absolutely cannot do that. Are you mad?"

"Why not?"

"Because like most of the people in that building, he's desperate to arrest you, but in his case it would be particularly brutal. That's a one way ticket to Holloway, possibly via intensive care."

"Okay." I pretended to think about it. "I accept the risk, but there are a few things I need to clear up with him. Can you set it up for me?"

I didn't expect him to say yes. He didn't disappoint.

"Fuck you," he spat instead. "I'm done for tonight, and you can go to hell."

I watched him take the first few steps down to the car park then came to a decision. If Nick wouldn't do it for me, I'd have to do it on my own.

Chapter 37

DOUGIE, Nick or Jason Shelley. It was one of the three, and the state of Nick's face kind of confirmed which one. But I still wanted to put Dougie on the spot, in my own way and on my own terms. Because even if Nick had been terrorising me, there was still a chance that Dougie Compton was the man in the fedora hat.

So I phoned the switchboard, asked to speak to him, and a moment later I was put through.

"I hear you're looking for Clare Woodbrook," I said. I'm not great at accents, but I grew up in the North East of England, not far from the border with Scotland. Affecting a generic Scottish accent was a risk, as in reality there was no such thing. Was I more Glasgow? Edinburgh? Inverness? I had no idea, even though I'd done it before. I had to hope that despite his rather Scottish-sounding forename he wouldn't be an expert and immediately see through me.

"Who are you?" he said, in a tone that was neither friendly nor encouraging, but thankfully more estuary than Scottish.

"A former colleague."

"And how did you hear that I was looking for her?"

I almost giggled with the next bit.

"Because I was supposed to be meeting her today, to persuade her to turn herself in, but a couple of detectives turned up."

"I see. And they gave you my name, did they?"

"No, but like I said, I'm a former colleague. I work on the newspaper. I think I've met you before."

"Really?" His tone made it sound like there was zero possibility that had ever happened.

"Maybe," I said.

"And your name?"

Conundrum. I couldn't use Charlotte Sadler again. It was about as secure as a three-year-old's piggy bank. But whatever I said, he could check in an instant and know I was bluffing. Best to keep things simple.

"I'd rather not give you my name," I said.

"I'm not going to talk to you anonymously."

"Fair enough. In which case I'll leave you in peace to enjoy your evening. Actually, wasn't it that other one who was leading the search? DCI Terry Handley or something? Don't you worry. I'll give him a call and see if he's interested. Goodnight and sorry to bother you."

I didn't immediately end the call. Predictably, he rose to the bait.

"Hold on. What did you want to tell me?"

"It's more what I want to show you. I want to meet."

There was something akin to a harrumph.

"Make an appointment and you can come in to the station and show me whatever you have."

"Sorry, Mr Compton," I said, suspecting the omission of his title would make his blood boil. "I'd rather meet in private. Somewhere neutral. Just you and me."

"That sounds very unconventional."

"Call it paranoia. I don't want to be considered an accessory in any of this. I can give you information but I want to be able to disappear."

"And why would you do that?"

"Because, like you, I believe people should be made to pay for their crimes. And even though Clare and I are former colleagues, we're not exactly friends. I admit, we used to be, which is why I agreed to meet her, but that's the extent of my involvement."

He appeared to think about it for a moment. I suspected he was mobilising a team of detectives to turn up as backup.

"I'd need you to come alone," I said.

"You don't call the shots here, lassie." Maybe he was Scottish after all. Bugger.

"I think I do. It's up to you to accept them, though."

I gave him the address of the abandoned warehouse where I'd met Nick on Wednesday.

"How will I know you?" he asked.

"You'll know me. I'll introduce myself. But if you turn up with anyone else, I won't be there. Just you, Mr Compton, for both our sakes. What car are you driving?"

"A dark blue Volvo. What time?"

I checked my watch. I'd need at least an hour to properly scope the area for reinforcements before we met. But not so long that he'd have time to plan anything more elaborate than that.

"8pm," I said. "I look forward to seeing you there."

I ended the call. Then turned and saw Nick back at the top of the stairs, looking even more furious than before.

"What the hell do you think you're playing at?" he snarled.

I couldn't answer, because I was still working it out myself.

DCI Dougie Compton replaced the handset and smiled. For once there'd been some good news.

He pulled his mobile out of his jacket pocket and dialled a familiar number.

"You'll never guess who just phoned me," he said, when the call was answered.

"Well, I know it wasn't me," said Graham March.

"Your old friend Clare Woodbrook."

"Really? So I was right, then? She *is* back. And what? She just called for a chat?"

"She had a ridiculous accent and gave some bullshit about being one of her own former colleagues, but that was obviously bollocks. She wants to meet."

"She *what?*"

Dougie chuckled.

"I know. All very odd. Some shite about having information about herself. What's she playing at?"

"I don't know, Dougie. What are you going to do?"

"I'm going to meet her, aren't I? Bring her in, get promoted. I've got to admit, I was having a shite day but it's just perked up considerably."

"Is that wise, though? She's what I like to call a lunatic."

Dougie thought for a moment. It had crossed his mind that it could be a trap, but the potential reward was worth a calculated risk. Especially if Nick had been telling the truth and she was looking to turn herself in. In any case, he'd go prepared.

"She gave an address of a warehouse, and said 8pm," he said.

"Presumably you're not going on your own."

"She said if I took anyone else, she wouldn't turn up."

"That sounds high risk, my old pal."

"I'll go armed. What's the worst that can happen?"

"She'll shoot you?"

Dougie laughed.

"Don't worry. I'll be on my guard the minute I see her. I've got a quick call to make and then I'm on my way. I'll let you know how it goes."

Chapter 38

NICK stood there in all his leathers, holding his crash helmet, with two black eyes and a broken nose, waiting for me to justify myself. But I didn't owe him anything.

"I don't answer to you," I said, holding my ground.

"I don't give a flying fuck," he shouted, which was unnecessary, as I was no more than a couple of feet away. "I told you not to speak to Dougie for your own sake, not mine."

"That's what I don't get, Nick. Why? Why are you so bothered about my welfare? Presumably the worst that can happen is that I get arrested, but isn't that what you want in your heart of hearts? Or does it worry you that if I get questioned I might start talking? Telling people what I'm up to and what I've discovered about Eddie Whitfield."

"What *are* you talking about?"

On the upside, he wasn't wearing the crash helmet, so if I needed to punch him, I could actually knock him straight out. But he was holding it between us like some kind of a shield. Once whacked, twice shy and all of that, if it was him outside Suadela.

"Tell me what happened to your face," I said. "It really does look like somebody hit you. Have you been skulking around in dark alleys?"

"I told you. It was a football injury."

"I've seen *Match of the Day*. Footballers get broken legs, occasionally a pulled hamstring or a groin strain. Not a broken nose and a couple of shiners."

"Yeah? You've never seen a police five-a-side match then."

"It sounds brutal."

I couldn't help giggling at the charade. Why didn't he just admit it?

"Why are you so keen on me going home?" I asked. "What have you got to hide?"

"And again, what the hell are you talking about?" His eyes narrowed in fury. "I don't think you should be here in the first place, and God knows, as soon as you piss off back to whatever hole you crawled from, the rest of us will be able to sleep a damn sight more easily. But what the hell do you mean, what have I got to hide?"

I raised my eyebrows.

"Really? Okay."

I took a step back and turned away. He lunged forward, and spun me back round.

"Answer the question," he spat. "What are you trying to say?"

I pushed his arm away and rubbed my shoulder. His grip had been unnecessarily firm. It reminded me of how he grabbed my arm in the hotel on the first night. And it was a problem. Both times he'd grabbed me with his right hand. Life would have been so much simpler if it had been his left.

"Can you stop trying to molest me?" I said, which made him angrier still. "I'll tell you where I'm up to, shall I?"

"Go on, I'm all ears."

"Technically not *all* ears. You're partly a couple of black eyes and a broken nose, but let's not be pedantic. All right, so I established a link between Rex Dexter and Eddie Whitfield."

I paused, checking for a reaction, but to his credit, he didn't flinch.

"Rex met a journalist in a pub," I continued. "You know about that, it's in the file. But the thing that wasn't in the file was that he was a virtual paedophile with a fetish for sixteen-year-old schoolgirls. Not the journalist. Rex Dexter. Why was that missing?"

"I don't know that there was ever any evidence of that. I heard rumours, but nothing more."

"Okay." I took a step back into the darkness to let a couple of people pass. Thankfully they didn't look in my direction. I waited until they were out of earshot before continuing. "The other thing that wasn't in the file was the two other people in the pub. Do you know why that was?"

"From memory, no idea," said Nick, in a voice that was now more exasperated than confrontational. "I suppose you're going to tell me why it was important?"

I nodded, for what it was worth in the near darkness.

"One of them was Eddie Whitfield," I said. It was time to take a leap of faith, and make my theory sound real. "The other was a policeman. Shall I tell you what happened?"

"Go on."

"Eddie and the policeman had a conversation. They were planning something. The details aren't important for now, but the relevant bit is that Rex overheard them. He referred to it in a kind of oblique way on his radio show, and they silenced him."

"Interesting theory."

"Isn't it? So the issue is, who was the policeman? Any ideas?"

Again, he was poker-faced.

"How am I supposed to know that?" he said at last.

"I just thought you might have some inside information," I said. "And if you don't, I'm hoping that Dougie does. Hence the urgent need to speak to him. If it was Dougie himself, then I can join the dots, and point out how Dougie committed the murder and then derailed the investigation. Equally, though, if Dougie, as a senior member of the investigating team, knew about one of his sergeants, for example, having clandestine meetings, then that would be fairly conclusive too."

I clenched my first behind my back, ready to strike first if Nick showed any sign of trying to silence me. Instead he took a step back.

"You want to know what I think?" he asked.

"I'd love to."

"I think you've got a death wish."

"Is that a threat?"

"A threat? Consider it a warning. I strongly advise you not to go anywhere near Dougie."

"Duly noted." I made a show of looking at my watch. "Have we finished?"

His eyes narrowed again, and he took a step forward and almost poked me in the eye with his outstretched finger.

"You don't know what Dougie can do," he said, in a voice so low it was much more intimidating than a shout. "I'm washing my hands of you."

And with that he turned and made his way down to the car park. A minute later, I heard the engine of a motorbike roar into life, and blast away at considerable speed.

I, meanwhile, was already running significantly later than planned.

The traffic was heavier than I'd expected and it took me nearly an hour to drive to the warehouse. Everything was working against me. I'd hoped to thoroughly scout the immediate vicinity, checking for backup, but as it was already past 8pm, the checks would have to be minimal, significantly raising the stakes. I opened my window as I approached, listening for the sound of a helicopter, but there was only the noise of distant traffic. On a first drive-past, I didn't notice any suspicious cars full of policemen. After a couple of circuits, I was as sure as I could be that the coast was clear.

Dougie's Volvo was parked outside the loading bay of the warehouse. It was possible that a battalion of armed officers were on the other side of the metal door, waiting to pounce. I parked up, out of sight, and made my final approach on foot, skirting the far side of the building first, peering through downstairs windows, looking for any sign of life. It was hard to see anything without a torch, but as far as I could tell, the building was empty. I wished I'd brought the SIG. In my rush to depart and catch Nick, I'd left it in Farringdon. And Dougie himself might be armed. My only hope was that he'd prefer to take me alive.

When I was finally as sure as I could be that he'd come on his own, it was time to approach the car. My heart was pounding. This was either the bravest or the most stupid thing I'd ever done.

Keeping to the shadows, I got as close as I could without being seen. Dougie was in the driver's seat. There was nobody else with him in the car. It was now or never.

With a final sprint, I made a dash to the car and grabbed the passenger door handle, wrenching it open, hoping for an element of surprise.

I needn't have bothered. Somebody had been there before me. Dougie's lifeless body didn't acknowledge my arrival. Instead, the remains of his brain glistened on the inside of the driver's side window, the hole in his head leaking blood and gore all over his suit. A gun was lying on the passenger seat. I grabbed it, aware there was a killer in the vicinity, my survival instinct kicking in.

In retrospect that was an error.

There was a screech of tyres, skidding on gravel. Graham March appeared. He saw me, next to a corpse, and holding the murder weapon. And his face broke into a sickly smile.

Chapter 39

"**H**ELLO, hello," he said. "Back to your old tricks?"
For a moment I thought about turning the gun on him and emptying the chamber.

"What the hell are you doing here?" I shouted instead.

"Dougie rang and told me he was meeting you."

"And you turned up for what? The comedy value?"

"No, believe it or not I turned up to help you escape in case you needed to. Although lucky for you, somebody beat you to it. Not so lucky for Dougie, in fairness. I was just having a look around but came back when I saw you."

The man was unbelievable.

"Was it you?" I asked.

"Was what me?"

"Shooting Dougie, for heaven's sake."

"I'm not the one holding the gun." He walked towards me, then peered into the car. "Clearly, I know you just got here, and I can vouch for the fact that you didn't kill him, but a less informed person might jump to the obvious conclusion. You, with a history of shooting people, are standing holding the gun that just killed the detective who was about to arrest you." He took a step back.

"It's quite a sexy look. Lessened by the fact that it's you rather than somebody attractive."

"Graham, I'll shoot *you* in a minute if you don't tell me what happened."

"No you won't. I'm the only possible witness to your innocence."

"Did you see anything?"

He had such a smug expression I was tempted to shoot him anyway.

"No, I arrived just before you did," he said. "Saw the mess, phoned 999. Next thing I know, you turned up."

"You did *what?*"

"I phoned the police, didn't I? What I like to call my citizen's duty."

In the distance I could hear sirens. I needed to get out of there.

"In fact that's probably them, now," he added, taunting me. But before I could move, he grabbed my arm. His fingers digging into my flesh.

"You should hang around and explain what happened," he said, like he was enjoying every minute. "It's not going to look good if you make a run for it. If he told me he was meeting you, I'd imagine there's a fair chance he told someone else."

I shook my arm free, but in the process of doing that I was distracted. He moved fast for an overweight idiot, and before I could stop him, his hand had darted into my trench coat pocket and pulled out my car keys.

"Give me those," I said.

"What's it worth?"

"It's worth me not putting a bullet in your cock."

"Ooh, dirty talk. Though I understand why certain bits of my anatomy fascinate you. It's the same with all the ladies."

I was in too much of a rush to point out his delusion.

"Graham, stop being a twat. Give me the keys."

He started walking backwards, towards his car.

"I'm not an expert on acoustics," he said. "But judging by the fact those sirens are getting louder, I'd say you've got about thirty seconds before they turn up. Could be less."

I could see the blue lights flashing off the walls of buildings further down the street.

"Keys, Graham. Final chance."

As the sirens got ever louder, he held out the keys. Then I watched as he dropped them down a drain, my escape route disappearing forever.

"Oopsie," he said.

Chapter 40

WITH the sirens reaching an almost deafening pitch, Graham dragged me to his car, pushed me inside, and then powered off in the other direction – in the process causing me to bang my head on the window.

"What the hell are you playing at?" I shouted, once I'd taken a grip on the dashboard, my relief at getting away overwhelmed by sheer fury that I hadn't managed to do it on my own.

"Call it insurance, my dear," he said, with a chuckle. "They're going to find your car, find your fingerprints, put two and two together and get a resoundingly simple four. Which admittedly will be difficult for you to talk your way out of, so now you're reliant on me. Who'd have thought?"

I still had the gun. I really, really did think about using it. Only the awareness that we'd crash managed to stop me.

"I'm your witness," he continued, hitting the accelerator hard as we joined a main road. "I can get you off. This one, anyway, not all the other things they'll do you for. Although it might just involve a favour in return."

"If it wasn't for you, I'd be out of there, anyway."

Compared to being in debt to Graham March, twenty-five years in prison suddenly didn't sound so bad.

"Possibly," he continued. "But there might be CCTV, and if so, it'll show you leaning into the car, coming out, holding the gun, and that wouldn't look good either."

"If there's CCTV it'll show who actually killed him and I won't have anything to worry about."

"You'd have to hope so, wouldn't you?"

I didn't like the way he was grinning.

"What do you mean by that?" I said, feeling my temper rising again.

"Just that it'd be unfortunate if there was a problem, for example, and something was obscuring the camera while that happened, but then moved out of the way."

"What are you saying?"

"Nothing, I'm merely hypothesising. A giant spider on the lens, maybe. Or possibly bits of footage that got lost if that particular bit of the tape was faulty. Any number of things, really. What were you so keen to meet Dougie about?"

I fastened my seat belt. This looked like we were in for the long haul. I ignored him, trying to get bearings on where he was taking me.

"At the risk of repeating myself, what were you so keen to meet Dougie about?" he asked again.

"I can't tell you that," I said, spotting signs to the M11 – the main motorway leading out of London in the direction of East Anglia.

"I presume it wasn't to confess your sins and plead forgiveness, because believe me, if it was then Dougie wasn't your brightest choice."

I turned towards him, pointing the gun.

"Graham, I'm going to ask you again. Was it you?"

"Was what me? The subject of that erotic dream you had last

night? Quite possibly, and understandable if so, but believe me I wasn't a willing participant."

"Stop being a ... Did you kill Dougie?"

"No. And put the gun down. We both know you're not going to use it."

He had a point. I dropped it to my lap but still left my finger on the trigger.

"Did you see who killed Dougie?" I persisted.

"I'm the detective," he said. "I'm the one who asks the questions."

"Former detective."

"Very much still a detective, my dear, and when you announce to the world that you made up all those allegations about me, I shall certainly have a word with my detective colleagues and put them right if they're having any suspicions in regard to your involvement of the demise of poor DCI Compton."

"Oh, dream on, Graham."

He shrugged.

"Your choice. But if you don't, then, without wanting to overstate the issue, you're completely fucked. Although actually, saying that gives me a mental picture of some poor sod slipping you a length, and your face all scrunched up in some sort of hideous gurning expression during the heat of the action, not that anyone would spot the difference."

I sighed. So that was his plan. Recanting all the accusations I'd made about him and retracting all the evidence, in exchange for confirming I hadn't committed a crime that I really had nothing to do with. It was pathetic, and I'd make sure he'd suffer incalculable pain for even thinking I'd be a willing participant.

"You can drop me here, if you like," I said, still with no idea where we were. "I'll make my own way home."

Instead, he took a slip road to the motorway, then floored the throttle again.

"Here?" he said. "I don't think so."

"Where are we going?"

"We're going for a drive."

"Where to?"

"Wherever the road takes us. Anyway, back to your earlier point, you said you wanted to start being nice to me, yes? You wanted to take me for a drink? Now seems like as good a time as any and you can tell your Uncle Graham what made you meet Dougie Compton in a deserted industrial estate, with a gun in your hand."

"You know as well as I do, I didn't have a gun in my hand."

He reached out to grab the weapon, but I moved it away just in time. So instead, he let his hand drop to my leg for a momentary grope before I punched it.

"Ow!" he said. "What did you hit me for?"

"Because you were trying to molest me like some sick pervert."

"In your dreams, my dear. I don't think it's my fault if you moved the gun away."

"You're enjoying this, aren't you?"

"Being in a car with you? Christ no, though if you look in the glove compartment there might be a mint and that'd make it slightly more tolerable."

"No, I mean your whole pathetic, petty little game. It's turning you on, isn't it? Giving you a hard-on. Assuming you can still manage that in your condition."

He laughed, adjusting his legs.

"Do you want me to show you? Help yourself, my dear. But I must point out I'm not going to pay you a fiver like one of your normal punters."

"Oh, fuck off."

He laughed again.

"Your language really isn't up to scratch, is it?" he said. "I must admit, I'm disappointed. It's a sign of mental weakness to resort to profanity."

"Would you prefer *piss off*, then?"

"Hmmm." He paused for a moment. "On balance, no, because that gives me a mental image of you relieving yourself, with your nasty bits on open display. Just the thought of that makes my stomach churn."

This wasn't getting us anywhere apart from further away from London. We'd just passed the M25. I still had no idea where we were going.

"I'm going to ask you again: did you see who killed him?" I said, once I'd calmed down a touch.

"No, my dear. I only arrived just before you did. I'm going to ask *you* again: what were you meeting him for?"

"He's a friend of a friend and I wanted a chat, okay?"

"That's obviously bollocks."

"It's all you're getting."

We lapsed into an uncomfortable silence. I kept watching the road signs. We blasted past junction seven to Harlow. A few minutes later, he slowed the car and pulled over on the hard shoulder, before bringing it to a stop.

"You can get out now," he said.

"Are you being funny?"

He shrugged.

"The door handle's on the left."

"We're in the middle of nowhere."

"Your point?" He switched on his hazard lights but left the engine running.

"My point is, as I just said, we're in the middle of nowhere."

He turned to face me, with a nauseating grin on his face.

"You're quite partial to abandoning things at the side of motorways, aren't you?" he said. "Isn't that what happened to your car when you did your disappearing act back in February? I thought you'd be at home."

"I'm not even discussing that," I said. Leaving my car on the hard shoulder on the M25 was all part of my elaborate plan to disappear but leave enough clues for Danny Churchill to eventually find me. It was far from my proudest moment.

"Anyway, this is what you want, isn't it?" Graham continued. "A long way away from the scene of your crime. There's quite a gap between junction seven, which we passed a few minutes ago, and junction eight which is a bit further up. But if you walk for five miles in either direction you should come to one or the other. I should mention, for the sake of upholding the law, it's actually illegal to be a pedestrian on the motorway, so watch out for patrol cars. That'd be a bit Al Capone, wouldn't it? Of all the things you're wanted for, they finally nick you for going for a stroll."

"You're being serious, aren't you?"

"You could try to hitch-hike," he continued, oblivious. "There's a chance it wouldn't be a brutal rapist, although admittedly a small chance. Although to be fair, I'm not sure even the Yorkshire Ripper would have been that desperate. Out you get. But give me the gun first."

I took a deep breath.

"I'm not giving you the gun."

"That's an order."

"Graham, you're not a policeman any more."

"I will be once you clear my name for me."

I couldn't bear being in the car with him a moment more. I started to wipe my fingerprints off the gun, using the length of my trench coat as an emergency cloth. I didn't need the gun. I certainly didn't need to spend another moment with that idiot. I got out of the car, and a few seconds later he was laughing as he left me to my fate.

Chapter 41

I CLAMBERED up the grass verge to get out of the view of passing traffic, sliding on the mud, and trying to get my head together and begin assessing my options.

What had just happened?

Where was I?

What was I going to do now?

Why was Graham March such a bastard?

First things first. If Dougie Compton was responsible for the murder of Rex Dexter, and had been orchestrating a cover-up, it made no sense at all that he'd just been murdered.

But who killed him? Graham? And if so, why? That made even less sense. I could believe that Graham would turn up to watch me in an uncomfortable situation. I found it harder to believe that he would be there to potentially help me escape. It'd be the first time ever he'd actually been useful. Why would he do that? Perhaps because of our mutual German friends, or because – as he'd said – he was hoping that I'd somehow exonerate him. But I couldn't find any rational explanation for him killing Dougie Compton and then hanging round for me to see him there.

But if Graham wasn't the killer, then who? Who else knew

that I was meeting Dougie – and most importantly, when and where? There was only one obvious answer. Nick. Nick had overheard the conversation. He knew exactly where I was going because he'd been there before. And although he'd been standing at the top of the stairs when I made the phone call, he was travelling on a motorbike, and that would have been far faster through the traffic than my underpowered Astra courtesy car.

I thought of my conversation with him. *If Dougie, as a senior member of the investigating team, knew about one of his sergeants, for example, having clandestine meetings, then that would be fairly conclusive too.*

Nick had been onto me since day one. He was one of the few people who knew I was in London and where I was staying. He'd been on the original case and so could have derailed it. He'd prepared the file of evidence for me, so could easily have removed anything incriminating. He bore all the marks of being the person I'd punched outside Suadela. And if he thought that Dougie Compton might be able to confirm my suspicions, he had both the means and motive for silencing him.

I still didn't have any concrete, incontrovertible proof, but there was certainly no lack of circumstantial evidence. It all made sense. Instinctively I'd been wary of the bloke from the first moment I'd met him. High five for instincts. Now all I had to do was find the proof. The only problem was that Nick was neither short nor left-handed.

First, though, I had to somehow find my way home. I lit a cigarette to try to calm my mind, and then phoned Joe.

"We've got a problem," I said when he answered.

"Clare, I can't speak. I told you. I'm at a dinner."

"This is serious, Joe. Dougie Compton's dead."

"Jesus. How?"

"He was murdered."

"How do you know?"

"I was supposed to be meeting him but he was dead when I

got there. I'll warn you now, the police are going to be looking for me, but I didn't do it."

"Oh, for God's sake, Clare."

"Don't start having a go at me. I'm not having a good day. I think I'm beginning to understand what's going on, though."

"Where are you now?"

"That's the other thing. Graham was there too, and whisked me off, but he's abandoned me somewhere, about halfway between Harlow and Stansted Airport."

I could hear the sound of chat and laughter in the background. The chink of cutlery on china.

"What the *hell* is going on?" asked Joe.

"A big part of me wishes I knew. The rest has a strong suspicion that I already do."

Joe's voice was muffled as he spoke to someone else with his hand over the microphone. After a moment, he came back.

"Now is not the time to get into the details," he said, tension leaking into his voice. "I'll speak to you tomorrow. In the meantime I'll get somebody to pick you up. Exactly where are you?"

I looked for any distinguishing landmarks but it was pitch black in all directions, apart from the lights of passing traffic.

"About three or four minutes past junction seven of the M11, northbound," I said. "Aside from that, no idea."

"Wait there, then. I'll get someone to patrol the hard shoulder. Make yourself known when you see them flashing their hazard lights."

"Is that safe?"

"Safer than spending the night in Essex, I imagine."

He ended the call.

I had no idea how long I'd have to wait, nor who I was looking out for. If it was Nick it was going to be awkward. I didn't want to sit down and risk getting the trench coat dirty, so instead stood in the cold, feeling more incensed by Graham with every minute, and marvelling at the sheer amount of litter the British public throw out of their car windows.

Almost an hour later, I saw a car moving much more slowly than the rest of the traffic, its hazard lights flashing. For better or for worse, I made my way down the bank and waited at the edge of the road. It stopped beside me, and I opened the passenger door.

"Get in," said Emily, looking more serious than I'd ever seen her before.

Chapter 42

I WAS so pleased to see her.

"Emily," I said. "I've been worried about you."

I fastened my seatbelt as she indicated to rejoin the carriageway.

"Joe said you'd had a call," she said. "Something about me being kidnapped?"

"Exactly, from your phone. I spent half the day in a mad panic and the rest of it narrowly avoiding getting arrested. Apart from that, I was trying to make arrangements to take you to dinner."

"Well, I'm here." She moved up through the gears as she reached maximum speed. "And sorry about dinner. It's been a difficult day. Jonathan called in sick so I've been doing double. I heard about Dougie Compton."

"Already?"

"Joe mentioned it. Something about him being murdered? Joe said it wasn't you, though."

At least that was something. I didn't even know where to start.

"Yeah." I paused, looking out of the window, watching the

darkness pass. I hated being out of control of my own destiny. "I arranged to meet him but somebody got there first."

"How did you end up here?"

I gave her the summary, making sure she was aware of just how little I thought of Graham March.

"I've been desperate to talk to you anyway," I said, once I'd finished. "I've been making progress."

"Really?"

"There's been a lot going on. How well do you know Nick?"

"Not very, why?"

I still didn't know where to start. Without tangible evidence it was risky to start making accusations.

"Have you got any idea who took your phone?" I asked.

Emily shook her head.

"I left it on my desk when I went to get coffee. When I came back it'd gone."

"You didn't see anyone near your desk, looking suspicious?"

"I asked around. Nobody had seen anything."

"If you find out, let me know."

"Because of the call?"

"Precisely because of the call. Someone's been plaguing me since the moment I got here, telling me to go home."

"You mean the damage to your car?"

"Yes, that, but other things too." I told her, at last, about the letter with the bullet and then being attacked outside Suadela. "What I'm trying to work out is if there are two separate things going on here, or whether there's a link."

"You think the person who's been terrorising you is trying to stop you investigating Rex Dexter?"

"Possibly. Or maybe they just don't like me."

"I can't imagine someone not liking you."

That made me laugh for the first time in a long time.

"Oh, you've got no idea. I'm pretty sure nobody likes me, but some have a more passionate loathing than others. Anyway, the point is, the more I find out, the more I think there's a link."

"I like you," she said, with a sweet naivety. "I know I probably shouldn't say that out loud, but I'm off duty now, kind of, so I think I can get away with it."

She pulled off onto the junction 8 slip road so we could turn round and head back towards London. As she did so, I told her about the conversation with Michael Steward, and my theory about Rex Dexter overhearing a conversation between Eddie Whitfield and a corrupt policeman.

"Some of this is conjecture," I concluded, "but it fits. I'm trying to find out who the man in the suit and hat was. My strong suspicion was that he was the one who committed the murder."

"Because?"

"Because looking at the forensic reports, and the angle of the knife blade, it was most likely somebody left-handed, and slightly shorter. And that's what put me onto Dougie Compton, because he was both. But I needed to speak to him to put him on the spot. It just didn't go as planned."

"Are you mad?"

"Quite possibly."

"He'd have arrested you."

"That was always a risk. But supposedly Graham was there to make sure that didn't happen."

She shot me a look of confusion.

"Why would he do that? How did he even know you were there?" she asked, as we passed back under the M25.

"Apparently Dougie called him, if you believe that."

"Do you think Graham killed Dougie?

"I can't see it."

"But he was there. He could have done it."

"He was, but why would he? If you believe a word he says, which admittedly is a stretch, he's trying to clear his name at the moment."

"But why help you escape, then? No offence."

"That's complicated. We've got a mutual friend in Germany, which is kind of a long story."

She wasn't giving up.

"But what if Dougie had something on Graham? What if Graham was the person in the pub and Dougie knew about it? He was worried that Dougie would confirm it for you?"

"And then Graham killed Rex Dexter? Not a chance. He's too big for a start. Even assuming he was less fat eight years ago, he wouldn't have been any less tall. And he's not left-handed either. Graham's as bent as a malformed banana but I can't see him killing anyone. Apart from possibly me, at some stage."

"So what do you think?"

What exactly did I think? I thought it was Nick, in every respect apart from the height and the left-handed thing. Maybe he was ambidextrous. Something stopped me saying it out loud, though, because there was still the question of Jason Shelley. Or possibly somebody different altogether. Suddenly I had an idea.

"Do you know a DCS Terry Handley?" I asked.

"Why do you ask that?" That seemed to throw her off course.

"He's apparently the person responsible for arresting me," I said. "I don't know much about him, but he was also the DCI on the original Eddie Whitfield case. So if we could speak to him, there's a possibility he could tell us more about Jason Shelley."

"I've heard of him," she said, "but that's about it."

"You've not come across him, on a case?"

"Have you any idea how many people work within the Metropolitan Police?"

"I could take a guess, but I expect you could give me an accurate number."

"Actually it changes on a daily basis, but somewhere around 27,000. There are over fifty chief superintendents."

I sighed.

"I feel like one of those Americans who say *'you come from London, you must know my friend'*. It was just a thought."

Maybe it was all too late now anyway. In twenty-four hours I'd be packing my bags and preparing to go home. I was missing Germany more than I'd ever imagined possible, but then I missed my life in London too. Maybe I was destined to spend the rest of my life missing things. I certainly felt I was missing something with the case. It was like almost all the clues were there, but I needed one more to arrange everything in order.

"Why did you ask me how well I knew Nick?" asked Emily, interrupting my daydream.

"Oh, I was just wondering."

"Sure?"

"For the moment, anyway."

Now wasn't the time. We lapsed into an easy silence. I yawned. It had been another long day, with far too much excitement, if that was the word. I needed one more night to re-evaluate. Go back to the start, if necessary. If I woke up in the morning, still convinced it was Nick, I'd explain everything to Joe. In the meantime, though, I really, really had to stay out of trouble. It was following me round. So much for being low profile.

"So what now?" asked Emily as we reached the end of the motorway.

"Are you around tomorrow?" I asked.

"I can be."

"Good. And do you have a new phone yet?"

"I do. I'll give you the number. Enter this into your phone."

She waited till I was ready, then reeled off the ten digits.

"Perfect," I said. "Tomorrow is my last day. I'm not giving up, and there are a few things I'm still working on, but whatever happens I'll call you before I start packing up, okay? Or maybe we could do the dinner thing tomorrow night, to toast my failure. Though I understand if that's too high risk, especially now."

"It would still be lovely. I'm not scared. What time do you leave?"

"First thing Sunday morning, all being well. In the meantime, if you can drop me off somewhere round here, I'll get the tube, and let you get back to your evening. Huge thanks for rescuing me, though."

She shot me another look.

"It's no problem. And don't worry. I can take you back to the hotel."

"I moved out of there after the car thing."

"Sorry, I didn't know. Okay, to wherever you're staying."

Suddenly I had a terrible thought. It wasn't my car that was abandoned at Dougie's murder scene. It was the courtesy Astra. How was I going to explain that to the body shop? I could phone them and say it had been stolen, but that wasn't going to help. The police would trace it back to them in an instant, ask them who'd borrowed it. When they realised I was supposed to be turning up to pick up my Mercedes, they'd be lying in wait for me. The chances of me seeing my car again were pretty much non-existent, and how on earth was I supposed to get home? Bugger.

"You look worried," said Emily.

"Sorry, I just thought of something else that's bad."

"Care to share?"

"No, nothing to worry about. Just another little problem for tomorrow."

"If you're sure?"

The M11 had turned into the North Circular Road, and we flashed past Redbridge Underground station.

"Positive. Drop me here if you like," I said.

"Let me take you home."

"Honestly, don't worry. I've got other things to do tonight."

"But it's gone eleven o'clock."

It was kind of her to offer, but I thought back to what Anders had said about keeping the location of the safe house secret. It was tempting, but I had to respect his instructions.

Eventually, Emily gave up, although we were in Bethnal Green by the time she found a tube station that she could park close to.

"I'll call you tomorrow," I said, as I got out of the car.

"I'll look forward to it," she said. "I should be free for dinner, I think, if you have the time."

I smiled.

"That'd be fantastic. I'll call you as soon as I know."

I watched her pull away into the night-time traffic and then thought about making my way into the station, but the possibility of being caught on CCTV was far too much of a risk.

Instead, I walked to a minicab office, and asked them to take me all the way to Farringdon. As the car weaved through dark city streets, I closed my eyes and felt myself drifting, but I knew I couldn't succumb. It was a time to be more alert and more focused than ever.

DCS Terry Handley answered the call.

"News?" he said.

"She's moved out of the hotel," said Emily.

"Where to?"

"I don't know, but she's calling me in the morning. She wants to meet tomorrow before she goes home, so all is good. It'll be the last chance, though. She said she's still planning on leaving on Sunday."

"Best laid plans and all of that. Where are you now?"

"Heading home. I'll call you with details of the meet as soon as I know. And if not we just have to take the initiative."

"Excellent work. Better she comes to us. We're reeling her in."

Emily's mind was racing. She'd grown to like Clare as a

person, but needs must. And if taking her down called for a degree of duplicity, then that was exactly the sort of ruthlessness she'd need as she moved up through the ranks.

"Clare asked if I knew you," she continued.

"Really? Why?"

"She knows you're the one looking for her, and she's interested in Jason Shelley."

"Why him?"

"He's on her list of suspects."

Terry gave a short laugh.

"I thought she was supposed to be good," he said. "And you're sure it's not because she suspects a link between us?"

"One hundred percent."

"You always were the expert at numbers."

Emily said goodnight and ended the call, finding it hard to suppress a tingle of excitement. She knew that Terry would be feeling it too. He'd been waiting for this moment for a very long time. It was too tantalisingly close for either of them to allow anything to go wrong now.

Chapter 43

Saturday, October 30th, 1993

IT felt like I'd only just gone to sleep, but when the phone rang, I glanced at my watch and it was nearly 8am. Turning over in bed, I thought about ignoring the call, but then decided against it when I recognised Iglika's number.

"Clare?" she said. "You were asleep?"

"No, I was just about to step into the shower." Was it really that obvious? I don't know why I felt the immediate need to lie. I sat up, ran my hand through my hair, and tried to focus. It was too early for a cigarette but I had a sense it was going to be a stressful day, so start as you mean to go on. I reached for the packet. "Is everything okay?"

"Everything is not okay," she said, her voice betraying a shakiness that I'd never heard before. "It is urgent that you come back as soon as you can."

That sounded ominous.

"Why, what's happened?"

"I must not discuss it by telephone. Can you come today?"

I blew a thick plume of smoke.

"I wish I could. Is it really that bad? I'm back in Koblenz tomorrow."

"Not today?"

Was it just me, or were we going round in circles?

"It's not going to be possible today unless something dramatic happens. But I'll call you as soon as I set off. Am I still coming to Sofia on Monday?"

"Yes, but please come more early if you can."

"I'll try." What did I mean by that? No idea. This was the last thing I needed. "I'll keep in touch and let you know if anything changes."

I ended the call, and sank back into the pillows. How on earth was I going to get to Sofia within forty-eight hours and still manage to function? Never mind earlier. Even getting to the airport was going to be a challenge without a car. I loved my car. The thought of abandoning it forever was heartbreaking, but in the greater scheme of things, better that than missing Sofia altogether by virtue of a twenty-five stretch in Holloway.

I headed to the shower. The hot jet of water helped spur me into life, and by the time I'd made coffee and toast, I felt ready for ... well, if not action, exactly, then at least trying to work out where I could meet Joe without being arrested, now even more of his colleagues would be looking for me. In the end, I phoned him and suggested an archway under the railway line at the back of King's Cross station. It wasn't far to walk, it was vaguely out of sight, and if he was late, at least I'd be able to pass the time chatting to the prostitutes, sharing bitchy anecdotes about Graham.

I took the coffee and toast to the front room, and watched Eddie Whitfield's confession one last time.

"By the time you're watching this I may well be dead, but I want to go to my grave with a clear conscience, and make my peace with God. And before

I start to lose my mind, I owe it to all of the people I've hurt to clear up a mystery that has troubled the Metropolitan Police for the last eight years.

"On the night of Friday 26th July, 1985, the DJ Rex Dexter was killed with a single knife wound in the car park of his radio station, Sound Of London FM.

"I take no pride or comfort in this confession, but for the sake of passing into the next life with no more secrets, it is with a heavy heart that I must now acknowledge my guilt for that murder. I know this will come as a surprise. I know that I was never considered a suspect, and I know that I could have died without ever confessing, but I am a changed person to the man I was back then. I have nothing to lose by making this confession, but everything to gain. God will be my only judge and jury and it is my hope that by taking responsibility for my actions, it will help my quest for His forgiveness.

"I didn't know Rex aside from what I'd seen on TV. I'd never met him until that day. It was a chance meeting. It wasn't planned. I can't explain my state of mind eight years ago, but I would like to apologise to his friends and family for his death.

"I would also like to apologise to the Metropolitan Police for the amount of time and money they've spent investigating his murder. I know I should have come forward earlier, but I had other things on my mind back then. But over the last eight years, I've had a lot of time to consider the sins in my past and while I cannot bring the dead back to life, I can at least hopefully give some peace to the living by finally revealing the truth.

"May God bless you all. Amen."

I knew it almost off by heart. And yet after the events of yesterday, I heard it in a way I'd never heard before. Suddenly I had a tingle of excitement. Suddenly everything made sense.

Joe wasn't late. I was. If I was going to go out in a blaze of glory, I might as well be well dressed for it – but I was running precariously low on clean clothes. I tried to remove the worst of the Essex mud off my boots, found one last shirt that wasn't covered in pen or debris from a punch-up, one last pair of tights that wasn't laddered, and a dark navy skirt because the beige one was looking a mess. By the time I'd brushed the dust off my trench coat and fixed my make-up, I had less than fifteen minutes to do the twenty-minute journey.

Joe started walking as he saw me, heading in the direction of Camden.

"You do realise you've just made it look like I'm hanging round, waiting for a prostitute?" he said, when I caught up and fell into step.

"Sorry about that," I said. "Although in fairness, it probably looks even more like that now we're walking off together." I meant it as a joke, expecting him to point out that I looked like nothing of the sort, but he didn't, so maybe I did. Add soliciting to my list of charges while you're on.

"What happened last night?" he said, making it sound like an accusation.

"With Dougie? I wish I knew. I turned up to meet him, but somebody got there first. Then Graham did what Graham does, and acted the twat. Thankfully Emily came to my rescue."

"You do know it doesn't look good?"

"I'm very well aware it doesn't look good. But trust me, I had nothing to do with it. Has there been any news?"

He shook his head but the frown didn't lift.

"I've not been into work but I suspect they'll have already identified a chief suspect."

He really wasn't helping.

"I've got a few issues, Joe, I'm not going to lie," I said.

"Trouble does seem to follow you around."

"It does but this time none of it is my fault. I'm supposed to be in Sofia at the moment, doing my day job, but instead I'm here trying to help you."

"And what exactly is your day job?"

"You know about my day job."

"I'm not sure I do."

It was definitely time to change the subject.

"And on top of everything, I've lost my car," I said.

"How have you lost your car?"

"Because it got vandalised and I took it to a body shop and they gave me a courtesy car, but thanks to Graham that was left at the crime scene last night, covered in my fingerprints, so it'll be getting impounded. I'm pretty sure they won't give me mine back if I've lost theirs."

The most annoying thing was that I'd gone out of my way to help Joe, thinking that if I could prove I was somehow useful, he'd feel more inclined to turn a blind eye to my previous indiscretions. But it hadn't exactly gone to plan, and I had a strong sense he was regretting ever asking me.

We reached a small play park and sat next to each other on a wooden bench in front of the swings.

"Do you know what happened to the gun?" he asked.

"Which gun?" As if I didn't know.

"The one that killed Dougie."

I wasn't looking forward to this.

"I picked it up," I said, and watched as his expression turned even more worryingly hostile.

"Why, for God's sake?"

"Because it was on the car seat, and, yes, I know it was a stupid thing to do, but as far as I was concerned, there was somebody out there killing people and I wanted to be protected."

"But if they'd left the gun behind they were unarmed. What were you scared of? That they'd give you a frosty stare?"

"It was a spur of the moment thing."

"Jesus. And where is it now?"

"Graham took it off me. I don't think he trusts me with guns. Has he not handed it in?"

"Not as far as I'm aware." He closed his eyes and shook his head.

"On the upside, I'm pretty sure I've worked out what happened with Rex Dexter and Eddie Whitfield," I said.

He sighed as he turned towards me.

"Go on."

I recapped my meeting with Michael Steward, and the theory about the overheard conversation.

"Interesting," said Joe. It wasn't exactly the glowing praise I'd hoped for.

"Anyway," I continued, undeterred, "I've been concentrating on looking into the senior police involved in the original investigations into both Rex Dexter and Eddie Whitfield."

"I hope you haven't gone anywhere near Terry Handley?"

"I haven't needed to."

"You do realise that after last night you're back to being number one on his hit list?"

"I can imagine, but that does seem terribly unfair."

"Clare, I've only got your word for it."

"And Graham's."

"This is the remarkable thing. Relying on Graham as your alibi."

"I know, and I prefer not to think about it. But anyway, back to the point. I rewatched Eddie Whitfield's confession. He said he was responsible for Rex Dexter's death. He didn't say he'd killed him."

"That's a question of semantics."

"No, I think it's a pivotal point. His actual words were: '*It is with a heavy heart that I must now acknowledge my guilt for that murder.*' He's taking the blame, but at no point does he actually say that he was the one who plunged in the knife."

"So why would he confess, then?" asked Joe, with a flicker more interest.

"Because he was deeply religious and he was carrying the burden of guilt. As far as he was concerned, he *was* responsible. Had that conversation in the pub not happened, Rex would be with us now. But it did, and then the person he was with acted, and he blamed himself."

"Maybe."

"It's more than maybe, Joe. He didn't name the actual killer. He wasn't a grass. But my theory is that he knew he was going to die, so he thought he'd clear things up, take the blame, because as far as he was concerned he'd been responsible, even if it wasn't actually him who pulled the trigger. Obviously that's a metaphor and I know knives don't have triggers."

A bus stopped opposite and a mother with a young child got off and then started walking in our direction. I hoped they were there to use the swings rather than being some undercover police double act. Joe didn't flinch, which was a good sign.

"The point is," I continued, "who was the other man? We know he was wearing a suit and a fedora, but aside from that we don't know what he looked like. But we also know that the person who killed Rex Dexter was possibly both slightly shorter and left-handed."

"Possibly."

"Exactly, but it's all I had to go on. So in the simplest sense, I was looking for someone senior on the original case who might have been up to no good with Eddie, and my attention turned to Dougie. Hence the meeting." It wasn't yet time to air the alternative Nick theory because I had a much better one.

"Which got him killed," said Joe.

"I'll take responsibility for lots of things," I said, "but you really can't pin that on me. Anyway, Dougie fitted the bill. He had the means, the potential motive ..."

"But now he's dead."

"He is. It doesn't mean he wasn't involved, though. And then I remembered something Graham said last night. *'If he told me he was meeting you, I'd imagine there's a fair chance he told someone else.'* I think there's one obvious person that would be. And that person had to silence him in case he said something he shouldn't."

"And they are?"

"Terry Handley. Because not only is he looking for me now, but he was also the SIO on the original Eddie Whitfield case."

"I can see how that would be convenient for you, but it wasn't Terry."

"Why?"

"For starters he's about six foot four, definitely not left-handed – and like Brian Dalton, he was with me the night it happened. He was telling me about his marital problems."

That took the wind from my sails. I watched another bus drive past, then shivered, feeling the cold for the first time.

"Okay, let's go back to the original investigation team," I said, after a moment, thinking on my feet. I still felt I was close to the answer "You vouched for Brian Dalton, Trevor Covington, and Alex Ward. Dougie Compton is dead. That leaves four other possibilities: Graham March, Neil Fearon, Kenny Mason and Jason Shelley, the undercover guy."

"Kenny's dead too, remember," said Joe. "Wrapped his car round a lamppost."

"I thought it was a signpost?"

"Figure of speech."

"Okay, but it doesn't mean he wasn't involved."

"Agreed. But he wasn't around to kill Dougie last night, was he? So Graham?"

I sensed Joe was getting impatient.

"I can't believe it's Graham," I said. "I'd love to think it was, but again, too tall and right-handed. In any case, I know Graham. I investigated him at length when I was at the newspaper. I uncovered all sorts of things that he was guilty of, but nothing like that."

"So Neil Fearon?"

"I thought it might be but I can't see that either."

"Because?"

"I went to his office. He locked me in but I managed to escape.

Long story which you've probably heard already. And then I went looking for evidence of any drug-running or the like at Suadela but as far I could tell, he came up clean again. Yes, he's probably the correct height, but he's right-handed."

"How do you know?"

"I checked in his office. The computer mouse was on the right of his keyboard. A pen was on the right of a notepad."

Joe checked his watch. The impatience was definitely getting the better of him.

"So you're no further forward?" he said.

It was time to forget about the Jason Shelley dead end, and play the Nick card.

"Well, in the words of Spandau Ballet, to cut a long story short, there is one thing."

"Which is?"

"You're not going to like this, but I keep coming back to Nick."

Joe sighed in exasperation.

"Bear with me on this," I said, before quickly explaining the Nick theory, and telling Joe about the terror campaign against me.

"Nick was on the original case," I concluded. "He could have hidden evidence in the original investigation and certainly excluded anything important from the documentation you gave to me. He's made no secret about the fact he isn't happy that I'm here. He knew where I was staying, so he could easily be the person who vandalised my car and sent me the bullet."

"So could Emily, for that matter."

"Yes, but the person who called me to say Emily had been abducted was a man. The person who attacked me outside Suadela was a man."

"But you didn't see his face?"

"No but I think I can tell the difference between a man and a woman, and it was someone about Nick's height and build. Then I met Nick yesterday and he looked like he'd been beaten up."

It was time to play the trump card.

"And – here's the clincher – he knew I was meeting Dougie," I continued. "He overheard me making the arrangements and then went racing off on his motorbike. That would be a far quicker way of getting there than a car." I felt utterly triumphant. "Again, for whatever reason, Dougie had to be silenced. Nick had the means, motive and opportunity. Think about it. Nick's your man. He has to be."

"That's awkward," said Joe.

"Why is that awkward? Because you trusted him?"

"No, It's awkward because for the last few seconds he's been walking up behind you, and he doesn't look very happy. And it very much looks like he's holding a gun."

Chapter 44

BEFORE I'd had a chance to panic, Nick came round to the front of the bench, pointing the gun at me. But then he lowered it, and Joe shuffled up, so I did too, creating space for Nick at the other end. I was the rather uncomfortable filling in a policeman sandwich.

"So you think it's me then?" said Nick. "I've got to say, I'm disappointed."

"Did you hear all of that?" I asked, a tiny bit sheepishly, but equally trying to calculate how I could disarm him so Joe could perform the arrest.

"Enough of it," he said.

"I suppose you're going to deny it?"

"Of course I'm going to deny it, because it's a lot of bollocks."

"But you turn up here with a gun?"

"Unless it's escaped your attention, my boss was murdered last night. I'm firearm trained and you're the chief suspect, so if you had a gun I had to come prepared." Nick had never been particularly friendly, but this was new ground. "And I suppose you're going to deny it?"

"What? That I killed Dougie?" I said. "Of course I am."

"Despite your fingerprints on the passenger door handle?"

"I'm not denying I was there. You knew I was going to meet him. I told you that before I ever set off. Do you think I'd have done that if I was going to ambush the man?"

"I don't think any of us know what you're going to do any longer."

I glanced at Joe for support, but none was forthcoming.

"But your face?" I said, turning back to Nick.

"I told you. I got hit playing five-a-side football, for God's sake."

"And can anyone else confirm that?"

"The other nine players. And before you ask, I'll just reconfirm that it was a police team."

"I've heard the police are occasionally happy to offer a cover-up."

"If that's the best you can do, I suggest you do go home, before my patience runs out completely."

I turned back to Joe. He looked more disappointed than ever.

"Nick's a good detective," he said, shaking his head. "I'm sorry the two of you don't see eye to eye, but I'm inclined to agree with him. If that's the best you can do, I think we write this one off to experience."

I let out a tiny scream of frustration.

"I'm so close, Joe," I said, causing Nick to snort, and me to turn and glare at him. "Seriously, though, I am. I can feel it."

"Are we done here?" asked Nick, directly to Joe, bypassing me completely, the condescending bastard.

"No, we're bloody well not," I said.

"I think we probably are, and I think you'd better disappear before Terry catches up with you," said Joe. "Oh, talking of which, I got a description of your man Jason Shelley, for what it's worth."

"And?"

"It's not much but he had ginger hair and big cheek dimples, apparently. I don't have a picture, sorry."

Why did that sound important. Had Michael Steward said something about ginger hair? No, he said he couldn't see the hair colour under the hat. It meant something, though. My head was beginning to hurt.

"You look fed up," said Joe, softening for the first time.

"I am. But really, I'm so close."

Nick snorted again and then stood up and started walking away. Before I could give him a piece of my mind, I was interrupted by my phone's ringtone. I recognised the number.

"Sorry," I said to Joe. "I must get this."

And as I hit the button to connect the call, I remembered why the ginger hair and dimples rang a bell. Jonathan Hubbard. Emily's colleague/part-time boyfriend, in the car.

"Is that Clare?" said Michael Steward when I answered, my brain still trying to work out the implications. Was it just a coincidence? Or was it Hubbard? Shelley had to be working somewhere. He'd gone back into the police under his own name. It had to be. Didn't it?

"You said to call you if I thought of something," Michael continued, snapping me back to reality.

"I did. Thank you. I really appreciate it. Has something come up?"

"The man in the hat," he continued. "I've been thinking about what you said. Did I see his hair colour?"

"It wasn't ginger, was it?"

I was ready to leap for joy. I crossed my fingers and Joe shot me a look.

"What? No. That's the point. I remember I said I couldn't see anything because of the hat, and you asked about the back of his head. That was what I was thinking about, trying to picture it, and then it came to me. He was bald."

Definitely not ginger then. Every time a door opened, it slammed shut with brutal predictability.

"How bald?" I asked, trying to suppress a sigh.

"Complete Duncan Goodhew. Because that was the thing. It was the 1980s. Goodhew was a big star then, after winning gold at the Olympics, and I remember thinking, what is Duncan Goodhew doing in a pub like this? Except it wasn't him, obviously, but I'm pretty sure your man was completely bald. Does that help?"

Despite the disappointment, the neurons in my brain were re-energised. Who'd been completely bald in all of this? Nobody. Nobody at all. Unless ... Unless ...

"Ooh, Michael. It definitely does," I said, feeling a deep tingle in my stomach that morphed into a full-blown flutter.

I thanked him again, ended the call and turned back to Joe, trying to stay calm.

"I need to go back to the *Echo*," I said to him. "I need to look in the archive. There's something I want to check."

"Because of the call?"

"Precisely because of the call. Give me till this afternoon. Please. If I haven't got back to you by then, I'll call Terry Handley myself, tell him where I am and ask him to pick me up. But if I do, can you do me a favour? Promise you'll be there to take the credit?"

"Are you being serious?"

"You know what. I really think I am."

Chapter 45

I ALMOST ran back to Farringdon, slowing down only to phone Derek.

"Are you calling to say goodbye?" he said.

"No, not yet. But you know that thing I said about not asking any more favours?"

"Oh God."

"There was one tiny little one."

"Oh God."

"I need to go back to the library. Just for a few minutes."

"Oh double God."

"Derek, I don't want to be critical here, but I'm thinking maybe you need some other turns of phrase. You're a wordsmith. How about: *yes of course, it'd be lovely to see you again after such an excellent evening on Thursday.*"

He laughed.

"It was an excellent evening and it would be lovely to see you. But I'm still standing by the 'Oh double God'. And it's Saturday. I'm not at work."

That wasn't going to stop me.

"I'd offer to come and pick you up, but I've lost two separate cars in the last three days," I said.

"So you want a lift as well?"

"I'd happily get a cab, although if you were passing ..."

"When do you go back to Germany?"

"Tomorrow."

"Am I allowed to unplug my phone between later this afternoon and Monday, to be on the safe side?"

"Derek, if you can get me into the library I'll let you do anything you want."

That sounded a bit more risqué than I'd intended it to.

"If you'd said that to me twenty years ago, my imagination would be going into overdrive," he said, not letting me off the hook.

"Derek, if I'd said that to you twenty years ago, I'd have been eleven."

"You wouldn't have had to be twenty years younger too. Although maybe one year younger so I could talk you out of doing what you did."

"You don't know how often I wish that too. But is that a yes?"

"Where are you?"

"Heading towards Fleet Street."

"I'll meet you outside in an hour."

That gave me time to collect the time-honoured dark glasses, before making the dash to the *Echo*. Derek was there, good as gold. This time he came into the library with me, and I was glad of the company. There were far fewer people around, and I looked a lot more conspicuous.

"This won't take long," I said, partly to reassure him, and partly because, if my suspicions were correct, I had a busy day ahead.

He followed me to a computer, and then watched over my

shoulder, searching for any information at all on Kenny Mason, and specifically the night he was killed. I'd read the stories once, but now they were more than just a sideshow. They were central to everything.

It didn't take long to find the *Echo's* story, but there wasn't a picture. I checked the other newspapers, but the archive didn't go back that far.

There was only one more place it could be. I moved to the picture library and that's where I found him. Michael had a point. The likeness to Duncan Goodhew was uncanny.

I knew who the man in the hat was. I also knew he'd been killed in a car crash.

But what if the accident – wasn't an accident?

What if someone had arranged for it to happen. Kenny had been on a night out with police colleagues. One of them could have spiked his drink. One of them could have tampered with his car.

Kenny Mason had been a DS on the Rex Dexter case. What had he known that cost him his life? Was he corrupt? Or was he an innocent victim in all of this?

And what if the answer had been staring me in the face all along?

Chapter 46

I GAVE Derek a hug as we emerged back on the street.

"Are you sure that's everything?" he asked. I think he was secretly enjoying the excitement of it all, although for me it was less about the excitement and more about working out how to deliver the truth to Joe without a personal catastrophe rather taking the shine off. Joe would need proof. He wouldn't be interested in just another theory. But that was easier said than done when everything happened eight years ago and evidence was in short supply.

"I am," I said with a smile.

"Can I go now?"

"You have my permission."

"Oooh."

"What?"

He was grinning.

"Just the way you said that. *You have my permission.* It was kind of kinky. But thank you, Mistress. Glad to be of service."

He bowed and I laughed, holding out my hand so he could kiss the back of it.

"I'm seeing another side to you, Derek," I said, "and I have to be honest with you, I'm not sure it's healthy." I gave him another hug, and finished it with a light tap on his backside. Despite what I'd seen at the Schloss parties, I wasn't yet an expert in the dark arts of pain.

The day was passing far too quickly. It was nearly 2pm by the time Derek had left me, and I still had lots to do. I called Emily, hoping she'd come to my assistance. Thankfully, she leapt at the chance.

"I'm just trying to think where to meet," I said. "The coffee shop thing isn't going well." Then it came to me. Close to where I used to live in the Docklands, there was an old brick storage building. Both the building itself, and the cobbled street on which it stood, would inevitably soon be bulldozed to make way for a development of new apartments that most normal people couldn't afford. Unless, of course, they did a bit of art fraud or similar, but the less said about that the better. Until that happened, it was empty, and I was confident I could find a way in.

"What about dinner as well?" asked Emily, once I'd given her the address.

"If everything goes to plan, I should have the whole evening free," I said. "We've just got a few things to wrap up in a bit of a brainstorm this afternoon and then I need to hand everything over to Joe. Once that's done, I'm off the hook, and aside from trying to work out how I'm getting home, I'll have the night off."

"I was forgetting about your car."

"Worst case I can speak to someone who can fly me."

"Really?" She sounded surprised.

"Perks of the day job, in some respects."

"Well, make sure you turn up this afternoon, rather than just disappearing on someone's Learjet."

I chuckled, and decided against pointing out it was actually a Cessna. Some things are best kept private.

"Don't you worry," I said. "I'll definitely be there. I'm thinking of your spectacular career prospects when this gets resolved."

"Indeed. It's exciting. I'm thinking of that too."

There were just over two hours before I'd need to set off to meet her, and I still had to find a branch of Ryman, the stationery shop, and then make another phone call to Joe, to tell him I'd solved things. I didn't tell him quite how, as I still needed the evidence, and I was going to need Emily's help with that. He sounded jaded, but came round when I gave him a suitably mouthwatering teaser.

"Where's Nick?" I asked him, once he'd decided to give me the benefit of the doubt.

"At this moment, I don't know," he said. "You're not still thinking he has anything to do with this?"

"Joe, you have to trust me. Just make sure you know where he is."

"Because?"

"Because I'm worth trusting."

"Don't even start me on that."

"You're not still sore about the other thing?"

"I'll always be sore about the other thing."

"If it's any comfort, my entire criminal proceeds have been invested in phone calls on your behalf this week, so I think that makes us even. Probably makes you an accessory, now I think about it."

He didn't seem to find that as funny as I did.

"You'd better go before I change my mind," he said, after a pause.

"We'll speak later." I ended the call before I talked myself into trouble.

"We're meeting at 5pm," said Emily, before giving DCS Terry Handley the address.

"Perfect," he said.

"Is there anything you need me to do?"

He paused for a moment.

"Are you firearm trained?"

"Not officially."

"Okay." He sounded hesitant. "Look, I'll be honest with you. I'll have a weapon and I'm going to have armed officers on standby at the entrances and in the streets outside, but time is tight. She's unpredictable. If she comes quietly then everything is okay, but the first sign of trouble I want you to get the hell out of there. Leave it to me and the backup. Understood?"

"Understood. But she trusts me. I'm fairly sure if I'm there, she won't turn violent."

The DCS laughed.

"Believe me, constable, you cannot rely on that. She might trust you now, but when she realises what's just happened, she's going to turn. The number one objective here is to make sure everyone gets out alive. You especially. Whatever happens, keep a distance away so she can't use you as a human shield. Is that clear?"

"It is."

There was still one thing bothering Emily. It should have been discussed at the start, but now it was urgent.

"Can I just clarify the situation with DSI Joe Leyland?" she said.

"In what regard?"

"He's still a powerful person. I know I've done this for the greater good, but if he thinks he can't trust me, I don't want it causing trouble."

"I don't think you need worry about that."

She wasn't convinced.

"Because?"

"Because we've got enough evidence that he's consorting with a known criminal. He'll be going down with her. If it makes you happy, get her talking when you get there. Get her to confirm she's been working with Joe. Once she's said enough to incriminate the bastard, that's when I'll give the order and we'll strike. Understood?"

"Perfect."

Emily ended the call and checked her watch. The next couple of hours couldn't pass soon enough.

Chapter 47

THANKFULLY, the Docklands warehouse was still there. The entrance was on a deserted alleyway, out of sight of the main road, and breaking in was as simple as picking a couple of padlocks. Best of all, there was still electricity. Once I'd negotiated a narrow corridor, I flicked on the lights, causing a yellow glow to fill the open space of the main room, and spill out through the barred windows to the cobbles outside.

I didn't have long to get organised, but I found a couple of chairs in an old office. Like everything else, they were covered in dust, but I wiped the worst of it with the top sheet of the flipchart pad I'd bought in Ryman, then carried them through to the main room. I then hung the rest of the pad on a nail poking out of the crumbling plaster of the walls, and put my remaining shopping on an old wooden desk at the side.

Just before 5pm, a car engine rumbled then died in the alleyway. By the time I got to the door, Emily was walking towards me. I led her inside.

"What is this place?" she asked, looking around and taking in the general sense of decay. She wrinkled her nose at the strong aroma of damp.

"It's been here years," I said. "I used to live a couple of streets away. I apologise that it's not the most salubrious, but the last time I tried to have a meeting in a coffee shop I nearly got arrested, so I thought this would be a bit safer. Anyway, come in, take a seat, make yourself at home."

There was no question of removing coats. The air seemed colder inside than out.

"What have you got, and how can I help?" she asked, once she'd tentatively taken one of the chairs. She moved it away from the other so there was a big gap between us, which was strange. It wasn't like there was a shortage of space.

"It's like I said, I want to have a brainstorm. We need evidence." I paused, thinking I'd heard a noise from the corridor. But before I could stop and check, a bat swooped across the roof void, evidently not happy about being disturbed. Emily shrieked, and I only just managed to stop following suit. There was another creak, this time from the exposed rafters. Part of me wanted to get out of there as quickly as possible, before the whole place collapsed. Emily shuddered, and I couldn't blame her.

"I've got a flipchart," I continued, moving to the wall, once we'd both calmed down. "What I want us to do is write the key facts of the case on it, and then see if we both spot the same pattern. Then we can focus on gathering the proof. Because I'm pretty sure I know what happened, but I want to get your take and see if you agree. Does that sound okay? I'm working on the basis that you're the expert analyst."

She nodded and smiled.

"And then what? You take it to DSI Joe Leyland?" she said.

It was odd that she used his full name and title. So far we'd only ever called him Joe. Maybe she was just being hyper-professional.

"That's the plan," I said.

"And do you think this is what he asked you to do?"

"I hope so."

"And you think it's Nick?"

That stopped me.

"What makes you think that?"

She shrugged.

"Nothing, really. Only that you asked me last night how well I knew him. I thought maybe you'd uncovered something about him. That he was your number one suspect."

"Well ... " I paused. How best to explain it? "I don't really want to say too much and cloud your judgement."

"Have you gone through this with Joe?"

"Not yet."

"But you're meeting him?"

"If we can think of a way to prove the theory, I've said I'll speak to him before I go home."

"Is Joe helping you do that?"

"What? Prove the theory?"

"No, is he helping you go home?"

Why did I feel like I was being interviewed?

"Hmmm." I frowned. "I haven't asked him. I like to think I'm self-sufficient. Anyway, moving onto the chart."

But Emily hadn't finished.

"Do you think he would, though?"

"What is this?" I asked. Again there was a noise from the corridor. Maybe just wind, blowing on the open door.

"I'm only trying to clarify exactly where you're up to," she said. "Making sure that Joe Leyland is helping you."

And there it was again. His full name.

I moved away from the wall and took a step towards her.

"Why are you acting strangely?" I asked. "Is there something you're not telling me?"

"I'm not acting strangely, am I?" she said.

I took another step.

"Some people think I'm paranoid," I continued. "But I prefer to think it's a well-attuned instinct for self-preservation."

As I took a third step towards her, she stood up, suddenly looking nervous, and moved away to the side. I don't know what she thought I was going to do.

"Where are you going?" I asked, edging ever closer. But with every step I took, she took one of her own to keep the distance between us.

"Nowhere, I was just getting cold sitting down."

"You look nervous, though. If you don't want to be here, you're free to leave. Why do you keep moving away? What do you think I'm going to do?"

"I'm not moving away," she said. "I'm trying to get circulation in my legs."

"Come this way, then, and it'd save me having to chase you."

I meant it as a joke, but it backfired badly. A look of panic shot across her face.

But before I could apologise and reassure her, the door burst open, and a man I didn't recognise entered at speed, pointing a gun at me.

If I hadn't had months of training, I might have panicked.

"Who are you?" I asked instead, trying to sound outwardly calm.

"Clare Woodbrook – we meet at last," he said. "DCS Terry Handley, and you're under arrest."

I smiled, despite myself.

"Terry, lovely to meet you. I've heard so much. Actually, that's not strictly true, I haven't heard much at all, except you've got my picture on your wall. I hope I'm not a disappointment in real life."

Emily pulled out a set of handcuffs and started to approach me, which I thought was brave. Terry was keen to get a move on.

"Clare Woodbrook. You do not have to say anything unless–"

"Oh come on, Terry," I interrupted. "Do you really have to do all that? Come in and we'll have a little chat. Look, I've even got a flipchart so if you want a detailed confession we can write it all up, and at the end, I'll sign it for you. Does that help?"

He didn't look the type for levity.

"Hands out where I can see them," he continued.

I reached my arms out in front of me like I was about to dive into a swimming pool. Emily cuffed me. I nearly asked her what the hell she thought she was doing, but in truth it was obvious. The traitor. She didn't even have the decency to look me in the eye as she did it.

"I still need to read you your rights," Terry continued, still pointing the gun at me.

"Oh, go on then, if you must," I said. "But you can drop your gun before someone gets injured."

"Clare Woodbrook," he started, ignoring my suggestion, "you do not have to say anything unless you wish to do so, but what you do say may be given in evidence."

"Is that it?"

"We'll do the rest at the station."

"Fine. I'm glad that's out of the way, but let me make a better suggestion," I said. "Emily, there's a bag on the table. You'll find a bottle of Champagne and three glasses. Be a darling and pour, would you? I think we all deserve one."

Chapter 48

EMILY shot a glance at Terry, as though seeking his approval.

"Oh come on, humour me," I said. "I appreciate what you're here to do, and I'm making it easy for you."

"You need to come with me," said Terry.

"I know, but there's no rush. And you might be interested in what I've got to tell you first, before this all gets unnecessarily formal. I'll have one, anyway, Emily, if you'd do the honours."

She didn't move, which was more frustrating than the handcuffs. It was a good bottle. For his part, Terry seemed on edge, as though he didn't quite know what to make of me. I doubted he'd thought it would be this straightforward. From the corner of my eye, I noticed movement from the far side of the window. I turned to see an armed police officer, holding a machine gun. So, Terry had brought backup. What was he expecting? I'm nice.

"Let's get the nasty bit out of the way first, then, shall we?" I continued, unperturbed. "Yes, I was responsible for an art fraud. I confess. I'm really sorry but what can you do? And yes I shot my former business partner, but it really was self-defence, even though I appreciate that you and everyone else keeps telling me otherwise. And yes, I did fake my own demise in a helicopter crash in the mountains of Switzerland, specifically so the wreckage and bodies would never be recovered, but I'm here, as you can see. Absolutely, one hundred percent guilty of all of that. Happy?"

He continued to stare at me, still pointing the gun at my chest. At some point he was going to wonder why there were three glasses. It was almost as though I'd known he was coming.

"But none of that's what I'm here for today," I continued. "So before we go off to the station, let me at least explain how I solved the Rex Dexter case for you. I presume you don't want Joe to get all the glory. And this is a one-shot deal. I'm doing it because I'm a good person, but if you stick me in a cell before I have the chance to tell you, there's a strong likelihood I might stop being quite so helpful."

"I'm not here to piss about," he said.

"Neither am I, Terry, but believe me, you'll want to hear this." I turned to Emily. "If you're not doing the honours with the Champagne, can you at least write things on the flipchart for me? I'd do it myself, but it's a bit awkward in handcuffs."

Again she looked to him for approval. This time, eventually, he nodded. Emily moved to the chart, took the top off a marker pen and got ready to write. I thought about sitting down, but he'd only try to stop me, purely for the hell of it.

"So," I began, then turned my attention to Terry. "Eddie Whitfield. I believe you were the person who put him behind bars, yes?"

"As part of a team."

"Indeed. And you know he confessed to Rex Dexter's murder. Joe asked me to cast a glance over it because – and apologies to Joe if this betrays a confidence – it all seemed a little bit odd and he thought fresh eyes might help. So now I'm going to give you two for the price of one. Let's get the flipchart going. Emily, are you ready?"

She nodded, still looking nervous, or maybe embarrassed. Either way it would be good to give her something to think about other than her treachery. No wonder she'd been excited about the effect this meeting would have on her career prospects.

"Write these bullet points, as I tell you," I continued, "and we'll stop when the evidence is overwhelming, okay? But try to write quite small, please, so we can fit them all on one page, as there are quite a few. We'll begin with the confession, so let's start the list with just that: 'The Confession'."

She wrote the words and took a step back.

"That okay?" she asked.

"Perfect. Now add: 'Eddie Whitfield'. Below that 'Rex Dexter', then 'Radio DJ' because that was his job. And then finally for now, we need to think about when this took place, so put 'Year – dash – 1985'."

By the time she was finished there were five lines on the chart, and Terry looked like he was about to lose his patience.

"Trust me, Terry," I said, wondering how long it would take him to tell me off for not using his title. I was surprised I'd got this far.

He edged further into the room, which was a start, but he still didn't drop the gun.

"So," I continued, deciding to summarise for his benefit, "I've been trying to find a link between Eddie and Rex, because in the original investigation there wasn't one, at least not in the evidence I saw. But I found one. Rex Dexter met a journalist in a pub called the Seven Crowns in Islington on the afternoon of the day he died, not for an article for a newspaper, but because he wanted someone to ghostwrite his autobiography. There were two other people there. Eddie Whitfield, and a mysterious man in a hat. I'll come back to the hat, but based on the recording of his final radio show, it seemed likely that Rex overheard them speaking, and made a reference to it on air that night. He implied he'd keep it a secret, but as we know, he liked a gossip, and that pretty much signed his death warrant. Or so I thought at first."

I paused, to check Terry was still following.

"Continue," he said.

I nodded, wishing I'd had the foresight to have a cigarette before Emily arrived. It was going to be awkward now, but sod it, I fancied one.

"Before I do, can someone get me a cigarette out of my pocket please?" I said.

Terry scowled and shook his head.

"I don't know what the hell you think you're playing at, but keep speaking before the cold gives me cramp in my trigger finger."

"Fair enough." I sighed, then turned back to Emily. "Anyway, I spoke to Michael Steward, the journalist, yesterday. He gave me some useful details about that day in the pub and about Eddie, but he also gave me an even more valuable tip, though neither of us realised it at the time. He was telling me why he wasn't interested in ghostwriting the book. He thought it was the worst kind of vanity project. Rex wanted to tell the story of his luxurious lifestyle, full of pop stars, TV shows, and glamorous women. But Michael had heard rumours that there was a darker side. Rex, as you know, was a womaniser. But as Michael pointed out to me, the use of the word *woman* was perhaps overstating it a bit. Rex liked them young. Not as young as some of his contemporaries, by all accounts – and I strongly suggest you look into Jimmy Savile – but young nonetheless."

"Can I just point out," Terry interrupted, "if you're making slanderous accusations about living people–"

"It's only slander if it isn't true. But getting back to the point, despite some of his friends and colleagues going for as young as possible, Rex apparently liked them at sixteen, believing that that made it legal. I'd argue the point, but let's not get sidetracked. And not sixteen minimum, but sixteen. By seventeen he'd lost interest. Actually, Emily, add these to the list please, in case we forget: 'Islington', and 'Seven Crowns', and then 'Mysterious Man' and finally 'Young Girls'."

I paused while she did as directed, grateful that she was at least trying to be helpful.

"So Rex Dexter was a pervert?" said Terry, suddenly interested, which made me wonder if he had leanings in that direction as well.

"He was. Exactly that," I said. "Emily, you said you used to listen to his radio shows. Did you ever pick up on anything along those lines with anything he said?"

"No," she said, shaking her head.

"Okay. Maybe he kept it hidden. Anyway, I've been trying to work out who the man in the hat was. All we knew was that he was wearing a suit, and a fedora, and that he was possibly a policeman."

"On what basis do you think he was a policeman?" asked Terry, scornfully.

In a bizarre way, I was enjoying myself.

"I'm glad you asked me that," I said. "On the basis that when Eddie confessed, someone high up in the police was keen to accept it at face value, without really looking below the surface to see if it was true. And that implied a cover-up, which would imply police involvement. There's a point, actually, Emily. Could you add 'Fedora' and 'A Potential Cover-up'. How many rows have we got so far?"

"Eleven," she said, without pausing to count them. She really was remarkable.

"Perfect. Not many more."

"Is this some sort of game?" asked Terry, again sounding impatient.

"No, it's more of a mind map word association thing. Keep bearing with me. Anyway, back to the point. For the avoidance of doubt, Eddie Whitfield did not kill Rex Dexter. I do believe that he thought he was *responsible*, but it wasn't Eddie who wielded the knife. But that got me wondering: why did Eddie believe that to be the case?"

I paused, casting a longing glance in the direction of the Champagne. This was thirsty work. The other two ignored me.

"This is where it gets complicated," I continued, when I realised it was pointless. "I thought the man in the pub might be Dougie Compton, but I was wrong. I arranged to meet Dougie to put it to him, but when I got there he'd been murdered. Not by me, I hasten to add, and thankfully there was a witness to that, although the less said about that the better. But the point was, someone killed Dougie. Why? And if it was linked to the original case, was the person who killed Dougie also the killer of Rex Dexter?"

I let that hang in the air for a moment, expecting a question or comment, but none was forthcoming.

"Meanwhile," I continued, "I've been getting plagued since almost the moment I arrived in London. Emily can tell you. Someone sent a bullet to my hotel, vandalised my car, tried to beat me up outside Suadela – which is a nightclub, by the way – and phoned me threatening to kill young Emily here unless I went home to Germany. Was any of it linked? And do you know the answer?"

"Enlighten me."

"First, the next line, Emily please. 'Threats'."

She had to stoop down slightly to write by now. I waited until she'd finished before continuing, aware that I really needed to up the pace.

"Yes, it was linked," I said, "but no it wasn't the same person.

It was still all a bit of a mystery. So let me take you back to the man in the pub. He was wearing a hat. Why was he wearing a hat? Well, it transpires that without a hat he was very recognisable. As the journalist said, he was as bald as Duncan Goodhew. And as soon as I found out that particular nugget, I knew exactly who he was, and everything fell into place."

Chapter 49

TERRY still looked scornful, but at least he hadn't snapped and put me in the back of his police car.

"Who was he then?" he asked, when it became apparent I wasn't going to continue unprompted.

"Kenny Mason," I said.

"What? But Kenny's dead."

"He is. But he wasn't back then. He had a tragic car accident, a year or so later, actually after a night out with you I believe."

I looked Terry in the eye, testing his reaction. He didn't flinch.

"We were celebrating closing a case," he said.

"You were. And can you remember the name of the pub?"

"Christ, it was years ago."

"I thought you'd say that, so let me tell you, it was the Halfway House in Edgware."

"If you say so."

"I do, because apparently that's the truth, so Emily, please: 'Halfway House' and 'Edgware'."

Finally his patience cracked.

"I've had enough of this," he said.

"I'm sure you have, but trust me, we're nearly there. There's only one last thing to put on the board: 'Real Killer' followed by a question mark. Then, Emily, you can sit down if you like, your work is done for the time being."

That seemed to buy me a moment. She wrote the final line and then stepped away.

"So, to summarise, let's all read the chart, in order," I said. All eyes turned to the page.

The Confession
  Eddie Whitfield
  Rex Dexter
  Radio DJ
  Year – 1985
  Islington
  Seven Crowns
  Mysterious Man
  Young Girls
  Fedora
  A Potential Cover-up
  Threats
  Halfway House
  Edgware
  Real Killer?

When they'd had a moment to study it, I continued.

"We're going to come back to the board, but Emily, you're the analytical genius. See if you can spot an initial pattern, and let me know if anything jumps out at you."

She nodded and I turned to face Terry.

"Okay, so back to Kenny," I said. "Point number one. It wasn't an accident. I've been reading the newspaper coverage today. Not only were there pictures of Kenny in the archive, who did indeed look a bit like Duncan Goodhew, but there were question marks over the crash itself. An inquest discovered that the car had several mechanical problems, and in the hands of someone who had had too much to drink, it was lethal. Nothing was proven, of course, but no surprise there."

Again I looked for a reaction, but again Terry was unmoved.

"But then I looked at the time of the crash," I continued "and it wasn't even particularly late at night. And while I know policemen can put the pints away, the amount he'd have had to drink led me to one big conclusion. Kenny's drinks were spiked. His car had been tampered with. Net result, Kenny was murdered. And now I suppose you want to know why?"

For the first time, Terry was starting to look edgy. But what threat did I pose? I was unarmed and in handcuffs. My only weapon was my voice.

"Kenny was meeting Eddie Whitfield in the pub the week before he got arrested on the vault job," I continued. "Was Kenny giving him a warning? Obviously not, because Eddie went ahead with it and got arrested. In fact, Kenny didn't know anything about the undercover operation at all, which was unfortunate for him. Why unfortunate? Because he was bent. He'd been supplying information to Eddie on other potential lines of enquiry, and getting a cut for his trouble. But when the undercover op came to a head, Kenny was exposed. Really, he should have been arrested there and then, but you let him run free, didn't you Terry?"

"I heard rumours but nothing that was ever substantiated." He'd started to sweat.

"You heard rumours? That's interesting. Because I found out that you heard more than rumours. Remember, you had an undercover guy right at the heart of Eddie's organisation."

He took a step towards me.

"I think I've heard enough. If you're going to spout ridiculous accusations, we can call a halt to this now."

"I'd agree. If the accusations were ridiculous. But they're not. In fact the very word accusation implies an element of doubt, and believe me, there's no doubt about any of this. So back to the point. We know it was Kenny in the pub. We know he was corrupt. We know he should have been arrested, and if he had, that might have stopped him being murdered. But he wasn't arrested so now we have to ask why."

I glanced at Emily. She was studying the board. I didn't think it would take much longer, and struggled to suppress a smile.

"So let me wrap this up for you," I said. "A deal was struck. Kenny was more use on the outside, and believe me, I know how that feels. Although the difference in my case is that I'm helping to solve a murder, rather than orchestrating misdirection. Because that was Kenny's role. He knew who'd killed Rex, and his mission was to make sure that nobody else did. A cover-up for a cover-up. Are you all right, Emily – you've gone a bit pale?"

She'd gone more than a bit pale. She'd broken out in a sweat. And then, from her coat pocket, she pulled out a gun.

Chapter 50

"**B**ITCH," she snarled, pointing the gun at me. Terry, to his credit, looked shocked.

I looked beyond him to the doorway, where Joe was now standing, next to Nick, and flanked by two police officers, their guns trained on Emily rather than me. She saw them and panic leapt across her face.

"Drop your weapon," shouted one of the policemen.

Emily didn't drop her weapon. She kept it pointing at me. Terry rushed across the room to join her, but didn't drop his aim either.

"Are you going to tell everyone the pattern, or shall I spell it out for them?" I said, my voice calmer than it should have been with two barrels pointing in my direction.

"Very fucking funny," spat Emily.

"Because here's the thing," I continued. "We know the killer was slightly shorter and left-handed. I thought I remembered you were left-handed when you passed me the notepad, back at the beginning of all of this, but I've just watched you write your own downfall on the flipchart and confirmed it. And in case anyone hasn't got it yet, I refer you to the first letter of each line. TERRY IS MY FATHER."

Behind Joe, another couple of armed officers appeared. The stakes were rising exponentially.

"I'll tell you what I believe happened, and stop me if I'm wrong," I continued, taking a step back, not that it would help much if either pulled the trigger. "As you told me at the start, you used to listen to Rex Dexter's radio show. You and all your friends. You loved music, you lived in London, you wanted to get close to pop stars. So, you'd been in the audience at a TV show with a friend and met Rex Dexter, and you were exactly the sort of girls he liked to prey on. Rex liked you, but you were still just fifteen. You didn't turn sixteen until a couple of weeks later. Your friend, though, she was slightly older. Only by a couple of months, but that was all-important. So backstage, Rex took her off and, for want of a better word, he assaulted her. You heard what had happened, and quite rightly you decided to do something about it."

I paused, giving her a chance to protest, but she knew that the game was up. Her face was flushed, veins pumping in her temples.

"Of course, you didn't intend to kill him," I continued. "You approached him at the end of his radio show because you wanted to put him on the spot. As you told me, your father was a policeman. I suspect you wanted Rex to turn himself in. You took a kitchen knife, partly for your own protection, and partly so you could threaten him. But Rex wasn't impressed. He certainly wasn't going to bossed around by someone he viewed as merely a little girl. I expect he insulted you, made you angry. Maybe even asked you if you wanted the same as your friend. And somewhere along the line, in a fit of rage, you plunged in the knife. Am I right?"

"He deserved it. He raped her," she said, visibly furious at the memory.

"You know what, I don't disagree with you," I said. "But the fact remains, you killed him. And Terry, the last thing you wanted was for your own daughter to be convicted as a killer."

He looked like he was about to throw up.

"Of course, since then, Emily, you joined the police yourself, and nobody knew Terry was your father. You told me yourself, your parents had split up. In fact they were never married, which is why your surname is North, which comes from your mother. Terry still loved you, though, and he wasn't going to see you be tried for murder. So to go back to the original point, he tried to suppress the evidence, but it wasn't his investigation, and it was difficult to do without raising suspicion. Kenny was on the case, though, and when he started to work out what had happened, he became suspicious, and put his theories to Terry. A deal was struck. Kenny buried the evidence, and in exchange you, Terry, hid the evidence of Kenny's corruption. However, my guess is that Kenny was a chancer. He'd decided that he could blackmail you and that's why you had to kill him."

"And what about Dougie Compton?" It was the first time Joe had spoken. I glanced in his direction, but quickly returned my attention to the gun barrels aimed at me. They tend to have that effect.

"Ah yes, poor Dougie," I said. "As we know, he called someone to say he was meeting me. That was Terry. My guess is that he'd discovered things but had been forced to keep them secret for the sake of his career. But when it looked like the truth was about to emerge, it was the classic two-birds-one-stone thing. Terry killed Dougie to silence him, then made it look like it was me, destroying my credibility even further in the process. I can see the logic, but it's horrible how things spiral, isn't it? There were lots of secrets. But no matter how hard you work, some secrets never die."

"And Eddie Whitfield?" asked Joe.

"Eddie thought he was responsible because he assumed Rex

had been killed on account of what happened in the pub, and Kenny's cover had been blown. But in fact, Eddie had it all wrong. Rex hadn't recognised Kenny as a cop – how could he? He thought they were both low-lifes, ripe for a dig on the air. In reality, Rex died for a sin that was far worse. So Eddie's guilt was real, if misguided. It was based on religion. But like I said, he acknowledged blame for the murder. He never said he'd actually committed it."

"And how do you explain the man who attacked you outside Suadela? Or called from my phone?" said Emily, her voice a near whisper.

"That was easy. That was Jonathan," I said. "For a time I thought he might have been the mysterious Jason Shelley, but then the more I thought about it, if that was the case, someone would have known and been able to tell me. But you brought Jonathan to my hotel. I saw the way he looked at you. He was smitten. I doubt you told him all the reasons why, but you asked him to do you a couple of favours, to scare me off. I don't scare easily, though, and when he jumped out at me at Suadela, I think he was trying to frighten me rather than actually hurt me. His heart wasn't really in it. He wasn't up for a fight. Believe me, I've been attacked by plenty of men before and he put up minimal effort. And of course when I smashed his face, he ran. Which is why he called in sick the next day."

I paused for a moment to let that sink in.

"Only three people knew I was in London. Four if you include Graham March. You knew what I was capable of. As you said, you'd read a lot about me. Not wanting to blow my own trumpet, as it were, but I think you were scared I'd discover the truth. With good reason, as it happens. Sorry, Nick, for doubting you, but if one day you learn how to smile, you'll do yourself lots of favours. Joe, you might want to pick Jonathan up. He'll corroborate when he learns that Emily is a killer."

That was the moment she snapped, pulled the trigger, and fired a bullet straight into my chest.

Chapter 51

AS I fell backwards I was aware of the sound of gunfire. The first duty of the police is the preservation of life, but when a known killer starts firing bullets, they tend not to hesitate to intervene.

A couple of minutes later, I opened my eyes, to find Joe leaning over me, looking terrified. I wasn't sure if it was because he'd just seen me get killed, or because I was a corpse who'd opened her eyes.

"Make yourself useful and undo the handcuffs," I croaked. The shock on his face would have been funny in other circumstances.

He helped me sit up, and once my hands were free, I undid my trench coat and inspected the bulletproof jacket beneath. It had done its job, but by God I was going to have a bruise in the morning. My topless modelling career would have to wait a while, and my favourite coat was ruined.

All around was chaos. Radios were ablaze with activity. Sirens were getting louder. Both Emily and Terry were down. I feared the worst, though judging by some of the shouts and urgency of those rushing around, there was a chance they were still clinging to life.

"The ambulance is on its way," said Joe, his voice almost tearful.

I moved backwards to prop myself against the wall. I needed to get my breath back.

"You do know that's not an option," I whispered.

"It bloody well is. We need to get you checked out."

"In an ideal world I'd agree with you, but trust me on this, I think I should probably take advantage of the opportunity to make myself scarce."

"You're not going anywhere," he said.

But to his credit, he didn't try to stop me as I gingerly got to my feet. And then he started barking orders, distracting his colleagues, as I made my way to the corridor.

I took a final look at Emily and Terry as I left. There was a lot of blood, but both were getting CPR. I hoped they were going to be okay. Nick nodded in acknowledgement as he saw me head for the door. He didn't need to say anything. He didn't try to follow. I emerged onto the alleyway, into the flashing lights of the approaching ambulance, its siren blaring.

There was no point trying to run. In any case, I wasn't sure where I'd be running to. I headed to the street and flagged down a cab, wanting the night to swallow me whole.

Chapter 52

Sunday, October 31st, 1993

DESPITE only having one head, I woke up with two headaches. The pounding physical pain from the bottle of wine that had helped blur the trauma of yesterday, and the logistical challenge of getting home to Koblenz. The former wasn't helping with the latter.

Worse still, I faced the immediate problem of finding enough clean clothes to look respectable for a final meeting with Joe. The trip hadn't been a sartorial success, but at least the central mission had been accomplished. I forced myself to get out of bed and hit the shower before attempting a speedy West End shopping trip. The benefit of being back in London, rather than Germany, was that at least some of the shops were open on Sundays.

Joe had called and suggested taking me out for lunch. It was a risk. I was still on the wanted list, but he suggested a restaurant in Covent Garden that was popular with tourists so he thought we'd be able to mingle. My bigger concern was having enough time afterwards to get packed and head home, so instead I suggested a small pizzeria I'd noticed in Exmouth Market, not far from my house in Farringdon. Even though we were on the phone, I could sense his raised eyebrows, but he was polite enough to refrain from interrogating me. Either that or he knew it'd be pointless.

Thankfully he agreed to the suggestion, and by 2pm, I was ready, in my new dark grey dress, black sheer tights, and new royal blue woollen winter coat. The shoes were an extravagance, but who ever had too many shoes? And thankfully I wouldn't have to walk far in them. Make-up did a reasonably effective job of hiding the bags under my eyes.

"Any word on Emily and her dad?" I asked, once we'd shaken hands on the street, and once he'd given me what he probably thought was a subtle appraisal. His downfall was the extended gaze at my legs. I've always thought they were one of my best features, and while I wasn't attempting to seduce him, I must admit I thought they looked more than passable, especially accentuated by the rather sexy suede heels.

The head shake was telling.

"They did what they could," he said, looking particularly downcast.

"I'm so sorry."

And I really was. Yes, Emily was a killer, yes she'd double-crossed me, and yes she'd tried to kill me. But despite all that, I liked her. I'd learned to look upon flaws as an asset, and she was unique and brilliant in her own way.

"I'm teasing you," said Joe, suddenly failing to hold back a grin.

"*What?*"

"They're both in a bad way, but they're expected to pull through."

I nearly hit him, but I'm glad I didn't as he could well have flown through the restaurant window.

"Joe, you don't joke about things like that," I said, giving him a stern look instead.

"You should be happy. It makes it a damn sight easier if they're still alive. They can be tried and convicted, whereas if they'd died, you'd be even more in demand as the key witness to carnage."

"Even so, I was very sad for a moment, just then."

"She shot you."

"She's not the first, and I doubt she'll be the last."

Joe sighed. His expression began to change, from mischievous to forlorn. Things had changed. I didn't want that any more than anyone else, but I didn't have an option. I was the architect of my own malaise.

"Why do you do it?" he asked, his voice dropping.

"Do what?" As if I didn't know.

"All this violence?"

I shook my head, more out of a sense of resignation than anything.

"I don't. I just work in a dangerous world. Case in point: when have I been violent this last week? I haven't. I've been helping you. I keep telling you, I'm a nice person."

"You broke Jonathan Hubbard's nose."

"That was self-defence. He attacked me."

"You put two detectives in hospital when you attacked them in a coffee shop."

"Also self-defence."

"You beat up one of Neil Fearon's security men, smashing him over the head with a gun, shortly after you shot your way out of his office. Then broke two of Neil's fingers."

Awkward.

"You heard about that?"

He nodded.

"That was self-defence too, and it was just as well I did, or I wouldn't have been able to solve your case for you."

His face began to thaw.

"I'm never going to change you, am I?"

"Should we see if they've got a table?" I said, keen to change the subject, taking a step towards the entrance. Joe, to his credit, stopped talking and followed.

"How did you work it all out?" he said, once we'd placed our orders and the waitress had delivered a bottle of sparkling water for me and a Peroni for Joe. The restaurant was small and busy, but we had a table at the back, beneath a row of hanging wine bottles and plastic grapes. I was fairly confident we wouldn't be overheard.

"Some of it was logical, some of it was guesswork," I said. "It was primarily a question of looking again and again at the evidence. Laterally rather than literally. It's like the thing with the bullet, the Mercedes, and all of that – it wasn't you, it wasn't Nick, I decided it couldn't be Graham, and on the face of it, the only other person who knew where I was was Emily. It wasn't her, either. But then I remembered she'd turned up at the hotel with Jonathan Hubbard, so suddenly there was another suspect. Once I started trying to work out what possible motive he could have, it all started to fall into place. Have you arrested him, by the way?"

Joe nodded.

"We have. He's been suspended, pending a disciplinary, but he didn't try to deny it. He was actually more involved than you thought. He'd been to see Alfie Pattison before you got there, and asked him to report back if you turned up. Tell him what you asked about."

"And did Alfie do it?"

"Apparently."

"Wow." That was a lesson learned.

"You can't blame him. He thought he was doing the right

thing. He didn't want to get in trouble with the police."

The pizzas arrived and looked delicious. I asked for a bottle of chilli oil to add a bit of extra kick.

"What about the thing with Emily and her friend at the TV show?" asked Joe, after a mouthful.

I shrugged.

"Lucky guess, kind of. I knew she was a fan of Rex Dexter's radio show. She'd have been about the right age. The rest was a theory based on what Michael Steward told me. It could well have been wrong, but I thought it was worth a try."

"I think that's amazing."

"It's like I said to Emily. I'm not a detective. I'm a journalist, or at least I was. I never had to worry about the Police and Criminal Evidence Act. All I had to do was compile enough evidence to convince an editor – not a jury."

"And the Kenny Mason thing?"

I finished a bite of the pizza while I thought about that one.

"I suppose it started with Terry," I said after a moment. "You told me you were with him the night it all happened, and he'd been discussing his marital problems. That rang true with the theory about him being Emily's father. She told me her parents had split up, but her dad was a detective. I don't expect she thought I'd work out exactly which one. The fact that she told me her parents had never married explained how she had a different surname."

Joe frowned.

"All well and good, but Kenny Mason, though?"

"I'm coming to that. Be patient. Heaven's sake."

I decided to have a bit more pizza to punish him for his impatience. It was all a game, really.

"The man in the hat," I said eventually. "I was convinced he was a policeman. It made sense on lots of levels, but I had no idea who. The hat thing bothered me. Then I had a call from Michael Steward who remembered he was completely bald, so I went to the archive at the *Echo* and looked up news stories about Kenny Mason. I found a picture of him in the photo library."

"They let you back into the *Echo*?"

"They didn't know. Long story. I've got a friend there who made it happen."

"Danny Churchill?"

I shook my head. There was a time when I'm sure Danny would have done anything for me, and vice versa, but that bridge still had to be rebuilt.

"No, one of the subs. Anyway, once I knew it was Kenny, I set to working out why. There was a quote from Terry Handley in one of the press reports of the crash. That was a link. Then it was just a question of working out how it fitted together."

Joe smiled, and shook his head.

"You're wasted. You know that?"

"I was last night."

"What?"

"I had a bottle of wine and not much food."

He laughed.

"No, I mean, wasted as in you've got more to offer the world than just getting into trouble."

"Haha, I know what you mean. And that's very kind of you to say. But that's a good point. We were discussing my amnesty."

"Were we?"

"I think you said that if I did this for you, you'd have a word with the Queen or something."

"I very much think I didn't."

"Maybe not the Queen, then. But I'm pretty sure you said I would serve my debt to society so much better if I were allowed to stay free."

"And again, you have a vivid imagination."

"I'll take that as a yes."

"Just be grateful I undid the handcuffs last night and turned a blind eye when you walked out of the door."

"Ooh, you're so mean to me."

He laughed.

"My job is to take people like you off the streets."

"You literally just did, and brought me in here. And now I'm treating you to lunch, so everyone wins."

He sat back, once the pizza was finished, and looked at me with something approaching fatherly affection. At least, I hoped it was that. Could have been anything, really.

"How are you getting home?" he said, after a moment.

"I'll see if I can get a flight. It might involve a couple of phone calls." I looked at my watch. "That's a good point, actually. I'm supposed to be in Sofia tomorrow."

"Ah yes. You were going to tell me what you were doing out there."

"Pretty sure I wasn't."

He reached into his pocket and produced a Mercedes car key.

"Yours, I believe," he said.

I was so happy.

"How did you manage that?" I reached out for it, but he moved his hand away.

"Luckily for you, the Astra was far enough away from the crime scene that it didn't get impounded. I had someone open the drain and get the key, then took it back and swapped it for yours. Nice car, by the way. They've done a good job with the paintwork."

"Where is it now?"

"Parked about two streets away."

Still he didn't give me the key.

"I thought I'd never see it again," I said.

Eventually, he put it on the table and pushed it over.

"Don't say I don't do anything for you," he said.

"Thank you." I wanted to give him the biggest-ever hug. "We make a good team, Joe."

"I don't even want to think about that," he said.

Chapter 53

THE ferry crossing was rough, and not the best preparation for a five-hour drive, through the night, back to Koblenz. But with every passing mile I had time to reflect on the last week, grateful, above all, for my freedom, but deeply nostalgic for my former life.

In my heart, I knew I still had a long way to go to convince Joe that he could trust me. And I still had Graham March to deal with. Mutual friends in Frankfurt wanted us to work together, on some as-yet-unspecified project, but I could barely think about the man without being overcome by a deep sense of loathing. I'd considered popping in to see him on the way to the ferry, purely to give him a broken arm, but decided against. His time would come.

I was no further forward in coming to terms with my own inner turmoil either. I thought of Emily, lying in a hospital bed. Of Nick, who had annoyed me from the moment I'd met him but had turned out all right in the end, even if I'd failed to make him laugh. And above all, of Derek, and all the good people I'd left behind, in a moment of self-indulgent madness.

Still, there wasn't much I could do about that now. And by the time I pulled into the driveway of the Schloss, all I could think about was bed, and hopefully catching a few hours of much-needed sleep before the long journey to Bulgaria.

It was nearly 4am by the time I killed the engine and made my way to the entrance. Maybe it was the tiredness, but I didn't begin to question why light was coming from the downstairs windows. But as I opened the door, I suddenly felt very wide awake.

Anders and Birgit were waiting for me, their faces grave.

"Everything all right?" I said.

Anders shook his head.

"You'd better come with me."

I dropped my bag in the hallway and followed him into the front room. Birgit followed, and closed the door behind us.

"What's wrong?" I said, a mounting sense of panic playing havoc with my stomach.

"You were supposed to be going to Sofia tomorrow," said Anders. "Meeting Iglika."

"I still am." Were they about to tell me off for being back so late?

Anders shook his head again. Birgit looked ashen.

"There's not an easy way to say this," he said. "But her body was discovered tonight. Throat slit, and left on the steps of the National Palace of Culture. I'm afraid we appear to be at war."

The end.

SPECIAL THANKS...

Secrets Never Die was a lot of fun to write and kept me sane in a year of madness and mayhem.

As ever, it was written with the assistance of late nights, candlelight and music - with special mention to Massive Ego, Ashbury Heights, Endless Shame, Sonic Reunion, She Hates Emotions, Blutengel, Adam Is A Girl, Seelennacht, Vaylon, DayBehavior, Empathy Test, Tenek, Kirlian Camera, Mesh and Blume. Bonus points if you like them too.

Special thanks, of course, to my editor Carrie O'Grady for tolerance over deadlines, seeing things I'd missed, and adding the polish that makes so much difference. Thanks also to Caroline Vincent and Carol Lewis for spotting remaining typos. And finally, to Mary Cafferkey for encouragement, Angela Menné for biscuits and wine, and to you for reading this far. I really hope you enjoyed it.

Clare will be back soon...

If you enjoyed *Secrets Never Die*, don't miss *The Blood Of Angels* - book 1 in the Clare Woodbrook series!

Trust no-one. Especially those who promise to save you.

Former investigative journalist Clare Woodbrook has committed the perfect crime, but it's come at a terrible personal price. So, when she's offered a chance at redemption, she grabs it with both hands.

But it means joining an organisation rooted in the espionage of the old East Germany. It's a world of secrets and lies, in which old allegiances and rivalries count for nothing, and everyone has a sinister hidden agenda. Worse still, she's being hunted by a psychopath, intent on bloody revenge. As Clare embarks on her first mission in London, Paris and Frankfurt, the bullets begin to fly, and she has to face up to a stark yet terrifying truth.

***The Blood Of Angels* is available now in print and ebook formats.**

You'll also find Clare in the Anna Burgin series of mystery thrillers. *Cold Press* is the story of her disappearance. **And the ebook is available FREE at Amazon, Kobo, Apple, Google and Nook!**

London. 1993. Investigative journalist Clare Woodbrook goes missing on the brink of unveiling her biggest-ever story. Is it kidnap? Murder?

Worse still, the police investigation into her disappearance is being headed up by a corrupt DCI - himself the subject of one of Clare's current investigations.

Clare's researcher Danny Churchill sets out to find her, and enlists the help of his flatmate - feisty fashion photographer Anna Burgin. But they soon realise that nobody can be trusted. And as the search becomes ever more desperate, suddenly their own lives are very much on the line.

Packed with intrigue, twists, conspiracies, and dark humour, Cold Press is a hugely entertaining British thriller, with a sting in the tail.

After *Cold Press*, the story continues in **Out Of the Red** and **Fade To Silence** - two more gripping mystery thrillers with breathtaking twists, and dashes of dark humour.

All three are now available in a great value box set for less than the price of two!

The full Anna Burgin series:
1 Cold Press
2 Out Of The Red
3 Fade To Silence
4 Court Me Kill Me
5 Illusions Of Warsaw

FEEL FREE TO SAY HELLO... :-)

If you enjoyed the book, have any queries, or just want to say hello, I'd love to hear from you via www.davidbradwell.com. While you're there, you can also download a **FREE copy of the Anna Burgin series prequel** - In The Frame:

Photography student Anna Burgin didn't expect to be arrested, but she's the only suspect for a series of crimes, and the Police have found damning evidence in her room. But Anna has no recollection of doing anything wrong. Was it a moment of madness? Or is somebody setting out to destroy her? And is the stranger in the bar really trying to help, or just part of an evil conspiracy?